Notice
Me

Emem Uko

ISBN: 1984257676
ISBN-13: 978-1984257673

DEDICATION

To my family
Wherever I am, you bring me home.

CONTENTS

ACKNOWLEDGMENTS

Thanking:
God for this gift of words that form into a bigger picture
My family for their unwavering support
Anders* for trusting me to weave a web of storylines on his tale
Uche Ekhator for her love of learning and incredible know-how
(you make me want to go back to school)
Patricia Dawson for her ability to make things sound better
Debbie Chibuzor for being a receptive wall I've bounced off
questionable ideas
Christian Coker for designing eye-catching book covers
Boybands with hardworking and talented members

*not his real name

Prologue (Accept)

It all started with a message alert on my phone. When I clicked on it and realized that I didn't recognize the sender, I almost deleted it and only stopped short when I saw a glimpse of the message. It was a compliment about one of my books. It said something like, "'Said book' is a page-turner that..." I had to accept the sender's "request" to read the whole message. In excitement, I accepted it. I got the chance to read the message, but by the time it ended, I was hot with temper and had already called him a dozen awful names. Who did he think he was?

His message had actually started out with great compliments. He'd really understood the nuances of the characters in my book and mentioned how much he'd enjoyed the reality of the story. But then, just like that, the compliments disappeared, and it seemed to become critiques unfolding into distasteful words toward the protagonist. I was mad. Yes, the protagonist is not the likable sort, but he had no right to distort the character as to how he understood her. His understanding of the protagonist was lacking, and I sensed him to be an "egotistical nonentity" of a person. I actually wrote that phrase as a response to his message.

For the sake of privacy, and the fact that this book is based on true events, I will not reveal his first message to me. Just know that my response was fiery and insulting as well, an action that I might have regretted, if it hadn't formed into a friendship that I so much cherish even unto this moment.

When I responded to his message with insults of my own, I became remorseful because I wasn't the kind of person to fall for cheap shots like that. I knew that publishing my work would come with admiration and criticisms, and I was supposed to be ready. This person was clearly a troll, who had read my book, no doubt. He seemed to have thought deeply about it though. I should have been happy about that. I guess I wasn't in a mood to tolerate someone who cheapened the actions of a character who temporarily forgot her life plans for love. He bashed her every move, even going as far as mentioning chapters and paragraphs. He called her names that were so disrespectful that I clenched my teeth to keep from screaming. I justified my reaction, but I should have known better. I fell right into his trap. In hindsight, we're both glad I did.

Chapter 1 (An Unlikely Friendship)

The "you've got a message" icon was lit. He'd responded to my lengthy insults, and I could not have anticipated his response for the life of me. It started out with multiple smiley faces, a few sentences replying to my earlier response, and then another comment about another book of mine.

I'm not exactly sure if I can explain the mix of emotions that swirled in my head, but I can say that seeing his reaction convinced me that I was chatting with a mad person. But I was curious, so I made myself a cup of coffee first, and then opened the message he'd sent me and read everything word for word. This time, I was in control of my emotions and although his second message to me was less harsh, I believe it was because he genuinely enjoyed the second book.

After the smiley faces, his message had expressed enjoyment for being scolded for the first time in a long time. He dropped a hint that in real life, no one had the guts to do that anymore, and he usually got hate messages on his social media from trolls. But he'd never gotten a response like this, because he'd never responded on his social media comments or messages. All he did was post things that his fans liked, and those who weren't fans let him know what hateful thoughts they harbored toward him. I was the first person he'd ever written to on a social media page he'd just created for this purpose. He'd thought about this for over three weeks, because he wanted to let me know that I did have a talent for writing and room for growth, but he also wanted to share that I shouldn't waver from my unique style of writing. I shouldn't follow trends, and I should keep my voice alive. Even so, he wouldn't take back what he'd said about the other book. It was after this explanation that he'd critiqued the next book.

My mind raced beyond any speed limit. *Who is he?*

My response to his second message started out with an apology for my previous message to him. Then I thanked him for what he'd written about the second book and I asked who he was. I didn't get a reply to this until after a month; yes, you read that correctly. But I continued to check his profile, which was active, but made 'private.' It had one follower, me, and also followed one person, me. The name used was a generic male first and last name and that was all there was to it.

The third message I finally received after a month said, "Well done. I like how she's developed." That meant he'd read my newest book, which had just been released a couple of weeks ago. I was happy that I'd gotten a fan in such an avid reader, but I was uneasy about who he might be.

"Yay, welcome back," I said sarcastically. "You didn't have to disappear just because you didn't want to tell me who you were. You should have just written, 'no comment.'"

"Missed me?" he replied.

"Don't flatter yourself. It just made me wonder about the weirdo I was chatting with."

"I'm glad you wondered. Weirdo, I am. A handsome one, too."

"Sheesh, there's no proof."

"It's better that way."

"For you maybe. This is weird for me. I don't feel comfortable chatting with someone I don't know. No face, no followers, too weird."

"I'm not a creep."

"Can't prove that either. Anyway, I'm grateful that you took the time to read my books. That's every writers' dream. Thank you so much."

"I liked your writing style when I read your book for the first time, even if I absolutely couldn't stand that character."

"Hey, can you stop now? Anyway, thanks again. Gotta go."

"Hold on."

I saw the message before I closed my page. Another message came in.

"Do you want a story? I'll tell you who I am eventually."

My hair started to itch with the mix of curiosity and excitement. My fingers started to tap the table in a fast tempo, just as fast as my mind was racing. I wanted to know who he was. I didn't have to write the story if I didn't like it. I wouldn't tell him this, of course.

I typed, "I'm in."

Chapter 2 (Who Am I?)

"I just wanted to tell someone because if I continued to keep it in, I knew I'd burst. I don't know you, but I like what I've learned about you from your social media accounts. You strike me as an honest person and I feel like I can trust you. It doesn't hurt that you have a friendly face, too."

"Lol, friendly face? I'm told I have a death stare that actually makes people pee their pants."

"Really? That's funny. I guess I can't see that through your photos."

"Nope, my photos are usually cute and smiley. Real life is different. I'm super tall, too, so imagine how imposing I'd look."

"That's quite hard to imagine. I just see a tall doll-like person with so much hair."

"Lol. So I guess my approachable face made you choose me to be your ghost writer?"

"Actually, my original intent was not to write a book. I was just bored and thought you'd be a nice person to chat with."

"Ah, gullible me."

"Haha. Well, I didn't think you were going to respond to my message. When I tell you my story, you can do whatever you want with it. It doesn't matter to me, as long as I can stay anonymous. I just think that you might want to write it, because you're obviously a good writer, and because it would be too good to pass."

"Braggart."

"That's my middle name."

"*rolling eyes emoji*"

"Haha. But I'm really glad you responded."

"That makes one of us."

"You don't mean that *sad face emoji*"

"Not a hundred percent. I'm still wondering what I've gotten myself into, considering that I have no clue who I'm chatting with, and the person is claiming to be someone that no one would dare talk to disrespectfully in real life. That's what you wrote earlier. Are you some kind of dictator?"

"Hahaha, are you scared? Just think the opposite."

"Okay, a chubby-faced underage girl?"

"Close."

"Funny. Tell me something? I'm guessing you're very popular since you said you get hate messages from internet trolls and you don't respond to comments."

"Gold star!"

"Stop it. Anybody can guess as much. I just want to know what you do."

"That's easy. Music."

At this, I couldn't stop myself from imagining who he could be. Possibilities from ballad to rock singers flashed across my mind. But I couldn't imagine which one would get hold of my books, read them, and write to me about them. Which popular singer had that kind of time? Which popular singer could find books that weren't on display on the shelves of Barnes & Noble?

But I reasoned that I followed a lot of musicians online, and I usually commented on their pages when they posted interesting photos. It was possible that one of them had seen my comment and curiously clicked on my page. Maybe that's how he'd gotten to know that I was a writer. Or, I could just ask him.

"Musician? Wow! But that doesn't help me because I follow many musicians online."

"You don't follow me."

"Wait, what? Then how did you find my books?"

"*Smiley face*

"No, seriously I'm curious. How did you know that I was a writer?"

"Through a blog."

"Which blog?"

"Sorry, can't remember. I just recall seeing the book cover and ordering the ebook."

"You Celebs order things online by yourselves?"

"Haha, very funny."

"Okay, and then you read the book and decided to be mean about it."

"Not exactly. I read the book and searched for the author, and learned about her other book, purchased it and read it. Then 'watched out' for more of her works, since her website advised keeping up with her on social media."

I rolled my eyes involuntarily. "Cool. So one day you decided to write to that author?"

"Precisely."

Who is he? "Are you going to give me another clue as to who you are? If I don't follow you, then there's no starting point for finding you."

"That's actually preferable."

"Well, I need to know who you are."

"You will, in due time."

I exhaled impatiently. "I have to be honest with you. I don't feel comfortable chatting with you."

"That is harsh."

"It's the truth. You're a popular musician that I don't follow online. It means that I have no interest in your music."

"You don't follow every musician that you listen to, do you?"

"True."

"But I know that you enjoy my music."

"How is that?"

"You've mentioned us somewhere."

"Really? 'Us?'"

"My band."

"You're in a band? Hmm, I guess we're getting somewhere."

"Yes, we are. It's a four-man band and that's where I'm going to stop for today. Like I said, you will know more in due time."

"Four-man band. That's like every band. Oh well, thanks for giving me some clues. I just hope you're not a weirdo, because, like I said earlier, I don't feel comfortable chatting with you."

"I understand that, but try not to be too concerned about me. I'm not going to jump out of the screen and bite."

"Sure, if you say so."

"I say so. Anyway, something just came up. I have to stop now, but I'll be sure to chat with you tomorrow."

"Sure. Have fun."

"I'll try. I can't wait for you to hear my story."

"Can't wait either."

Chapter 3 (Stunned At First Meet)

I've had sleepless nights in my life, but this time it was due to an overactive mind that just wouldn't stop cooking up ideas and scenarios. The fact that I could possibly be talking to a famous person, who had something juicy to share with me, sounded like a far-fetched dream. In fact, I found myself looking at my phone multiple times a day just to make sure that I hadn't make up the online encounter in my head.

It became a habit to just mutter, "who is he?" and then I would regain my composure and smile apologetically to someone who thought I was asking them the question.

Sometimes I would find myself giddy with excitement, as I wondered why I was the person chosen by this mystery musician to be his chat-buddy.

But as days went by, I started to regain my usual sense of normalcy and told myself that it was just a new wave of scam. The scam artist knew that there'd be some sad individual out there who would respond to unbelievable tales just to feel good about themselves. *Pathetic.* I shook my head.

And then out of the blue, another message. "Hi."

"The thing that came up actually took you seventeen days?"

"Oooo, someone missed Mr. Wierdo."

"I'm just saying. Your last message said we were going to chat the next day and then that didn't happen. Not even the day after, or the day after…"

"You should have sent me a message if you missed me that much."

"Well, I just figured you were busy being a musician."

"I was. We had a 'fan-meet' in Europe with my band."

"Fan-meet? So, you really are a popular musician?"

"You're still skeptical, I see."

"I'll continue to be until I know who you are."

"You will. Nice dress by the way. It's a good color for you."

"What are you talking about?" I asked as my eyes widened in confusion.

"The picture you posted yesterday."

"Oh, that, thanks."

"Hahaha. What did you think I meant?"

"Nothing! Are you going to start your story or what?"

"Are you mad at me?"

"Nope. I just think you're dragging this out. I'd like to get something before you disappear again."

"Aww, don't be mad. I won't disappear again, I promise. Even if I'm busy, I'll say hi."

"Whatever. Waiting for the story."

"*sad face emoji* I feel like you're just friends with me because of my story."

"It took you a while to realize that. The story, please."

"*shocked face emoji*"

"Fine. I'm leaving."

"Wait. I'm just thinking of the best way to narrate it. Texting will be too tedious. I'll use voice messaging."

My excitement ramped up so high that I feared it would burst from my head. I'd get to hear his voice or would he use those robotic voice things? Sheesh, I rolled my eyes. "Okay," I responded.

I saw the prompt that showed me that a message was being recorded. I waited patiently, watching my phone and breathing quietly, as though any sound would impact his recording. I get to hear how he sounds, I mused. This is actually real. This is actually happening.

After about three minutes and a few seconds, I got the voice message. Then an accompanying text message that said, "There you go. Let's begin from the first time I saw her." My eyes popped wider. "Her." Ooooh, this is going to be good.

I clicked and listened.

He had an accent...

It was loud. There were flashes from all corners, phone cameras, and real cameras. He was concentrating on the photos and memorabilia that were placed in front of him for his autograph. His band would be playing at the Arena in the evening, but first, was the fan-meet. They had greeted the fans, he had crooned a verse of one of their popular songs, "*She's mine*," which was currently at number two in the country's top-fifty charts. The fans had gone wild with excitement, and he'd blessed them with his signature wink and lip-bite.

Then came agenda number two, autograph time. They'd finished signing for the VIPs. This time was for the next expensive ticket holders. He'd mastered the art of autographing with the noise and blinding flashes. He knew that it would be rude to put on earphones or plugs, because he needed to give his fans his attention. He was very good at drowning out sounds. He also had a rule of keeping eye contact. He focused on the faces of his fans, and not on their phones or cameras, which tended to produce lightning sparks in the form of flashes at hundred miles per hour.

But on this day, he was a bit nervous. He'd fumbled twice on the lyrics earlier during rehearsals He knew that there was nothing to be nervous about, because he'd written those verses, but the Arena had given him quite a shock, since it was the largest venue they'd ever performed in. It wasn't his first time here, but it was the first after major reconstruction had made the venue even bigger. So as he signed autographs, he realized that he had to remind himself to smile, make eye contact, and listen intently in order to answer the questions that his fans asked him during their turn. But when the next person in the line came forward, a photo was placed in front of him without a word. His eyes were focused on the thighs of the pair of jeans that faced him, and smiling at the red dyed patch that was the shape of a heart, he looked up.

It was when he got stamped on his foot by his bandmate sitting on his right-hand side, that he realized that he'd been looking at her face all along.

Paralyzed, was how you could describe him in that moment. It was the unusual shades of brown colors in her full, neck length hair. It was her large almond-shaped eyes that held the largest and darkest irises he'd ever seen. It was the oval-shaped face with a tiny nose that rose up as though she'd just argued with someone. It was those bare lips that looked too full for a face so angelic and innocent. Her long neck held a black choker with an "R" alphabet pendant, and he'd just been looking at her clavicle when he felt the thud on his foot. She'd just stared back at him, straight-faced and emotionless.

He cleared his throat, "What's your name?" He asked as he readied his pen to autograph the photo. This photo, he noticed excitedly, was one of just him. Most fans had brought the recent photo that the band had taken together in their latest magazine shoot. A version of that group photo was being sold outside the Arena.

But she'd brought a photo of him, one of his favorites, he might add, that was taken when he'd had a solo performance a couple of years back in Thailand. He'd liked that haircut, and that was a very good year for him and his band.

"Make it to Mabel-Agatha."

His widened eyes weren't caused by the interesting nature of both names together. It was her voice. It was the deep hoarseness of her voice, which didn't fit the immaculate image that stood right in front of him, dressed in an Elmo T-shirt underneath a jeans jacket a darker shade from her pants. This girl was unusual and he was whipped.

He cleared his throat again. "Nice names."

She shrugged. "I don't think they go well with each other, but I love my roommate so I can't tell her that to her face."

He was smiling sheepishly at the face that wasn't smiling back, and trying so hard to look at what he was signing at the same time. He had to think twice before spelling "Agatha" and then he unknowingly started composing a poem too.

It was as one of the security men came to push the line ahead, that he noticed that he'd caused quite a holdup. He reluctantly gave her back the photo, and then watched her move to his bandmate. That was when she smiled, and his heart gave a lurch of awe and extreme disappointment at the same time.

She didn't look his way. She had eyes only for Twine, the band's muscular drummer.

He knew he had to concentrate on the autographs of the other fans, but it was difficult. Then she smiled again, so widely this time that he thought he was going to die because he couldn't breathe. Twine lingered when he gave her the photo, and that made him a bit furious, but he tried his best to hold it in.

It was when she disappeared into the line that he replayed their conversation in his head. "Mabel-Agatha wasn't her name, but her roommates. Why didn't she ask for him to sign a photo for her? A thought brewed in his head, but he quickly dismissed it. Even if she liked only Twine from the group, it didn't make sense to just ask for only his autograph, did it?

She didn't attend agenda three, photo ops. He searched the crowd frantically, looking for a girl with height at approximately five feet six inches and so many shades of brown in her hair, an Elmo T-shirt, a dark jean jacket and a gray backpack.

She wasn't anywhere.

"Hey T, what was the name of the girl that looked like a doll with a cracked voice?"

"What girl?"

"The one you signed for who had really full lips and was very, very happy to see you."

Twine raised an eyebrow. "Uh, they were all very, very happy to see me."

"Ass," he muttered in anger and walked away.

Chapter 4 (I'll Find You)

When I heard his voice, I had that feeling where your brain overworks itself trying to place something, but coming up short despite your great effort. I knew the voice with that accent, but being a recording, it wasn't crisp enough for me to guess correctly. But when he called Twine's name, that was it. I knew the band. I knew who I was chatting with and I almost collapsed in shock. When I came back to my senses, I was glad that he wasn't making me wait forever before telling me who he was.

I had been chatting with the lead singer of "For-Runners," one of the hottest bands to grace our ears for almost eight years since their debut. I could not believe it. No way. How on earth? He was nicknamed "cool mystery" for a reason. Unlike the playful bass guitarist, Alphonso, or the shy electric guitarist, Trance, or the out-going playboy drummer, Twine, Anders was the cool, sexy, winking, lip-biting, black- and-gray garbed singer that only said five words in every interview.

He's always rumored to be gay because of the thin line he treaded between being a rock star and effeminate. He is known for his fashion gender-bender styles, and somehow pulls off many trends in the black and gray color scale. There is also one thing he does that fans usually look out for. He adds one article of primary color to his outfits. It might be his scarf or wrist-watch or shoes, or even the hairband with which he'd tied his long hair before he'd cut it last year. I honestly thought he was gay. Not that he had openly talked about being in a relationship with a guy. I mean, he never refuted the rumors when he pecked his bandmates or was so close and touchy with his other guy friends. He always just shook his head and narrowed his guy-lined eyes with a smirk on his face. That was it. No words, no arguments.

Hearing him talk so passionately about a girl, took me off-guard. Picturing him with her was 'interesting,' but I could see it. Re-wiring myself to see him with that girl was easy, because he had struck me as a man who would be really into whoever he loved, because of his ability to focus intensely on his fans with his stare and body composure. He is famous for causing a female fan, who'd been normal while she spoke with Trance, to buckle and faint when she looked into his eyes. That was world-wide news that made fans jealous of the attention she got, his fellow musicians jealous for that ability to make someone swoon for real, and religious people speculate that he was possessed.

I couldn't believe in a million years that I was chatting with Anders. No way, I said aloud. No freaking way!

"Anders?" I typed.

"Yes." He responded.

"It really is you."

"In the flesh, or rather, on your screen."

"I'm assuming you gave away your identity on purpose."

"Right. I just thought, why not?"

"And you're confident that I'm trustworthy-enough for that?"

"I've never trusted anyone, because people tend to change when they're desperate. But I'm not worried, because what I'm doing here isn't going to cause me or my band any problems."

"I could tell people about our chats and that you read my books."

"You could, but it all boils down to the evidence."

I thought about it. There was no way I could prove that he was the real Anders, even with that voice recording. Anyone with a talent can imitate him. In fact, a fan known as "doppelganger Andas," is known for impersonating him, from his looks to how he sounds. I could be chatting with him right now, but my gut-feeling said otherwise. I'm chatting with the real Anders.

"Dang! I wish I had proof. Just imagine all the people who'd purchase my books because of you."

"Well, you could call my agency and pay for my services. All I to do is be seen holding your book and that's it."

He was right. Everything Anders wears sells out. *Gosh*, I imagined. "I'll be sure to get in touch with them when I can afford your services."

"Your books will fly off the shelves. You don't need me for that."

"The imaginary shelves, but thanks for the vote of confidence anyway."

"Have more faith in your writing abilities."

"I do. I really do. But it's just getting the word out for people to give them a chance."

"They will. Very soon."

And just like that, I believed him, and somehow was satisfied, and confident that I was doing very well as a writer. If Anders could get hold of my books, then I should be more trusting that anything can happen.

"Are you still searching for her?"

"No. I've found her."

"Whoa! Really? I haven't heard anything in our universe that you're dating anybody."

"You're hilarious. I wouldn't make my relationship public if she doesn't want it that way."

"Aww, beg her, please. Gosh, I need to see this girl that Anders of all people has fallen for."

"Well, we're not dating."

"Hold on, but you said…"

"I was just giving you an example of why you may not hear about my relationship. I've dated a girl that preferred to protect her privacy. You may recall an instance where I said I wasn't dating the girl with the bright red hair."

"Yeah, she was a family friend of sorts."

"No, she wasn't, but we made it that way."

"Yikes. How did she take it?"

"It was her idea. That way, she could be around me during our agency programs without too many questions, rumors, and fan hate."

"It makes sense. I remember seeing the photo of you two holding hands and then other photos; you guys were always with people. I heard you're into 'PDA', but I never saw you do anything like that with her. So I accepted that she was a family friend. But there was this photo, and the way you looked at her was a bit weird if you two weren't dating. It now makes total sense."

"That was a difficult relationship. We had to try to be smarter than every onlooker and the paparazzi, and I was still young, so those were some reasons why we broke up."

"So, you don't mind people knowing that you're dating somebody?"

"Nope, not anymore. But I'm not going to be out there advertising my relationship for it to be scrutinized by the media."

"They'll do it anyway. You're just a bag of news wherever you go."

"*smiley face emoji* that's new…never been described as a bag of news before."

"I'm just saying that I kind of understand why your ex-girlfriend wanted to keep your relationship hushed."

"Well, that's impossible if the relationship is to work. We should be free with ourselves no matter what."

"Hmm, your female fans are going to hate it."

"They love me."

"They'll forget that when a girl is involved. They prefer the idea that you're gay."

"Well, they may not get the chance to hate her."

"Because you're not dating."

"No, we're not."

"Did she say 'no' to you?"

"No, because I haven't asked her."

"Wait a minute. So she doesn't know that you're interested in her?"

"No, she doesn't."

"Are you crazy?"

"Apparently."

"Or is she in a relationship and you're trying not to meddle in it?"

"No, she's single, E, I just can't have her."

"Why is that?"

No response. I waited for over ten minutes before I tried again.

"Why is that, Anders?"

"Her life is perfect, and if I step in, I'll cause chaos."

"You don't know that."

"Yes, I do."

"Are you just making excuses because you're not sure if she's going to say 'yes' to you?"

"It's not an excuse, but you may be right. I don't think she'll say yes."

"You should give her the opportunity to either say yes or no. Don't make the decision alone. What if she absolutely adores you and you're depriving her of what could be?"

"You sure are an author. I can tell you that she doesn't absolutely adore me. That role has already gone to Twine."

I was taken aback by what I'd just read. "What? Twine wants to date her?"

"No, he doesn't. He's not interested, or I should say I don't think he'll be interested.

Twine does have a type, and based on Anders' description of this girl, I didn't see a compatibility with Twine. But who knows, things happen.

"So, this girl hasn't met any of you after the fan-meet, and you are not going to meet her?"

"No."

"Why? Why? Why?"

"Like I said earlier, I think she'll be better off without me in her life."

"What about you? Are you going to be okay?"

"I think so. I've done it for years. I'll give myself a few more years to adjust to the idea. I'm getting better at not thinking about her all the time, or stalking her online *smiley face emoji*.

I looked incredulously at my phone. I thought that I'd misunderstood what I'd read.

"Anders, how long have you known her?'

No response for five minutes, and then, "Going on three years now."

Air whooshed out of my nose and mouth all at once in my shock. He's been pining over a girl for this long and she has no clue that he likes her?

"What's her name?"

"That's not necessary."

"It is, Anders, because I'm going to write a story, and I need to know exactly who I'm writing about. Sometimes when somebody describes someone they like, they're blinded by only what they want to see. If I know what she really looks like, then I can get the right feeling across to the reader."

"I can describe her."

"What's her name?"

"Reva Santana."

"Thank you."

Chapter 5 (Who Are You?)

He didn't think he was good-looking; that's why when he'd been approached by a talent scout from FFQ Entertainment, he was sure he was being scammed.

"I'm not interested, thank you."

"Just take my card," the lady persisted, "and give it a thought. You'd be a wonderful addition to our company. Have you heard of FFQ Entertainment?"

Of course, he'd heard of FFQ. They were one of the biggest foreign entertainment agencies that signed big music names and popular actors. He didn't understand why the woman had given him her card though. As far as he was concerned, he was plain-looking, with a large nose and a pimple in the middle of his forehead that wouldn't go away. Maybe it was because he was skinny and tall. That had to be it.

"Yes, I have."

"Then you know that this is a wonderful opportunity. Those who get scouted have the best chance in the industry. How old are you?"

"Sixteen," he blurted out.

"Oh," her eyes widened. "That's good," she said silently as her forehead scrunched. "I thought you were older, but sixteen is a great age. You just have to come to our office along with your parents or guardian."

He nodded and wanted the conversation to be over. He didn't want to be late for the delivery he was making.

"Make sure you give it a thought, Anders. I'll look out for your registration form," she said as he walked away with a nod.

His mom was already in the school courtyard waiting for him. She didn't look pleased.

"I'm sorry," he said as he caught his breath. He had sped up when he saw her from the gate.

"You're always late. I've told you that I don't have a long lunch break."

He rolled his eyes inwardly. Why did his dad insist on making her hot lunches on Saturdays, and turning him into errand boy? His mom taught private lessons on Saturdays in a high school that was ten minutes away from his home. His dad was a bakery owner. He was the only child and best friends with his mom. They'd just moved recently to a new state, and he was having trouble making friends because of his accent, and his being gangly and noticeable among much shorter classmates. He didn't find it too bothersome though, because he spent his free time at home in the makeshift recording studio his dad had set up for him. One day he planned on being a professional songwriter, composer, and producer. His father liked the idea because "there was money in that business."

He fetched the business card from his pocket and gave it to his mom with the lunch bag."

"What's this?"

"Look at it when you get another break. Bye now," he said, running off as he memorized a line of lyrics that he desperately needed to write down and not forget.

There was a knock on the door. He didn't need to respond, as it was a habit for his parents to open the door after two knocks anyway.

His mom was back from school and she was still upbeat for someone who'd just taught high school students. Her wavy hair was still in place and her eyes were bright as ever. Maybe the ones who took weekend lessons were serious students and had no time to wear her out. There was always that one student who was forced to take extra classes against their will because their parents said so and…

"What do you think about it?" His mom asked, cutting his wayward thoughts short. He straightened on his bed, putting aside his comic book, as his mom sat on the sofa that had all kinds of clothes strewn over it. She didn't even bother moving the clothes aside.

"Has dad seen it?" he asked.

"Not yet."

"I don't know," he answered sincerely, studying his mother's face to see any inkling of doubt that would help him make his decision, but there was none. She had on her famous no-emotion face. The facial expression that had been responsible for making him confess his guilt of wrong-doing even before his parents discovered it. That face disarmed him. He had never seen his mom really angry, and he sometimes suspected she was a robot. Her students liked her and thought she was funny, because she liked to say the most absurd things with a straight face.

She nodded. "So, do you want your father and me to make the decision for you?"

"That'd be great," he answered nonchalantly. That certainly got a reaction from her, a fleeting appearance of a line in the middle of her brow before it disappeared like it had never happened. He noticed. He always noticed the minutest things. He always paid attention to any and everything.

He swung his legs over the side of the bed and sat at the edge near the foot of the bed. "I'll go find out what it's about, if you and dad think so. The woman didn't say anything in particular, but I suspect it'd be modeling."

She nodded, looking at the business card again. "This FFQ, the headquarters are abroad. I have heard good and bad things about them, same as all agencies out there. I haven't heard you say you're interested in something like this, ever, but it's you. You never say anything."

"Yeah, I know, Mom. That's because I haven't really thought about anything."

"That's not worrisome at all."

"You know what I mean, Mom."

She sighed. "I'll talk to your dad," she said as she rose to leave.

"Mom,"

She turned.

"Happy Birthday."

She rolled her eyes and left. He smiled because her reaction to it never got old. She had a rule about birthdays in their house. Everyone was free to celebrate theirs, but not hers. "Birthdays do nothing good for me. You just make me count my numbers, and place limits on myself because of those numbers. I don't like it." The agreement was to celebrate her birthdays in their minds, and her present was for them to make the best of whatever they found themselves doing on that day. His present to her was to accept what she'd want him to do concerning FFQ Entertainment.

He had allowed his mother to brush his hair since he'd refused a haircut. He wore his usual color scheme, gray jeans, black T-shirt with white graphics and his beat-up Converse. His mom wanted him to wear something else of course, but she gave up when he acted as though his ears were blocked.

They got there fifteen minutes earlier than the time Mrs. Yolanda Swift had mentioned on the phone, but they were soon ushered into her small cube-like office crammed with many black folders on white shelves. She greeted Anders with a wide smile, which made her face light up like she had just gotten the best news of her life. He smiled awkwardly and trained his eyes on the papers that were on her desk. She shook Anders' mom's hand and they introduced themselves.

"Yolanda Swift, senior talent scout for FFQ Entertainment."

"Everest Quigley, Anders' mom."

"It's so nice to meet you and I have to apologize for approaching your son without your consent. I thought he was older."

Anders frowned. He'd never been babied, so Mrs. Swift's words made him feel like a toddler, and that made him uncomfortable.

"He gets that quite often," his mom responded.

"Please follow me to one of our conference rooms. It's much airier than my office," she said as she picked up a folder from her desk, a clipboard and a couple of pens.

She opened a glass door and it lit up as they entered. She was right that it was more spacy and airier than her little office. There were a rectangular table and eight chairs, but they all sat toward the head of the table by the back of the room. Mrs. Swift took the seat at the head, Everest sat next to her right and Anders took the seat next his mom.

"Would you like anything to drink?" she offered.

"No, thanks."

"Yes, coffee." Everest had expected his response and just shook her head as she heard him.

This prompted a smile from Mrs. Swift, who looked like she was having a lot of fun. She wanted to get to learn more about this interesting kid and his mother: a kid who looked absolutely nothing like his mother. Everest had had to introduce herself as Anders' mom since he was a baby, because he was a fair kid with an unusual reddish-brown hair color and light brown eyes, while Everest was darker-skinned and had dark brown eyes. People used to mistake her for Anders' nanny and that had really hurt her for a while. She used to introduce herself as "Everest Quigley, Anders' biological mom." But over the years, she'd gotten used to the assumptions people made, and simply introduced herself as, "Everest Quigley, Anders' mom."

Anders shared a resemblance to his dad's facial and body structure, but nothing else. His dad was also darker than he, had black hair, and brown eyes. But there was no doubt that Anders was his kid, because he looked like his dad's older sister, who had died before Anders had ever met her.

Mrs. Swift picked up the telephone on the table and rang for coffee. Anders felt like an important guest and had a sheepish smile on his face. Everest swatted his thigh with her index finger and that was code for "behave."

Anders was surprised as he watched Everest raise a lot of questions during the meeting. Of course, this was his mom, and any good mother would be concerned about subjecting her child to a life that was so demanding both physically and mentally. It didn't matter if the child thought that that was all he wanted. A parent had to look out for her child.

Everest talked about the responsibilities that were placed on kids at an early age to conform to standards that could be difficult for them. She wanted assurance that FFQ looked after their overall well-being.

Anders was no doubt mature, but he was still a kid who needed guidance and protection. If they were going to sign a contract, Everest wanted to be sure that there was a provision for Anders to test the waters, and return if things were too hard for him. She made sure he understood that he wasn't obligated to live that life and could change his mind. But she knew her son to be one who would persevere, so she wanted to make sure that he was choosing wisely.

She questioned how they trained and prepared the kids. She seemed to be happy with the language school in which Mrs. Swift said FFQ enrolled all their foreign kids. She saw photos of the dorms and other facilities. She saw documents of courses and schedules for a typical trainee, who would eventually become a singer or actor. She noticed that according to their mission statement, FFQ wasn't too harsh on extreme changes of appearance like other agencies that encouraged starvation and plastic surgery. They focused more on the talent of the individual. All in all, FFQ wasn't a sweatshop for idols and celebrities, and Everest wasn't too nervous anymore about letting Anders try out.

Anders heard Everest's sigh and smiled because it was her usual sigh of satisfaction.

Chapter 6 (To Give Up or Not To Give Up?)

Not long after the contract was signed with FFQ Entertainment, Anders was saying goodbye to his parents at the airport. His mom looked too happy for the occasion, considering the fact that she wasn't going to see him for months. He was suspicious about her emotional balance. His dad looked like he might cry. That's how his mom should look, he thought.

He was headed to a different country on another continent, and while he was thrilled about his impending adventure, he wasn't looking forward to the language barrier. He did take some preparatory classes and was assured that he was going to take the language course as part of his training, but he still had a bit of anxiety knowing that communication was going to be difficult. It was already difficult for him presently with his first language, he mused. He threw the thought aside when he boarded the plane.

Many long hours later, the people looked and sounded differently. The surroundings looked different. Even the air smelled different. He was far from home, and he felt his chest tighten like he might wail in sadness. Anders had never been one to be emotional. He always found his place wherever he went and was okay being alone. He didn't need much to satisfy himself, as all that mattered to him was good food, music, and great comics. His mom used to say that if every child were like Anders, the world would be a slow, quiet level-minded place, and only saved from being boring because of music. Everest was somewhat happy with the kind of child he was, and his independence at an early age had made it possible for both parents to live more freely and do whatever they wanted. He always seemed to adapt easily.

There was a worrying factor though, and that was Anders' inability to care about things other than his core loves, music, comics and wrist watches. Although Anders wasn't socially awkward and could hold his own in a room full of his mates, Everest would have been happier if her son acted like a real teenager once in a while. She'd wanted some opportunities to scold him about parties and girls, but what she scolded him more about was for him to do his school work, and leave his music studio to get enough sleep.

Anders' dad was just happy to have a reasonable son who didn't cause trouble and who helped out when he was needed. Anders was happy to be let be.

He was greeted by a short, thin, balding man who held a small white sign with his name written in bold black letters. Anders could not have missed the man in the crowd, because he was so colorful that he would be noticeable even in a crowd of people who wore multi-colored outfits. The man looked at him and smiled as he approached him. He said hi to Anders, who was uncertain as to whether he was supposed to stretch out his hand for a handshake or bow. The man smiled widely and shook his hand. "Welcome," he said. "I hope your flight wasn't too stressful."

The trip had been very long with a connecting flight, but Anders, being a person who avoided small- talk, just shook his head and said, "No, it wasn't. Thank you."

He put on his backpack and pulled his large suitcase behind him, as he followed the man outside to a garage-like area which was bustling with vehicles and people. The black van was in a somewhat secluded spot, and another man came over, nodded to Anders who did the same, and then opened the trunk. He lifted Anders' suitcase like it weighed nothing and put it in. The short man had already opened the side door and beckoned for Anders to get in. The short man then went to the front to sit with the driver. In no time, they started their journey out of the airport. Anders, after taking a sip of water from one of the bottles that were lined up on the side of the van door, took out his earphones and put them on. This would have been a good time to look out of the window, admire and ask questions about the brand new country, but it wasn't like Anders to do that.

One thing Anders didn't fail to notice about his new environment was the number of people. People seemed to be everywhere. When the van slowed down, it was evident that they had reached their destination, and as the van waited behind other cars that were waiting to be directed to their parking spots by uniformed men, he could see high school aged kids trying to peer into the van window. No doubt, they suspected that whoever was inside was an interesting person because the van had the popular FFQ Entertainment logo on it. He was glad that the windows were tinted.

When it was their turn, the driver followed the directions of the uniformed man who waved his hand to a parking spot that was large enough for the van.

The van came to a halt and Anders took off his earphones and strapped on his backpack. He stepped out when the short man and the driver did. The driver handed him his suitcase and nodded again. He did the same. "Let us go there," the short man said, as he pointed toward one of the tall buildings that was no doubt the headquarters of FFQ Entertainment, since it was clearly labeled on the side of the building with super-sized block letters in the English alphabet. Oversized photos of musicians and movie stars were displayed on the walls of the massive buildings. These were photos of some of those who were the success stories of FFQ Entertainment. For a moment, Anders saw his face on the building and then wiped out that vision as quickly as it came. It didn't pay to get ahead of ones' self, he thought.

The short man then said something to him in his native language, realized it and apologized immediately, looking embarrassed. Then he cleared his throat and tried again. "Are you hungry?"

Anders had been sitting in a large room that looked like a multi-purpose room, because there were chairs stacked against the wall on one side, a table on the other side that held drinks, and a high ceiling curtain that looked like it was used as a room divider.

The room was so large that it had multiple doors and they were all wide open. While seated, he'd seen people pass by. A few had stopped and peered curiously at him, but they didn't say anything to him. He'd just continued to listen to music, and sometimes fumbled with his suitcase beside him to make sure he hadn't forgotten some essentials at home. Home, when he felt the sense of loneliness creeping in, he tried his best to shove it aside. The short man had taken him to the cafeteria in the large building and asked him to take whatever he wanted. He'd settled for a grilled cheese sandwich since it was a safe option, and he'd wanted to avoid conversations about the foods that were displayed enticingly, but looked scary to him.

Since the short man had left, he'd spent over two hours seated in the room and nobody had shown up for him. He knew where the restroom was and he hadn't need anything else at the moment. His plan was to wait awhile more, and if no one came, he was going to ask the first person he came across for the name that was written on his phone, a Mr. Ju Robert.

Someone peeped into the room from the door at Anders' far left side. Anders saw the face fleetingly before it disappeared. Not long after, the person showed himself fully at the door entrance and then slowly made his way toward Anders. He was a skinny boy wearing too-tight black jeans and an oversized white T-shirt. He'd packed up his hair, making it look like he had a small palm tree attached to his head. He walked as though he was readying himself to dash out any moment, and Anders thought it was funny, because he didn't think he was so threatening looking that the boy should act the way he did. *Maybe he was just the shy sort.*

When the boy finally got near where Anders sat, Anders took off his earphones and the boy said, "Hi, are you, Anders?" He was soft-spoken and said it in English.

Anders nodded.

"I'll take you to Mr. Rob now. He's in his office waiting to see you."

Anders got up, hung his backpack on his shoulder and took along his suitcase. The boy stopped abruptly like he'd just remembered something, and turned around to Anders with his hand stretched out. "My name is Trance."

Anders shook his hand and nodded and continued along as Trance led the way.

Wherever they were headed proved to be a long way away. They'd passed through hallways that were cramped with shelves and dodged people walking slowly and talking loudly. Some stared at Anders and did nothing to hide that fact. He stared back at them with his face as blank as he could manage. Trance met a few boys along the way who called his name and all he did was smile in response.

Then they took a turn that led them to a revolving door with a bridge-like entrance made of glass from which the outside could be seen. Anders was momentarily in awe as he saw the high-rises that were around the building where he stood. He looked forward and noticed that Trance had stopped to give him time to admire the view.

Anders continued on with Trance, and soon they were at another revolving door that led them to an open space that looked like the middle of a mall with shops flanked around. Only, it wasn't a mall and they weren't all shops. They were offices and stores, and then it dawned on Anders that FFQ Headquarters leased out spaces to other businesses.

"We're almost there," Trance blurted out.

They got into an elevator and Trance pushed number fifteen.

"Sorry for the long walk. I couldn't find a golf cart."

"No worries," Anders said.

Soon the elevator doors opened up to a hallway with dimmer lighting. Anders followed quietly and Trance halted at the first door. It was a glass door and a receptionist could be seen behind a desk that faced the door. Anders found himself swallowing continuously, because it seemed that the girl behind the desk had caused some sort of blockage in his throat. The first thing he thought of when he saw her face was that she looked like a doll. Not the scary kind, but the kind that could make a teenager forget how to respond to a greeting. Her hair color was obviously not natural, but that fire-red mane made him travel to a land that should only be visited in bed at night.

He thought he heard Trance say something. Trance had said something. Trance's grin was enough to bring him back to reality.

"I'm sorry, what was that?"

"She said you can take a seat over there and Mr. Rob will see you in a moment."

"Thanks," Anders mumbled, and sat down with a sigh that didn't mean he was tired, but just relieved that he didn't have to look directly at the girl's face.

Trance said some things to the girl, and then told Anders that the house manager would arrive later to take him to his residence.

For the second time that day, Anders' chest was heavy. When he heard 'residence' and remembered that it was going to be where he would be living with other trainees, he wasn't excited. He wanted to head home in that moment. He wanted to step into the kitchen and bite into a piece of warm bread from his dad's bakery. He wanted to run out of the house into the hot sun while carrying his mom's lunch bag and trying not to shake its content.

"Anders Quigley," a high sing-song voice called his name making his heart lurch. "Mr. Rob will see you now."

He thanked her without making eye contact. He pulled his suitcase and opened the only door he noticed in the cube-like reception area. He was greeted by the light scent of lavender and a bright office. The room was large and seemed to have windows for walls. He didn't see anybody behind the large desk, and then he heard someone behind him, but he didn't jump.

Mr. Rob, he presumed, had just taken some bottles of water from a refrigerator that was in the corner of his office.

"Hi," Anders said as he bowed a bit. He thought it was weird after he did that, but he saw that it brought a quick smile to Mr. Rob's face that disappeared immediately. But he was sure he'd seen it. Mr. Rob said hi back and handed a bottle of water to Anders and pointed to a seat. Anders took the chilled bottle, leaned his luggage close to a bookshelf that was located on the only wall in the office, and walked over to take a seat, placing his backpack on the floor.

Now, Mr. Rob was not what Anders would have pictured in a million years. CEOs, to him, should exude an air of importance around them just because they were swimming in money. They were allowed to be fat and flashy, but Mr. Rob was thin, almost skeletal, and plainly dressed. Then Anders saw his wristwatch and nodded inwardly. No mere person would casually wear a Hysek like that, a watch that should be in a password-protected display case. Anders was a watch enthusiast, but one who couldn't afford any of the watches he admired. Maybe he'd be able to afford one if this FFQ 'thing' took off, he mused.

"I hope you had a smooth journey."

"Yes," Anders replied after he swallowed the gulp of water, and tried to act indifferent when he heard Mr. Rob's whiny-nasal voice. It was unexpected and all Anders could think was that he sounded like someone in pain. He tried to look at Mr. Rob again as covertly as he could, just to make sure he was okay, because his outward appearance was questionable. The good thing was though that Mr. Rob had okay coloring. He didn't look like a sick emaciated person. He just looked like he could use some flesh on his skin and some honey water for his throat.

"Good, good. Have you had something to eat?"

"Yes."

He nodded with satisfaction. "I am happy that you are here with us," he said as he opened a folder and peered into it. Anders recognized the photo of the person on the comp card in the clear sheet protector. His face looked like he was bored to death, but eager enough that he'd been particularly excited to have his picture taken that day. The photo's outcome wasn't all that surprising to him because his face just did that naturally.

Mr. Rob pulled an opened laptop toward him and scrolled something. He didn't say a word, but just continued to nod and look at both folder and laptop screen. Then, when it seemed like he was satisfied with whatever he'd searched for, he raised his gaze to Anders and said, "We'll have a group-pick in two days. This is when the coaches and I will find out your level and see how much training you'll need."

Level of what? Anders thought. He had no training whatsoever, but he nodded.

"Benny will be here shortly to take you to your residence."

"Okay. Thanks." That seemed to conclude their meeting. Mr. Rob was still looking at laptop screen and Anders took that to be the 'we are finished here' signal. So he stood up and went to pick up his luggage. When Mr. Rob said nothing or even looked his way, he decided to leave the office and go back to the reception area and wait for Benny there.

As he closed the door behind him, he was met with the side profile of doll face and her long fiery red mane. She looked at him and smiled with a nod. Anders thought he was going to burn on the spot. He nodded and averted his eyes quickly as he thought of where would be the best place to sit. The sing-song voice said, "Anders, you may wait in that room right there if you prefer."

He had no choice but to look at her to see which door she was pointing to, because he could have sworn that Mr. Rob's office door was the only one in the vicinity. He had been wrong. There was a door that could easily be missed if one was new because the door looked like part of the wall. The only thing that gave it away was a thicker square panel on it that was probably where people pushed to open it.

He said thanks to her, but stopped on his heels. Where were his manners? He turned around and walked closer to her. "I'm sorry I didn't get your name?" he said, as he looked into large half-moon shaped eyes with unusually large-sized green lenses that were definitely contacts. She looked unreal, like an anime character that had lost her way, because an office setting didn't fit her look unless she was on her way to an anime convention after work.

She chuckled softly. "That is my fault. I forgot to introduce myself."

Anders caught his grin and warned himself silently to behave like a normal person.

"My name is Jiju," she said.

He nodded and said thanks.

The door was pushed in and Anders looked up from his phone to see a boy or man, he couldn't tell from the face, but the mature look made Anders suspect he was older. This man was round, red-cheeked and seemed friendly. He wore shorts that were a bit too tight on his stomach and he had tucked in his shirt.

"Anders!" the man called out with a modulated voice as though they knew each other.

Anders got up as the man approached him with his hand stretched out.

They shook hands and the smiling face said, "My name is Benny and I am the house manager of 'F' House."

Anders nodded like he knew what the man was talking about. At least he could guess that there were A, B, C, D, E houses, unless the houses were only named after the Agency's initials, then it would just be F and Q. He didn't bother asking because he was going to find out soon enough anyway.

"Have you eaten?" Benny asked.

"Yes," Anders responded, noting that he would never starve here when people kept asking if he had eaten.

"We will take the elevator to the lobby. I have parked a cart outside that we will use."

This news was welcome because Anders was beginning to feel fatigued.

"You need help?" Benny pointed at Anders' suitcase after he'd grunted when he hung his back pack on his shoulders.

"No, thank you."

Anders made it a point to stare at Jiju this time when he entered the reception area. She raised her head and smiled at them. Benny said something to her in another language and she responded with a small head bow. They walked silently, Benny leading Anders, who vaguely remembered getting into the elevator, as his mind still had Jiju's baby-doll face up, front, and center.

He snapped off his fantasy when the elevator bell rang as it readied itself to descend. He knew he was going to see her soon so that comforted him.

"Jiju is Mr. Rob's daughter-in-law."

And just like that, bile rose in Anders' throat. He acted as though the revelation didn't faze him and just nodded.

Benny chuckled, forcing Anders to look at him inquiringly.

"You should see your face," Benny said.

"What's wrong with my face?" Anders asked with a measured tone, making sure to try his best not to sound disrespectful, because he didn't know Benny's age and he knew he was in a land where seniority was taken seriously.

"You look disappointed. I was too when someone said the same thing to me. I'm kidding. She's his sister- in-law. Mr. Rob is married to her sister."

Anders exhaled and nodded. "Really?" he asked with a hint of a smile.

"That's why she can get away with the way she dresses. Staff is not allowed to dress like idols, but Mr. Rob lets her."

Anders stirred and reviewed, Benny's statement as it dawned on him that he was going to get a makeover in order to debut with the Agency, and he wasn't looking forward to what they might do to his appearance. Urgh! He hoped strongly that they wouldn't change him drastically, worse, recommend plastic surgery. His dad would have a heart attack, he mused inwardly.

There was a ruckus taking place in the lobby just as the elevator doors opened. "Anti-fans" he heard Benny murmur. No one needed to explain to Anders what that meant. What he didn't understand was how they'd gotten in. This building had seemed excessively secured when he'd come in earlier. Someone must have left their post unmanned or the Anti-fans were just too clever.

Benny skillfully took some turns and Anders followed. Soon, they were looking at a light blue and pink colored cart. Anders didn't know what to make of it. It looked like it belonged to a toddler and would break down if they both rode it. Benny lifted Anders' suitcase and placed it in the back seat, securing it with a hooked belt. He pointed to the front and Anders took his seat. Soon, they were riding along paths between high flower beds, trees, and colorful structures. People were staring at Anders as though he were a fresh catch, and some who knew Benny greeted him as he cruised by. Benny was calling out names of places as he drove past. Anders didn't bother memorizing them. He just wanted a bed because he was beginning to get a bit light-headed and sleepy.

Benny rounded the cart into a structure that looked like it was built for small vehicles, and after he parked it, he jumped off the cart like he weighed nothing. Anders was impressed, but suspected that he had done that a thousand times and it was now a habit.

He pulled his suitcase behind Benny, who had just scanned a keycard on the door to a building that was much older than the office buildings a few blocks away. As the main entrance opened, they were greeted by a smell of cleaning essentials and artificial flowery fragrances. It seemed like the cleaning crew had just left the building.

Benny straightened as he walked in, as though getting ready for serious business. Anders didn't know what to make of it, but he walked quietly behind. Soon they were in a large lobby that had different facets to it. There was an area with a large flat-screen TV screwed on the wall, surrounded by sofas and loveseats and some cupboards. No one was there. However, not too far away was a pool table and, around it, three boys were arguing about something.

None of them paid any heed to Benny and he didn't disturb them either. A boy was carrying a large gallon of water on his shoulder and he bowed his head a bit toward Benny. He looked at Anders curiously, but continued on his way.

"I'll give you a tour of the house when you drop off your luggage. Let me show you your room."

Anders followed quietly as they made their way to the stairs. Benny turned to see if Anders needed help, but he shook his head no.

When they got to the landing, there were sounds of a video game coming from a room. Other doors were closed, and as they continued down the hallway, Anders peered swiftly into the rooms that were open. Clothes were strewn on the floor of some, just like a typical boy's dormitory.

There was a room that looked like a common sitting room with a TV, and on the far side was a boy with a blond-white Mohawk style haircut, hunched at a table writing. Benny stopped as though he wanted to say something to the boy, but he decided against it and continued on. Boys ran past them at speeds that would have caused damage if they hadn't dodged Benny and Anders in time.

Benny cursed under his breath in another language. Anders was sure it was a curse. He'd learned that one pretty quickly on the internet. They finally got to a room at the end of the hallway with its door slightly opened. Anders could hear laughter coming out from it.

Benny pushed the door ajar and the laughter ceased immediately. Two pairs of eyes were trained on them. One boy sat on the lower bunk bed and the other sat wide-legged on the floor with sheets of paper in front of him.

All traces of laughter had left the face of the boy sitting on the bed. Anders immediately felt a wave of dislike coming from him. This boy was slim but well-built. He was all muscles. Anders immediately sensed that he was a gym rat because his forearms where a bit veiny for someone so young. He had long straight dark hair to his neck and some blond streaks in it. Although his face had lost the roundness of youth, he couldn't be over eighteen or nineteen.

The other boy who sat on the floor was a bit smallish. He wore an oversized white T-shirt and sweats. His hair was buzz cut and dyed blond. His face was pudgy even though he was skinny. Unlike the boy sitting on the bed, this one had a friendly demeanor and looked up with an amused expression.

They both greeted Benny, and the boy on the floor got up and walked toward them.

"You're Anders?" he asked, sizing him up, but also addressing him with a silvery expression.

Anders nodded as Benny said, "Anders, this is Alphonso," and then pointing at the boy sitting on the bed, he said, "and Twine."

Twine ignored them and was looking intently at his laptop. Upon seeing this, Benny shook his head and Alphonso rolled his eyes.

"Welcome, Man," Alphonso said to Anders with a handshake.

Anders nodded as he tried to suppress the feeling of dread that was beginning to crawl over his body. He hadn't completely taken in the fact that he'd just moved to a different country, and was going to do God knows what, and now he had to share a room with an annoying roommate. What he didn't understand was why this boy named Twine was being an ass. The bedroom did look a bit cramped, but Anders was good at not getting in the way of people and things. Twine would soon realize it, Anders thought.

But Twine's attitude toward him was bothering him more than he'd expected. Thoughts of whether he should return home to where things were familiar were already moving in his mind. Benny snapped him back to reality by calling his name.

Anders acted as though he hadn't missed anything Benny had said earlier. "So, there is one more person who already shares this room. As you can see, there are two bunk beds. You have the top of that one," Benny pointed at the other bed in the corner of the room.

Anders secretly hoped that Twine's bed was the one he was sitting on. He didn't want to share a bunk with someone who didn't even know him, but had decided to act cold on their first meeting.

Benny went on to show Anders his own dresser and closet space. Then he asked Anders to leave his luggage behind and follow him to the box room, where he would keep his empty suitcase after unpacking.

"Twine finds it difficult to warm up to people," Benny said to Anders as they made their way to the box room. "Don't worry about his attitude, okay? If you have any questions, ask the others or give me a call with the phone in the TV room."

The box room was in disarray and Benny wasn't thrilled about it. In the short time from when he'd turned on the light of the room, to when he closed the door, a slither of curses had escaped his mouth. When he remembered that Anders was right there with him, he looked embarrassed, and explained that the boys never listened about putting their boxes and suitcases back where they'd gotten them from originally, and it was a lot of work to rearrange them all the time.

Anders nodded understandingly.

"Would you like to drop off your backpack in your room before I take you on a tour around the building?"

"It's fine," Anders responded. It had been hard enough for him to leave his suitcase behind. Not that he thought that the boys were going to steal from him, but he just didn't trust Twine not to try to do something to mess it up.

Benny started with their floor, which was the second floor of the residential building of F House. He gave Anders some background information about the house and all the superstars who were once trainees who'd lived in F House. He talked about how honored he was to be the house manager and how he thought he was doing a good job.

He showed Anders the bathrooms, laundries, common rooms, kitchens, but told Anders that it was best for him to eat in the cafeteria instead, until he got the hang of buying groceries and preparing food. He explained to Anders that there was a handbook in his dresser that he had to read. It contained the rules of the house and information about house meetings and outings.

The tour was so involved that Anders began to half-listen to Benny. Anders realized that Benny liked to talk, and he had done this tour so often, that words came easily to him and he didn't miss a beat. When the tour of the ground floor was done, and Benny had introduced Anders to some of the F housemates who'd met them during the tour, Anders told him that he could find his way back to his room.

Benny was impressed. "Have some rest and make sure you go to the cafeteria for dinner. Ask anyone or call me if you lose your way. One more thing, no cell phones allowed, so you'll have to hand it over soon. I guess you can keep it until the weekend." Anders didn't protest because he knew about the cell phone policy, but he wasn't looking forward to a life without it. "Did Mr. Rob tell you when you're reporting for group-pick?"

Group-pick. Anders remembered hearing that phrase. "I think he said in two days."

"That's great. You'll have a day of rest. Go with Alphonso or Trance to the auditorium."

Trance. That was the name of the boy who'd taken him to Mr. Rob's office. "Is Trance the third roommate?" Anders asked.

"Yes. He's going to perform with the boys this time. They're hoping to convince Mr. Rob that they're ready to debut. If you're to be part of them, then you'll have a lot of catching up to do. But don't worry about it. You must be very good for Mr. Rob to add you to their group, and you'll have great teachers too."

"Add me to what group?"

"I'm not sure yet. I'm just assuming that's why he put you in their room."

"Are they models?"

Benny blinked at his questions and chuckled. "Models? They're training to be in a boy's band."

Anders stopped. What? Okay, there must be a mistake, he thought. He was here to be a model.

"Well, I'll see you later. Call me if you need anything."

He watched Benny's retreating figure, and while still stunned, he thought that Benny was mistaken. Maybe there wasn't enough room and that's why he'd been assigned to room with the other boys.

When he got back his composure, he walked slowly to the stairs and took his time as he climbed up. He could hear someone singing and his musicality kicked in. If he were at home, he would have headed for the studio. Then he wondered again if Benny had been mistaken.

As he reached the door of the bedroom, he heard in clear English as Twine said, "I haven't trained so hard for four years for them to add someone to the group just like that. He doesn't even fit our image. It was hard when they added Trance, and now I've accepted that we're a good trio…"

He sounded temperamental and Anders imagined veins all over his face and twitches on his muscles. Twine wasn't pleased with the new development.

"When we were in *HeartB Entertainment* together, we agreed that we were switching to FFQ because they wanted to take us as a duo." Twine and Alphonso had apparently known each other as young boys, and Anders was beginning to understand why he was angry. They'd known what they wanted from a very young age, and it seemed like FFQ was mocking them by changing their concept.

"I understood Mr. Rob's vision as taking time to make us better, you know, making us learn to play instruments, too, because the fans would be thrilled. Fine, I got that. But how many voices do we need in the band? Or is he going to be a mime? I'll have to talk to Mr. Rob about this. I can't take it anymore."

Anders didn't feel good about what he'd just heard. He still hoped that there'd been a mistake, because he was here for modeling. That was what he'd signed up for, right?

He pushed the door open and walked straight toward his dresser, not looking at the faces of either Twine or Alphonso. In that moment, the thought that swirled in his head was to give up, pack his belongings and leave. He hadn't signed up to be in a band. He wasn't cut out for any kind of hate from someone who thought he was a joke. Why was he here, really? He asked himself again as he fetched the handbook from the top drawer.

Chapter 7 (Say What?)

Group-pick day. Anders was starved and in need of sleep. Since he'd moved in, a couple of days ago, he'd avoided leaving F House. Not because he wasn't good at socializing, but he'd found it difficult to know just where to start. For the first time in his life, he was clueless as to what he wanted to do with his time before training began.

He'd read the handbook and everything was straightforward to him. He'd gotten a short visit from Benny, who was satisfied to leave him alone, when he'd seemed to show he had a grasp on his new environment and the workings of things around him. Anders had answered all the basic questions that Benny had asked him about his timetable and schedule, locations of necessities, and if he'd needed help with anything.

It had all been an act of course, because while he knew everything that was on paper, he didn't know what he was expected to do with the information before group-pick day. And everyone had left him alone, including Trance, who seemed to always be by himself. Twine and Alphonso always came into the room and then left again almost immediately. Alphonso always nodded Anders' way, but Twine paid him no heed.

So Anders had stayed in the bedroom, snacked, and was always doing something on his cell phone. At some point in the day, he'd missed being asked if he had eaten. He knew where to go, but he didn't go. He seemed to be waiting for someone to ask him so he could say 'no, he hadn't eaten,' and then going along with that person. This was the same Anders who was independent, and liked being on his own and doing his own thing. It was as though since he'd arrived in this new country, his usual-self had disappeared. He now seemed to miss his mother so much, and needed a friend to talk to. He chuckled to himself when he remembered the saying, 'you never appreciate what you have until it's gone.'

He'd had a sleepless night on his first night at F House. The other boys had woken up in the morning, gotten dressed and left. Nothing was said to him other than a nod of acknowledgment from Alphonso and Trance. He'd taken a shower and just lain on his bed reading a comic. Everest had called him, and he'd had to clear his throat many times to stop from bawling. This would have raised an alarm and he was sure his mom would have asked him to return home. Anders didn't cry. He didn't always need his mommy. Something wasn't right. But his mom's excitement and words of encouragement over the phone, were enough to make him consider getting used to his new life and waiting to see where it would take him.

"Go and eat something," was his mom's last scolding before she'd said she was going to bed.

"Bye, Mom."

This morning was different. The energy in the room seemed to have changed. Even though Anders was hungry and droopy-eyed, he looked forward to leaving F House, and going to see what all the fuss was about regarding group-pick. He'd seen some videos online, and he'd seen how seriously they took both auditions and training. In fact, training wasn't automatically a ticket to debuting. Some people ended up not debuting even after training for many years.

One could call this molding process brutal because it wasn't easy. There were expectations that you had to meet and surpass if you wanted to have the full backing of the Agency. You had to be so good that the CEO wouldn't have any doubts about signing you to his company. Many had given up on this dream after years of hard work and not seeing the door crack open even a bit.

Anders had done his research and knew that this wouldn't be easy. He knew that training as a model wasn't as brutal as training for a band except for the issue of weight gain. So he knew that his underlying anxiety and his need to go back home, might have something to do with the fact that he might be training to be in a band. He said a quick prayer that that wouldn't be the case.

"Hey, Man," Trance said as he sat cross-legged beside Anders, who was crouched on the floor, tying his shoelaces.

"Hey," Anders responded, pausing what he was doing to hear Trance. Twine was already gone when Anders came out of the shower and Alphonso had just entered the room from the shower.

"We can hit the auditorium together after breakfast if you like. I know a shortcut."

Finally. Anders could feel his throat get hot and his eyes begin to well up. It was certainly a foreign emotion and he didn't want to embarrass himself, so he focused on his shoelaces and nodded. "Sounds good," he said.

Trance got up and went to pick up his backpack, which he opened and put some items on his dresser.

Anders was done with his shoes and he also went to pick up his backpack. Benny had called him and said he didn't need to bring anything to the auditorium but his energy and enthusiasm. He thought that was funny.

The cafeteria was buzzing with so many people there. Anders walked beside Trance, who'd said ahead of time that he only liked a cold breakfast, cereal, and the like, but he was going to take Anders to get some eggs and pancakes because he looked like he needed it. Anders didn't refuse it. In fact, the growl in his stomach was confirmation that Trance was right.

The lines moved fast, and in no time Anders was pointing at the food he wanted. Trance said he was going to prepare his breakfast after Anders got his food, just because he didn't want his cereal to get soggy before they took their seats. Anders' tray looked so full that Trance had a smile on his face when he saw it.

"You should be okay since you're not dancing," Trance said.

Anders looked confusedly at Trance.

"You don't want to have a full stomach if you're supposed to dance at group-pick."

Anders now understood. He took a look at his tray and decided to leave everything on. He hadn't eaten well in a couple of days.

"Also," Trance continued. "Watch your spending, unless you have a lot of pocket money."

Anders nodded. He knew he didn't have to worry about that, because his parents would gladly send him plenty of money if it was for food.

He followed Trance to a large table where a few people were already sitting. Those people were grouped on one end and Trance went to the other. Twine was not in sight.

The first bite of his scrambled eggs took him to a place that he had secretly longed for, the land of the living. He was beginning to feel his energy return, and in that moment, he swore not to take his meals for granted.

He watched Trance eat slowly while reading something in a small notebook.

"What's that?" he asked.

Trance looked up and saw that Anders was pointing to his notebook.

"A song. An uncompleted song. A song that is keeping me awake, because I can't get it perfect no matter what I do."

"Perfection? Is it the lyrics or what?"

"I have the lyrics down and extra lyrics," he chuckled. "I just can't get it to flow naturally. It sounds hitched in my ears."

"You can sing it to me sometime if you don't mind. I'm sure it's great. You just need someone else to hear it out."

"Mr. Rob also thinks the last verse isn't flowing smoothly and is too wordy."

"He's heard it already?"

Anders' surprised look made Trance laugh.

"I love music, Anders, but I don't usually bother so much on one song if it gives me problems. I'm only doing this because it's an assignment from Mr. Rob."

"So, you guys are required to write songs?"

"Not exactly. He doesn't give everyone the same assignment. I'm the only one of the three of us with the song-writing assignment. Twine is getting drum training, and Alphonso is working on editing and arranging songs in the studio. He's actually part of the group who is producing *The Stickers'* debut single."

Anders liked what he heard. It seemed like Mr. Rob was into discovering and honing talents. If this was the case, he didn't have to worry too much. If Mr. Rob noticed that he wasn't fit for a band, he'd have him train as a model.

"Well, I'll still like to hear what you've got later."

"Sure thing."

"Do you think I'm supposed to be in a band if I'm rooming with you three?"

Trance's face was thoughtful. "I'd think so. Or else you would have been assigned another room."

"I guess I'm asking because I thought I was here to be trained as a model."

Trance's eyebrows shot up. "I don't think that's the case, Anders," he said, laughing. "Do you sing?"

Anders sighed. "Yes."

"Then that's why you're here."

He had been expecting a very large room worthy of the name, auditorium, but when he entered, the room was what he'd call a large-sized conference room. He soon found out that not every potential artist was attending group-pick. No solo artists, hence the name, group-pick. Also, those who were supposed to attend were those who were potentially going to debut soon or those who still needed to convince the Agency that they were improving and deserved to be favorably looked upon.

Anders had the feeling that his three roommates were among those who would be debuting soon even though he hadn't seen them perform. Just looking at them, one could tell that they were seasoned trainees and ready to show the world what they could do. The fact that the CEO had already given them some important assignments was another positive indication. But one thing bothered him. Why would the CEO throw him among a mix that was almost ready to debut? Or was he mistaken and they weren't good enough?

His mind told him otherwise. They had to be good or else he wouldn't be added to their band. He took a seat beside Trance. They were at the back of some boys who sat cross-legged on the floor. People were seated around the room, creating a spherical shape in the middle that Anders guessed was the imaginary stage.

The CEO and those who were supposed to sit with him at a table in front of the stage weren't in attendance yet. Trance answered the question before he asked. "Mr. Rob usually does this with one of the executives, his assistant and the head music and dance coaches. They'll be here soon."

It was a wonder that even though there were a lot people in the small auditorium, it didn't get hot. Anders wondered if it was the powerful air conditioner or just the fact that he had felt a few goosebump moments. These kids weren't playing, he thought. They were all still young, yet they sounded and acted like people who've been in the entertainment business for a while. FFQ was certainly standing on a gold mine with its picks of talents. It was just a couple of groups that seemed off. One of them had one too many members in his opinion. One girl was over-doing it and making the others look out of sync. Mr. Rob didn't say a word. He hadn't said a word since he'd come in with the others. He was greeted, he took his seat, and his assistant was the one who reminded everyone why they were here

Anders wanted to ask Trance if this was Mr. Rob's usual manner, but he didn't need to. That seemed like the case because everything proceeded as it should. First, the assistant introduced everyone seated at the table. Then he talked about the Agency, its founding and mission. He went on ahead to mention the groups by the names of the people in it. This time, Anders was sure that he was meant to be with the three. He sighed silently. Their group was performing last, which Anders didn't like. The pressure was on after seeing what the others were doing. What bothered him the most, was that he didn't know what he was supposed to do. He hadn't seen his group perform, he hadn't practiced with them. They didn't know if he could add any helpful skill to their group, and most of all, he was not ready.

He had thought group-pick was going to be the formation of the groups only. He was shocked to see that it looked like a professional audition and a show of extraordinary talents for some. In the few short hours, he'd seen acrobatic moves with slick dance steps, heard voices with amazing ranges, and seen a show of instrumental skillsets. All the while, he sneaked peeks at Trance, who just seemed to be enjoying the show. Trance didn't seem bothered. Anders decided that there was nothing for him to worry about. He wished he could talk to Trance about it, but it didn't seem the time for chit-chat.

Anders located Twine, who sat on the end of their row. He watched the other groups with a straight face, as though he would have preferred to be somewhere else. It was a while before he found Alphonso, who was squatted in a corner, looking longingly at a trainee from a girl group. Anders looked away because it was embarrassing.

The group before Anders' was stopped midway. One of them had forgotten his lyrics and another member had slipped during a complex-looking dance move. Mr. Rob had raised his hands and the music had stopped. They all seemed to understand the gesture as the group left the stage. It appeared to Anders that he was the only brand-new trainee in the auditorium. Everyone had been with the Agency long enough to know how things worked. He felt uncomfortable about it and was dreading the fact that they were next.

When they all got up, Mr. Rob said, "Anders, return to your seat."

The quietness was eerie, but Anders was beyond thankful for the exception at that moment. He went back slowly to his original place, ignoring the stares from every corner of the room. Their reaction made it seem like he was in trouble, but that wasn't the case. How was he supposed to perform with a group out of the blue?

They started. It was Alphonso. He had stepped forward while Trance and Twine kept their original spots, all three dancing in unison. Then Twine started to rap. The next verse was picked up by Trance, and Anders couldn't hold his jaw in place. They were good. They were really good. Why weren't they out there selling out venues? If Anders had to answer his own question, it would be that Mr. Rob had a plan that no one else was seeing.

The reaction from the attendees after they finished could have brought down the ceiling. The cheers were loud and the whistles were piercing. Anders understood Twine's anger. There was no need for him to be part of their group. Trance's face was red with excitement as he made his way back to his seat beside Anders.

"Anders." He was woken up from his thoughts by the nasal voice that could only be Mr. Rob's. He got up and went to the spot that Mr. Rob pointed.

"You have an original song entitled, "*Notice Me.*"

Anders felt his ears begin to burn and his legs seemed like they would give way. How on earth did Mr. Rob know about *Notice Me?* He wondered if he'd been bugged by the Agency and watched back home. There was no way Mr. Rob could have known about the song let alone that he could sing. The only information he should have about Anders was that he was trying out to become an international model.

"Your mother submitted a rough cell phone recording of your singing this song, and even in that condition, your talent could not be denied. You enunciate well and your vocal range is very rare."

Anders didn't know when his hands went to his chest. He was sure that he was going to pass out. The shift in the room could only be that it was rare for Mr. Rob to compliment anyone without seeing them perform before him.

"I, I…" Anders stammered, clearing his throat and trying again. "I thought I was here to be a fashion model."

Mr. Rob's boney face took a squeeze like he'd smelled something foul. He looked at a list that was placed in front of him. The others on the table did as well. Then he looked up at Anders with a frown, sizing him up from head to toe. It was a long stare, which made sense because Anders was tall.

"Did you write a song called, *Notice Me?*" Everyone could hear the impatience and irritation brewing in my Mr. Rob's voice.

"Yes," Anders replied quietly.

"Have you ever sung it out loud?"

"Yes."

"I want to hear it."

He was sure that the air conditioner was definitely off. There was no way it could have been blowing like it had been earlier because now he was sweating profusely.

One thing was for sure. Anders now knew where the confusion originated from. His mom had taken it into her own hands to show the world what they'd been missing, as she usually said on the rare times he sang when she was in hearing range, outside his make-shift studio.

He relaxed his shoulders and parted his legs a bit, a stance he took unknowingly when he was about to sing. Mr. Rob's mouth twitched. It wasn't so much a smile as it was the satisfaction that he had found something rare.

He started low and then almost immediately jumped to a falsetto, a feat that can be difficult for singers because they could easily mess up the melody. Not Anders. Singing was just one of those art forms that he saw as a tool to aid in his practice of music recording. He had never pictured himself on stage as a singer. The closest he'd ever thought of himself being on a musical stage was maybe becoming a DJ. He had the voice to make the music, and the skill to mix and produce the music. He could easily have become a good DJ, but being in a band had never occurred to him.

Now he found himself in a room full of people who were going to be amazing musicians, pouring out his soul to them without his consent, just because his mom had decided to share one of the most emotional songs he'd ever written.

He raised his head up, not realizing that he had bowed, due to the emotion that the song created. The room was too quiet for comfort. He couldn't look anywhere but at the table with Mr. Rob and his counterparts. The music coach had his mouth shaped like an O. The assistant was rubbing his arms as though fighting off goosebumps. Mr. Rob's head was slanted, and his eyes were on Anders as though he were a hawk that had just targeted his prey. Anders didn't know what to do next. So he said, "Thank you," and was about to leave when Mr. Rob called his three roommates up to the stage.

"Take note. Anders, lead vocalist and focus instrument, piano; Twine, rapper and focus instrument, drums; Trance, vocalist and focus instrument, electric guitar; and Alphonso, vocalist, rapper, and focus instrument, bass guitar."

Chapter 8 (Formation and Transformation)

"The name of your band is "For-Runners," spelled F, O, R, not the number four." Mr. Rob explained, "The name is more of a play on words, and doesn't mean that your music is just for runners. The name came to me in my sleep, and I thought it was a strong name for a strong band with the talents that you boys have.

Benny was trying his best to paraphrase what he had written down in the meeting he'd had with the CEO, Trustees, and Managers of FFQ Entertainment. The four boys were in one of the small conference rooms in FFQ headquarters, and they were listening intently to the update about their group and the possibility for a potential debut date.

While Anders listened, he couldn't help but feel the dislike directed at him from Twine that had amplified after he was named lead vocalist. To be honest, he would have chosen Trance. Anders knew he was a good singer, but he thought that Trance deserved it for the time and training he'd put into yhe group. He didn't know how his voice would merge with the group and their style, but he tried not to think about that because he knew he had an adaptable vocal range.

Speaking of Trance, he was excited and didn't show any signs of disappointment in the pick. He had been waiting for this briefing from Benny, which proved that debuting was near.

Of course, that announcement was going to come from the CEO himself, but having a name made it closer to reality.

Alphonso looked and acted neither excited nor disappointed. He just kept calling out their group name, For-Runners, testing the sound of it and inserting it into sentences to see if it worked. He nodded his approval after chanting, "For-Runners! For-Runners!..." four times.

Benny eyed him and continued with his briefing. "At 2 pm today, wardrobe and makeup department managers will meet with four of you in the showcase room. Make sure you get there on time because Mrs. Jackson has a bad temper. They'll show you your band concept, so basically, they'll make you better-looking."

Alphonso snorted, "I want to keep my blond hair." Then he glanced at Anders and said, "Anders and Trance are the ones who need makeovers. Twine is fine."

Trance nodded enthusiastically, smiling too widely for Anders' taste. Anders started to pray silently that they weren't going to be required to wear any kind of body paint.

Okay, he would have preferred body paint over what he'd just seen in front of him. He and the boys were seated in a room full of racks and mannequins, and a large projector was on. Standing to their right was a man who'd introduced himself earlier, but Anders had forgotten his name. He was overwhelmed by his own thoughts, after a ridiculous-looking image was projected on the screen of how he was supposedly going to look when he debuted.

No, no, no, please…

"What's that face?" Mrs. Jackson, who'd taken a seat to the left of the boys, asked Anders.

Anders was still at a loss for words as he stared intently at the illustrations on the screen. The title was Anders' makeover, so there was no mistake as to the person who was supposed to look that way. His reddish-brown hair was going to be dyed pitch black. He didn't want to imagine what a contrast it would be to his fair skin. That wasn't as bad as his supposed style. He noticed that the tops looked like what girls would wear, shapely and tight. *What was that all about?*

He realized that the look that they were going for was broody and dark. For someone who never went through the 'emo' phase or particularly liked it, he was not a happy camper. The only things he seemed to like were his boots and the expensive-looking wristwatch. That's if they would actually give him something close to what the illustration showed.

It didn't end there. They were also going to be coached on mannerism and their public image. The man said something about Anders being the mysterious one, less vocal. It seemed like that was the only thing that was going to be true about himself because he wasn't one to be talkative anyway.

None of the boys made jokes or even tried to lighten the moment. It was dawning on them that this process meant a change of their identities. They were going to lose some of themselves and were they ready for that? Anders' change was drastic, they realized. So what was in store for the rest of them?

The next was Alphonso. They all noticed immediately that his hair color and length were different. The hairstyle was a side fringe with the hair dramatically falling on the front of his face and the color was brown. It would have sucked if Alphonso had to dye his hair to boring brown, but it seemed like that was his real hair color. The other thing that stood out was the style of the illustration on the projector. Alphonso was definitely going to lose his entire outfit because there was nothing baggy on that illustration. In fact, his style reminded Anders of the cool rockers, who paid attention and were particular about what they wore. He wouldn't have minded if that was the style that was chosen for him. He saw Alphonso's face and was glad that he had a partner in the sucky transformation.

Can anything anger Trance? He was too happy with his makeover. His hair was an undercut with blond tips and his tight pants were left be. The change he got was that his wardrobe had a lot of jackets without inner shirts. Instead, there were mixed pieces of necklaces that covered the exposed neck and chest slightly. Trance nodded as the man explained looks and what they were going for. Apparently, Trance didn't have to change his personality, but improve it. He was too shy.

Then came Twine's transformation, and it seemed like all the boys were looking forward to it, because they all straightened before the images appeared. Alphonso whistled and said, "I take back what I said earlier. Twine, you totally need this."

Twine, struggling to appear expressionless, could not hide the fact that he liked what he saw on display. His hairstyle was a pompadour haircut; the sides clipped close and the voluminous top styled upward. The other members knew it was the perfect haircut for his appearance and personality, and pairing that with the muscle Tees that were on the illustration, made Twine look like the super-star he truly was.

"The girls aren't going to know what hit them," Alphonso said with a grin.

"Hear, hear," Trance responded,

Anders didn't say a word, but he wholeheartedly agreed with what the others said.

Twine's jeans were black and distressed and his boots were full-on military style. What a drummer he's going to be, thought Anders.

"Mr. Kenny, have you heard anything about our debut date?" Trance asked.

Yeah…that's his name, Anders thought.

"No, Trance. For-Runners will be notified in due time. For-Runners," he repeated with a smile.

"Okay, my turn," Mrs. Jackson got up from where she had been seated quietly, looking at each member of For-Runners and accessing what she could do with their faces.

"You all are a beautiful bunch, thank goodness, but you two," she pointed at Trance and Anders, "need some work on that skin of yours."

Trance rubbed his face, Anders frowned.

"I'll be testing makeup shades for you all today."

"Makeup…" Anders grumbled and got a sharp eye from Mrs. Jackson.

"Yes, Anders, makeup! If you're going to call yourself a star, you had better look like one!"

Someone should lay off the caffeine, Anders thought.

Mrs. Jackson took a deep breath and then lifted a suitcase onto the table. "I will try to create perfect shades for you all, and document the numbers and mixes." Pointing at Alphonso and Twine, she said, "I know that you two tan easily so you'll visit me more often." She stared pointedly at Anders and said, "If you ask me, I think you need a bit of color."

Three months later and still there was not an official public announcement about For-Runners' debut. This was odd, considering that their group was perceived as a contender for a major following for FFQ, compared to other agencies which had started advertising new girl and boy groups. The boys, who had been more relaxed when they didn't have a band name, were now antsy and nervous. They knew they were a strong group and the CEO had acknowledged them, but no staff member, including their assigned manager, could explain why they hadn't gotten an official announcement as the others had.

It didn't make sense that preparations toward making them a band were going on, yet they were not being advertised and promoted. The boys had already started looking like the images that were forged for them, since makeup and wardrobe visited them before they attended any agency-held functions. Rumors about and the anticipation of the new boy band, had already started to blow up. People started to nickname them, and declare themselves fans of the pretty group that they'd gotten glimpses of at events of their senior label mates.

Twine still wasn't on speaking terms with Anders, but Anders, out of the corner of his eye, saw Twine acknowledge the fact that he thought a new method of promotion was being tested with their group. That was the only explanation that could fit what they thought FFQ was doing. Why would FFQ work so hard to make them look great, deem them talented, and then fail to promote them? There was no news that FFQ was lacking funds. It was impossible, with their power list of celebrities and idols, for them to be broke and not have enough funds to advertise their up-and-coming band. FFQ was trying another form of promotion and it had nothing to do with an advertisement, Anders suggested. FFQ wasn't giving any official statement about them, but they had them make small appearances here and there, and people noticed them, wondered about them, and talked about them. It could be a build up to their public announcement, but this method that FFQ was using for them was unfamiliar in the Agency's history. FFQ was known to do elaborate promotions and product captions in popular TV shows. But they had been weirdly mum about For-Runners.

Alphonso has been dancing as a backup for the senior label-mates for years as a trainee. That hadn't stopped after his makeover. People now noticed that he looked different, and the word about his debuting soon in a new band got stronger because of his new appearance.

Twine had gotten in a commercial as an extra with a speaking line. Trance was in a drama episode and was a scene stealer. These were done without a change in their contracts yet as trainees. Anders? Nothing. He tried not to think too much about it, because it would have been different if they had debuted under FFQ and he had no job to do. He still believed that something was off, but he knew the power of word of mouth, and decided to go with the belief that that was what FFQ was up to.

Anders couldn't believe how different things were. They were actually getting job offers and had real work schedules. Before their makeover, before they had a name, they'd just trained tirelessly, and only gone as far as being backup dancers and stand-ins at concert practices. It had been tiring and stressful, physically and mentally. Now they believed that they were as talented as they were told because they were working.

It was noticeable that, while the schedules included activities for Trance, Twine, and Alphonso, Anders' name wasn't there. He was still finding it difficult to grasp the new language completely, but other foreign idols were provided with language coaches and all they did was learn the lines they had to deliver and perfect the pronunciations and accents. Anders could do that if he had a TV commercial job. But he was assigned Trance's original assignment of song-writing. At first, he was worried that that was an indication that something was wrong, but he soon threw that thought out the window because he was enjoying his song-writing duty, which came with studio time privileges.

One day, Benny showed up at their room and asked only for Anders. This prompted frowns from Alphonso and Twine, but they said nothing. Anders had just taken off his 'girly top' and was already putting on a comfortable T-shirt, but had to change back into the top he'd just flung off. Mr. Rob wanted to see him at his office.

The boys had been taking photos earlier, which looked like promotional photos, but no one knew what they were for when the boys asked. Anders had had so much fun during the shoot, which proved to him that modeling could have been awesome. Due to his height, the photographer had played with his shape and angles, and made him do some extra poses and movements. He was asked to jump around with a guitar, and that was the coolest for him, even though his assigned musical instrument was a piano.

When they took a break to change outfits, Anders overheard comments from the photographer that he thought were interesting. The photographer said that it seemed that those made to look feminine, meaning Anders in particular, came off looking more masculine in manner. The photographer had wondered for a moment if wardrobe had made a mistake. Anders would have loved to be asked if he wanted to change his overall look, because being effeminate was posing difficulties toward his presentation. He looked at albums of other band members and saw how they favored poses like arms on their waists and jutted hips. These were mannerisms that would come only naturally to someone who wasn't too manly. It was funny when he heard the photographer call him the manliest of the group, yet he dressed the 'girliest.' Even Twine, and all his muscles, had a bit of softness to him that Anders was shocked to see.

Anders knew that culture had to do with the style and there was nothing wrong with it. He just had to get over the shock of seeing himself whenever they dressed him up. He had to admit that doing the photoshoot was one of the best times he'd had in his journey to becoming a musician. He would love to model more often if he was being honest with himself. But while doing the shoot, he admitted that singing was great, too, after he'd watched his senior label-mates perform at their concerts. He wouldn't complain, he thought, not after hearing his mom squeal in excitement when he told her about his makeover.

"I can't wait to see you in person," she'd giggled. "Do you look girly? You know I've always wanted a girl."

"Mom!" he'd screeched, red with embarrassment.

"I'm just saying. I have seen photos of idols and they wear makeup. They put on lipstick, too, did you know that? Did they put lipstick on you?"

"Okay, Mom, I think I'll have to stop this conversation because you're giving me the creeps."

She laughed heartily in the background. "All right, I'll try to tone down my excitement. Send me pictures. I need to see your makeover."

"Sure. I gotta go. Talk to you later."

"Don't forget…" He ended the call with a shake of his head, and a smile he couldn't stop from spreading over his face. His mother was going to have a swell time seeing her son with eyeliner and nail polish. "Eeeek!" he shivered. "Why, just why?" he groaned.

Mr. Rob was marking something on his table-top calendar when Anders stepped into his office. He greeted Mr. Rob, whose head rose up and looked at him for what seemed so eerily long that Anders started to shift his weight.

"Have a seat," Mr. Rob said, pointing to the chair that was opposite him.

Anders sat down and tried his best to look back at Mr. Rob, because for some reason he was nervous and was wringing his fingers under the table. He wasn't sure why Mr. Rob had asked to see him. He thought the office was unusually bright, but it was no different than his office always was with all the windows. Then he thought the lavender scent was stronger than usual, but he knew that wasn't the case.

"How are you doing, Anders? Everything okay?"

"Yes, thanks."

"Food good? No trouble, right?" It took Anders a minute to understand that the last word Mr. Rob had uttered was "right?" because of the nasal tone of his voice.

"All is well, thank you." Anders said, nodding with assurance.

"Good. I wanted to chat a little with you because as the leader of For-Runners, you need to know the basic direction we plan to go with your group."

Anders straightened up and listened attentively. Finally, what he and the boys had been wondering about, was going to be explained to him.

"The board of trustees and I have decided that For-Runners will work on a mini-album before debut. The idea at first was for the band to release a single before debut, a couple more songs after that and then work on an album. The change came about when we saw that your group seems to be gathering a large following without the first promotion push we normally do."

This was sugar in Anders' tea. So it wasn't bad news after all.

"I called you here as the leader, and as the person in the group whose song-writing skills have been applauded by our professional song-writing team."

Anders nodded, feeling his heart rate rise with excitement and anticipation about what Mr. Rob was going to say next.

"We have decided to record two of your songs and one of them will be the group's debut single."

Anders jaw dropped to the ground.

"Yes, it is almost unheard of. Only one solo artist has debuted with his own song in FFQ's history. But we decided that one of your songs is appropriate for your group's introduction to your current fans and potential ones."

Anders' mind started running a hundred miles per second, trying to figure out which song had been chosen. Then again he thought, two of my songs. Two! Then he wondered if they will be in English. Two! Two!

"Your group will be meeting for new contracts to be signed, and you will be presented with another contract for your songs. If you choose to agree with our terms, then we will certainly be using those songs in the debut mini-album. FFQ has the right to choose other songs, but yours was a favorite in our meetings and I wanted to let you know that your talent is not being overlooked. I'm sure you've wondered about your scheduling or lack thereof."

Anders nodded, still in shock.

"In coming weeks, you and the group will have various meetings about recording your album, and planning other group activities. Make sure you are working on your rapport with your group. I hear reports that you're still struggling with that. It can't be easy on those three to have someone new as the leader, a foreigner at that. But I had my reasons for choosing you, and I know that while you give off a quiet attitude, you are a good thinker and will do great as the leader."

Anders nodded.

"Get your group together and let them know what I have said today, excluding the bit about the songs you've written. That can only be made known to them when you accept the terms of the contract."

Anders nodded, realizing that that's all he'd managed to do since he heard the news about debuting.

"Benny will meet up with your group and give you more precise information about the scheduled dates for everything. Keep up your good work, Anders, and remember the FFQ mantra about being the better person. We cannot afford any scandals by a new group, so you have to step up as a leader, and pay attention to Benny's briefings about your behaviors outside the Agency."

"I will," Anders managed to say.

Mr. Rob flicked his hands, indicating that Anders could leave. Just as he got up and thanked him, Mr. Rob said, "One more thing. We are flying your parents down for a visit."

Anders turned around so fast that he got dizzy. Mr. Rob's eyes were trained on a sheet of paper on his desk and he didn't make a move to acknowledge Anders' presence or reaction.

"Thank you so much," Anders forced out, trying to hold back a well of emotion that was threatening to burst from his body.

There was the hand flick again and Anders closed the door behind him. He leaned on the door for a moment, until he remembered where he was and saw two large green half-moon shaped eyes trained in his direction. He gave her a small smile and resumed walking. His legs felt like lead, but it was for a good reason so he didn't mind. *I will wear a girly top for this,* he mused.

Chapter 9 (Hello Mom and Dad)

"Anders! Is that you?"

It all came rushing to the surface. He hadn't known how much he'd missed his mother until he heard her voice. Anders had been in the music studio listening to Twine rap in the recording booth. He had just told Twine over the microphone to repeat a certain verse that needed a bit of word enunciation and a trainee had interrupted him.

"Benny said it's important. You're needed in the downstairs living room."

The downstairs living room was where special in-house events took place. If the Agency wanted to celebrate a small scale event for an idol or a group or a staff member, they usually used that room. That room also served as conference room or informal presentation room for the board of directors. When Anders heard the venue, he knew it was indeed important and excused himself from the studio. The other music managers were there to continue with Twine's recording session, but Anders had wanted to be there for the whole session. After all he had written the song and knew what the outcome should sound like.

Anders followed the trainee, who was one of the best break dancers in FFQ. No one could mistake this boy with the rainbow-colored dye job and lightning fast moves. Anders couldn't remember his name and was hesitant to ask him because he had once introduced himself to Anders in the hallway. His closest friends called him Rainbow and it would be weird for Anders to call him that. He admired him a lot, especially because he was so young, but so good that no one could dispute it. In a perfect world, Rainbow would have debuted, but there'd been a rumor that until Rainbow agreed to fix his nose, which was a bit crooked as a result of a car accident, FFQ was going to leave him stuck as a backup dancer. Every lead representative of the Agency, solo artists or groups, were supposed to present a visual that the Agency was proud of. FFQ was known to go to great lengths to make their artists look perfect, but the rumor was a bit iffy because FFQ did not promote plastic surgery. A broken nose may be an eyesore for FFQ, but there was nothing makeup couldn't conceal, and FFQ had amazing makeup artists. There had to be another reason.

Anders sighed as he thought of this and glanced at Rainbow, who was looking straight ahead, oblivious of his thoughts.

Not long after, they saw Benny outside the elevator on the first floor. He saw them approach and straightened with a smile.

"Thanks, Rainbow."

Rainbow nodded, and gave Anders another nod, and was on his way.

Benny pressed the elevator button.

"What's his name?" asked Anders, pointing in the direction that Rainbow had gone.

"Kan Nam."

"Yes, sounds like it. Thanks. So what's the important occasion?"

"You'll see."

The elevator doors opened and they both walked in. Benny pressed the basement button. Soon the elevator bell dinged and the doors opened up to the hallway that was lit so brightly it was as though natural afternoon light flooded in. The living room was to the right and Anders could see that the door was propped open. There was no music, so he guessed that there was no party or get-together going on. The quiet events were usually meetings so that was a possibility. Maybe this had to do with meeting high personnel on the board, or probably a company that wanted him as a brand ambassador. Then he stopped short just outside the door when he heard the familiar laughter. *No way!*

He hurried in to see his father's back and his mom's wide eyes and ear-to-ear grin. "Anders! Is that you?" she shrieked and ran into her son's arms.

Anders held on tightly to her and before he knew it, he was shaking from hitched breathing as tears rushed down his face. He was happy and couldn't understand why he was crying, but he didn't care. He had his mom and that's all that mattered in that moment.

She still had her vanilla scent about her, funny she hadn't lost it on the long trip here. Her hug still felt the same as from his childhood, funny he still remembered that. The difference now as they hugged was she gripped her hands together so tightly that he felt his ribs protesting.

It was the clearing of throat that brought him back to his senses and he remembered they weren't alone in the room. In fact, his dad had been talking to someone. He loosened himself from Everest's arms and quickly wiped the tears off his face. She still had the weird grin on her face.

"Yes, this is my Anders," she said, looking incredulously with tilted head at his face. She stepped backward and looked him over and started to laugh. "Wow," she exclaimed.

The throat clearing happened again and Anders turned toward the sound. He walked purposefully to Feng and hugged him quickly. Not as intense as Everest's hug, but a hug all the same. Anders couldn't even remember the last time he'd done this with Feng.

Feng patted his shoulders. "Good to see you, Son."

He still hadn't found his voice so he nodded.

Feng had been talking to someone Anders knew him as the man who was always with Mr. Rob. He quickly looked around the living room to see if Mr. Rob was around, but he wasn't. Apart from Anders, his parents, that man and Benny, there was only one more person who was busying with a light fixture at the corner of the living room.

The man said to Anders, "Spend some time with your parents and show them around. Give Benny a call later when they're ready to go back to their hotel. They're at *The Imperial.* Mr. Rob has prepared a full tour day for them tomorrow and you'll be accompanying them as well."

"Thanks," Anders managed to say.

The man nodded, shook Feng's and Everest's hands before he left. Benny nodded toward them and left as well.

Everest let out a giggle that she had clearly been holding in. "What did they do to my son?" she laughed as she touched Anders' hair.

"Stttoooppp!"

"You look good, Honey, really. Don't you think so, Dear?" she asked Feng.

Feng narrowed his eyes, as though trying to make up his mind about something. But he ended up nodding. "Yeah, you look cool."

Anders' cheeks were red with embarrassment, since his parents were watching him like a baby goat that they were contemplating buying as a pet. He felt really uncomfortable and hurriedly changed the topic.

"When did you get in?"

"Just this morning. Your boss said we should have some rest, but I couldn't wait to see you," Everest said. If only she'd stop smiling, Anders thought. It was getting on his nerves.

"He's the CEO, Mom, not my boss."

"Same thing," she said as she sat across from him, folding her legs and touching her chin.

"You're making me uncomfortable, Mom," Anders said, frowning.

"I'm just admiring you. I didn't know you could look so cool."

"Urgh!"

Feng laughed as he took a seat too.

"You look healthy and your skin is glowing."

"Argh, Mom! It's makeup."

"Well, your makeup person is very skilled. I can't find any zit on your face. You know the one you usually get on your forehead? It's not there anymore."

Anders shook his head. "I'm glad you're happy."

"Aren't you also happy?" she asked.

"I'm okay."

"That's 'speak' for he's happy too," Feng said.

Anders was very happy indeed. It was so nice to see his parents, and the fact that they were so relaxed about seeing him after his makeover was great. He'd wondered if it would be a shock for them, but they were taking it way better than he'd imagined. Now, the sore subject. "Don't you think I look a bit feminine?"

"You do," Feng said without hesitation.

Anders' stomach sank. He knew he did look feminine, but hearing confirmation from his dad made it real. His dad wasn't one to beat around the bush and whatever he said meant a lot to Anders.

"But isn't that the look you're going for?" Feng asked.

"I like it," Everest said.

Anders sighed. "I guess so," I just wish they'd tone it down a bit."

"Can't you suggest it?" Feng asked.

"Sweetie, he's still new and shouldn't be making demands already. Baby, when you become really popular you can ask them. It's not as bad as you think. I think girls out there these days dig this look."

"Umm, I don't know."

"It's true. One of my students, Logan, comes to school in tight jeans and chains everywhere. He also dyes his hair all the time. Chicks dig it. I'm sure if I were in their generation and —"

Throat clearing.

"Anders, it's not as bad as you think. They're professionals and they know what they're doing. Just go with the flow and enjoy yourself."

"Son, if it gets too uncomfortable, say something. No, it's not your style, but you pull it off well."

"Really?"

"Really. You look like a rock star."

With that said, Anders took in a deep breath and decided to take his parents' word for it. They thought he looked cool and that wasn't such a bad thing.

Anders had to admit that Mr. Rob was a charming man, even though he looked sickly sometimes. He was surprised to see a different side of the CEO. He was smooth with Everest and his mom was falling for it. If Everest had had any worries about her son's new occupation, it was gone with the wind. Mr. Rob praised Anders' talents, talked about all the opportunities on the table for For-Runners, his group, and their potential as super-stars. Even Anders started to day-dream about what For-Runners would achieve in years to come.

Feng didn't look skeptical, but he wasn't as easily swayed by Mr. Rob as Everest was. He asked questions and made sure all was understood. In the manner of an over-protective father, he made sure all the lines in the contracts were explained, and he also asked Anders what he thought about certain things. At one point, Anders wondered how people without good parents faired in life; who looked out for them? He was definitely a lucky kid and he knew it.

Their tour had gone smoothly. It was a chance for Anders to see some new places as well. Since he'd become a trainee, he hadn't had an opportunity to plan a trip or an outing because his breaks weren't long. He used his break times for sleeping in and composing music.

Benny had accompanied them along with a driver from the Agency. Everest had shopped a bit and Feng had test-driven some impressive electric cars. When Anders was recognized by a group of teenage girls at the mall, he decided to put on his sun-glasses and hat. Everest thought it was hilarious and was teasing him as they walked over and asked for his autograph.

They later went to lunch with Mr. Rob at a popular fried rice restaurant, and it was after this lunch that they headed back to FFQ headquarters to take a look at some paper work.

Anders knew when his dad was a hundred percent okay with the contract terms because of a sigh. Just like his mom, the sigh was usually his sigh of satisfactory completion to whatever task he was doing. Anders had heard that a lot when his dad finished baking something perfectly or repairing something back into wonderful condition. Hearing that sigh assured him that all was well. Everest got the cue with the sigh, too, because she relaxed visibly after hearing it, taking a comfortable position on her couch.

When Mr. Rob put away the papers, he apologized to Everest and Feng for not being able to take them around personally, and not being able to see them off tomorrow when they would continue on to their next vacation destination. They dismissed his apologies and told him that they understood. He was a very busy man after all.

"Whoa! She's so beautiful," Everest said to Anders, who pretended he didn't hear her. She was referring to Jiju, who'd bowed and waved them good bye before returning to her computer.

Feng chuckled quietly.

Their next stop was F House. Anders wasn't going to take them to his dorm room. Parents and visitors weren't allowed there anyway. Everest wanted to meet his fellow band mates and Anders knew she wasn't going to forget. He'd left them to watch TV in the lounge on the first floor. Two female trainees had gotten up when they approached and Everest noticed how the girl with the light-blue-tipped hair ogled at her son. This made her pat herself in the back for making one hell of a good-looking boy.

Trance was the only one in the dorm room and Alphonso was picked up from the game room before they all headed downstairs. Although Alphonso said he'd seen Twine earlier playing video game, he didn't know where he'd gone. When they came out of the elevator on the first floor, Twine was standing on the opposite side with a couple of boys. One was a trainee, the other a cleaner with a broom.

"Hey, good, you're here," Alphonso said.

Twine frowned at him.

"My parents want to meet you all," Anders said.

At first Twine acted like he didn't hear Anders and was about to enter the elevator as the others filed out, but he stopped mid step, looked at Anders and asked, "Where are they?"

"Lounge."

The boys all walked quietly as though they were heading to a concentration camp. Good thing no one was there to notice them because it looked a bit disturbing. Anders wondered why. He hoped it had nothing to do with the fact that the other boys hadn't been visited by their parents in a while. But he was sure that they were visited when they were new to FFQ.

Everest's laughter could be heard when they got to the corner near the lounge. She turned as she heard approaching feet, got up and walked quickly toward them. She gave Twine a hug, which might have startled him a bit because his eyes went wide and his hands hung loosely to his sides. Then he hugged her back before stepping away. Her hands instinctively went to his face, like mothers did when they admired a young boy who'd grown up right before their eyes, only this was the first time she was meeting Twine. He clearly didn't know how to respond to this warmth and didn't know where to rest his eyes.

"You are such a good looking young man. How are you?"

"Fffinnne," he stuttered, looking pleadingly at Alphonso, who was beside him. Alphonso shrugged with a cheeky smile on his face.

"He's Twine, Mom," Anders said.

"Twine? Like the thread?"

Twine smiled. "Yes, Ma'am."

Feng had already walked to where Everest stood, and shook Twine's hand.

Then Anders pointed to Alphonso and introduced him to Everest and Feng. Everest smiled widely. "Such beautiful eyes."

Anders had never noticed it before. His mom was right. Alphonso's eyes were an interesting shade of brown, a little murky at the pupil, but warm-looking in the iris like the effect of a drop of honey in tea. Alphonso's ears were notably red and he looked down as he became shy.

My mom is out to embarrass everyone, Anders thought.

When she turned toward Trance, she cooed unmistakably like she had encountered a baby.

Oh my goodness! Anders covered his eyes with his hands.

Trance loved the attention. In fact, he hugged Everest so tightly that Alphonso pinched his back to bring him back to reality.

"You're so cute," Everest said. "You look livelier than your name, my dear."

Trance smiled widely.

Anders shook his head and interrupted.

"Trance plays the electric guitar, Alphonso plays bass, and Twine is drums."

"I'm so proud of you boys. It isn't easy at your age to take on such huge tasks, so well done," Feng said.

"Thank you," they all said in unison.

Everest's eyes were watering as she said, "I'm sure your families are proud of you, too. Kids your age are out there playing around, but you have decided to make use of your talents to create special gifts for your fans. Be good, okay. You all seem like a wonderful group here, and I know you'll look out for each other."

She now looked at Twine. "Please take care of my baby – "

"Mom!" Anders protested.

"I know, I know, you're not a baby, but you're my baby. Boys, please take care of him for me."

They nodded, Trance, marveling at taking care of Anders, who clearly looked and acted more mature than they did, well, maybe except for Twine.

"Feel free to get in touch with us if you need anything. Anders is your brother, which makes me your mom, okay?"

"Yes, Mrs. Quigley," Alphonso answered loudly, which drew laughter from everyone.

Chapter 10 (Friend or Foe?)

They were in the same group and working toward the same goals, but anti-fans just loved to pit them against each other. Anders had his core fans and Twine had his. Anders was immediately categorized as mysterious, yet delicate. Twine was seen as macho and a playboy. Anders' fans had a knack for accusing Twine of mistreating him, the group's leader. Videos never captured the whole truth and photos were even worse, but the fans were so disillusioned that they created a whole universe of the boys feuding with each other. If Anders had his expressionless face, it was equivalent to a "pity stare," or "sad pout" and they would immediately point their fingers to Twine, because he had to have been the cause of Anders' sadness. It couldn't have been Alphonso or Trance because those two were nice and supportive of their leader. Twine just wasn't.

The boys had officially had their first appearance as a band on one of the most popular talk shows in the country. This development came after a meeting with the group, management, and CEO himself. For-Runners was increasingly becoming well-known in the public and on bloggers-sphere, and FFQ decided to introduce the boys, in order to reduce the speculations and lies out there. People were confused as to who the new boy band was, and if they were stand-alone or a unit of an existing band. This confusion began when a popular blogger speculated that two band members of a veteran band were being replaced by Alphonso and Trance, when the boys were seen in a practice video with the popular band.

Also, it didn't help that For-Runners' name was being spelled wrong on websites and magazines, and the members were being misidentified. The first thing that FFQ did was to quench this fire before it started, by officially adding the boys to the Agency website as a group, with the photos they'd taken of them after their makeovers. A short bio accompanied their photos, and some behind-the-scenes photos of them hard at work were also included. It was time to introduce the boys the right way. FFQ's website crashed several times that day. The Board agreed that For-Runners was ready to be promoted widely, and the Agency did it with a bang with appearances on a talk show, a music show, and a variety show within weeks.

The boys had been warned to stay off social media for the moment. They were new, and new bands were always doused with criticisms even before they served anything to the public. The public needed to know the boys well, so that they could warm up to them and declare themselves fans. But Trance had mistakenly opened a webpage that made him gasp when he saw what was posted there. He looked at Anders and prayed silently that their group was going to survive the hate. Terms that spanned from 'foreigner' to 'skinny gay' were used to label Anders. As he closed the webpage, Trance assured himself that the vibes he'd sensed from Anders when they'd first met, made him confident that he was going to be fine no matter what. He was a strong, well-focused guy, and bad labels wouldn't bother him, he hoped.

Some people who were sensitive in nature wouldn't be able to take in hateful terms toward them. Bands have suffered disbandment due to issues like fan-hate, because the targeted member took the hateful words to heart, which caused rifts, and made them give up on the dream, or even worse, cause themselves harm.

So-called anti-fans, who were usually fans of other competing bands, would create false accusations and rumors to shake the band they were against. Sometimes they lacked empathy for the band members they disliked, forgetting that these were human beings with feelings.

A war of fans usually arises, as the fans of the targeted group fire back to defend their idols. Sometimes it got so bad that some idols attempted to take their own lives, as they are made to believe the hoax that they are hated by everyone.

FFQ tries to pay attention to fan wars and tries to quell the heat. They send messages for their bands to stay off the internet while they do this, because the cyber-world is notorious for horrible celebrity attacks.

It was with this warning that Trance placed a fake smile on his face and worked on distracting Anders, because he didn't want to find out if Anders could take the hate or not. People may appear strong on the outside, but some really aren't. There have been celebs that've ended their lives and hadn't looked weak outwardly. Trance drew Anders' attention to the roster.

For-Runners had been assigned more time on the roster of the large music room at FFQ. This music room was equipped with a sizeable dance choreography room, voice practice room, stage room, and studio. The boys were in the stage room with their musical instruments today. They'd finally finished recording the last music for their debut mini-album and listened to the final cut of all six songs days before. Trance and Alphonso had cried so hard, that if anyone had seen them they would have thought there was a death in the family.

This is real, Anders kept chanting. Twine was noticeably friendly and talkative. In fact, he commended Anders on his vocals, saying that he was happy Anders was a part of the band, and he'd known Anders was 'something' when he'd sung on group-pick day, and then he gave Anders a quick hug. This stunned Anders for sure.

"*Notice Me*," the song Anders had sung on group-pick day, the song his mom had shared without his knowledge, the song that he wouldn't have sung out loud for people to hear, was one of the songs that was chosen for the mini-album. Anders was at a loss for words when he heard the final cut of his song. They'd recorded it in English. It had been refined beyond his imagination, and he agreed that it was a really good song for their debut album. The other song, the one that was going to be their debut single, was one that he'd written recently, entitled, "*Where Are You?*" He'd written this song in one of his homesick, lonely moments in the TV room at F House. He'd heard one of the music coaches say it was 'hauntingly beautiful,' and he had to throw away his humbleness and agree with him. He was still shocked at the ease with which he'd composed it, but most importantly, he didn't understand why such a song would be chosen as their debut single. It had too many feelings in it, as people would say, and it just didn't seem like a song that should be sung first thing in the morning. But the Agency knew better. They'd been in the business for a while. They understood the concept they were going for, and Anders had no reason to disagree, since he had no experience and no say in the matter whatsoever.

"Ah, ah, ah," Anders warmed up his voice.

A jumble of musical instrument sounds went on as Twine, Alphonso, and Trance got ready. The sign on the door had said, "Practice in Progress." No one was going to interrupt them in the stage room for three hours, because they were practicing hard for their first TV talk show appearance. It was now known around the Agency that they were going to perform their debut music live on a popular talk show, and that the album was going to be released on the same day.

Some people felt excitement for them, while some thought that everything seemed a bit rushed, and wondered if the boys were ready and would be able to handle the pressure. But the boys were not complaining. They just had to focus. They'd trained for this moment for quite a while, and this was the right time for them to reap the rewards

Anders took in a deep breath and looked at the others. Twine nodded and hit his sticks together before giving the drum some soft thumps. Then Trance followed and then Alphonso.

When Anders had written this song, he'd written it as a piano piece. But it had been rearranged for the other instruments, and become a magnificent work of art. As the strings called for Anders, with his legs slightly parted, shoulders relaxed and eyes closed, he answered with a voice so smooth that his fellow band-mates had grins on their faces.

Where are you?
I can't see anybody
Are you there?
Noooo?

Can you hear my voice?
If you're listening please open the door
I can't see it is dark
Light it up and show me the way

Where are you?
I can see nobody
Are you there?
Say something

All you have to do is whisper
I need to hear you
I can't hear you
I can't see you
Don't need to scream
Just say a word
Whisper something

Open the door
Please turn on the light
I need to see you, I need to see you...

Where are you
I can't see anybody
Are you there?
Noooo?

On the morning of the talk show, the weather was unusually crisp, as opposed to the days before that had been non-stop rainfall. Anders took it as a sign that all was going to go well, and he didn't need to worry about the tense atmosphere at FFQ. Mr. Rob had disapproved of the order of the directors' planned programs, and a few entertainment companies had lost bids on getting the boys on their shows. There had been rumors that some companies had been promised the boys' time, and even went so far as leaving monetary favors on the table for some directors at FFQ. This caused much tension in the Agency, and it wasn't a happy time for some, but the boys couldn't help feeling excited. Their time was finally here.

Their van passed a crowd of screeching teens, mainly girls, as it went into the underground garage. Anders seemed to be concentrating on his tightly entwined hands, Twine's finger was drumming out a tune on the seat handle, Alphonso was making pop sounds with his lips and Trance was giggling. Trance seemed to be the only one not pretending to have noticed the crowd. The others were acting like it was a normal occurrence, which was far from the truth.

When the van stopped, Benny, who was seated at the back, told them to wait until they heard otherwise. There was a man who sat beside Benny and another man who was in the passenger seat in front and they were the hired guards for the group. Then there was the driver, too. Both guards left the van and headed to a corner that supposedly was the entrance. They were back within minutes and told everyone that they could exit the van. They were led to an elevator, which they took to a level labeled 'G2.' The elevator doors opened to reveal a tired-looking man with sagging shoulders who'd buttoned his shirt wrong. Twine caught Trance's collar when he noticed that Trance had taken a step toward the man. Alphonso snickered and Anders was expressionless.

The man greeted them, introduced himself and said he was going to lead them to the floor where the office of the talk show was located. One of the guards stayed behind as the man entered the elevator and pressed '8.' The door opened up to reveal two women standing with smiles that were too bright for that time of the morning. "Hi," they both shrilled in unison. It seemed so practiced and off-putting, that even Trance was a bit startled by this, because they sounded honeyed. One of them had a startling red dye-job on her hair that made it seem like it was going to drip red if water touched it. The other had the typical bowl-cut of a conservative woman who didn't like to waste too much time on how she looked.

They also introduced themselves and Miss red-dye said she was in charge of making them camera-ready, doing their makeup touch-ups, that kinda thing, while Miss bowl-cut was assigned to whatever needs they had. First, the group was supposed to be led to a waiting room, where the two talk show hosts were going to meet with them to have an off-camera chat. So the ladies led the way, with the guard next, the band members, and then Benny behind.

Anders had some tea out of courtesy while Trance went for yogurt and fruits. Alphonso was munching on soft rolls, despite Benny's eyeing him, and Twine didn't take anything. The male host, Michael Chowa and the female host, Francisca Opso were evidently an amazing pair. It was clear to the boys in a matter of minutes after meeting the hosts, why their TV segment was so popular. Michael and Francisca had personalities that complemented each other, and seemed to know just how to ask questions, connect the answers, and lead to the next question without over-stepping or even interrupting each other. Their conversations flowed effortlessly, and it didn't feel like interviewing or interrogation. Anders even said something, too, without feeling the need to censor his words.

The waiting room's atmosphere was relaxing, thanks to the hosts. The boys were asked about the instruments they played and why they liked them. The questions were not too personal as to make them self-conscious, or too constructive to make them think too much. Then Michael told them that the Agency had sent them preferred questions ahead of time to ask the group, so the boys needn't be nervous. Francisca said they would begin a run-through of the questions, and the boys would get a chance to warm up soon. Anders gulped the last of his tea, Trance ate a few bites of fruit before putting down the bowl, and Alphonso licked his fingers as he spotted Miss bowl-cut, and asked her if there were moist wipes available. She was back with a couple of small packs in no time.

They all stood, waiting outside the door of the studio. Miss red-dye and the guard stood with them, and Benny was behind them, discussing something with Miss bowl- cut. In the manner of the seriousness of a newsroom, the boys started to look stiff. They couldn't control the fact that they were nervous, even with the calm remarks from the hosts for them to relax. This is a talk show, not an interrogation room, Michael said playfully. His words did nothing to help with Anders' lip biting, Trance's bugged eyes, Alphonso's noisy breathing, and Twine's bouncing legs.

A man, who introduced himself as the stage manager, came out and spoke quietly to Francisca. When he finished, Francisca said,

"Boys, it's rehearsal time. Andrew says the stage is ready and you guys are up for your warm up. Don't worry about our excited audience. We'll calm them down, so do your thing, okay?"

Trance sped to the door of the studio excitedly, and the rest followed calmly behind him. Trance then stopped as he got to the door, waiting, and Andrew got the handle. They trailed behind Andrew as the door opened up to a wide expanse of monitors, cameras, wires, people and their screams. It was the unmistakably impressive studio of Live in Entertainment and the audience was obviously excited beyond measure.

The studio was so brightly lit that everyone seemed to look angelic, even though some were probably just waking up. There was a man who took the role of MC, as he tried to calm the audience and remind them of how they were supposed to react. They had obviously practiced this many times, because the voices wound down and only a couple of whistles here and there could be heard. The boys followed Andrew as he led them to a corner that was already set up for a band.

There were markers on the floor for where they were supposed to stand, and Andrew showed each of them where their spots were. Anders took his place behind the microphone in the center. Twine took his seat behind the drums as he felt the sticks. Trance was already tuning his electric guitar, while

Alphonso was searching his pockets for his pick. He didn't like playing with any guitar pick but his own.

Alphonso and Trance had hoped to bring their own guitars, but Live in Entertainment aka LE, which boasted of being one of the biggest TV talk shows, had told FFQ not to. They had a music station, after all, equipped with their own instruments, DJs, engineers, and producers. They were going to take care of everything, and all the boys had to do was show up in peak performance mode.

Andrew asked them if all was okay. Alphonso nodded, Trance also nodded as he seemed to admire the guitar he held. Twine took a swing at the drum set and also nodded. The audience went wild again and was calmed with the help of an announcement from Michael. He acknowledged that the current audience was made up of much younger people, a change from their usual audience, but he expressed excitement for their attendance, and reminded them that quietness would help with shooting a successful show. Some girls responded heartily with promises of quietness.

The boys all looked at Anders, who swallowed, took in a deep breath, and tested his microphone with some warm-up sounds. The sound guys said the bass needed a bit of tuning and they corrected that on their end. So the boys tested their sounds again and all seemed set.

Anders turned to his band-mates and said, "Can we just try the chorus quickly?" then to Andrew, "We want to do a quick sound check."

"Sure thing."

Anders request was communicated to the audience and the studio became as quiet as a graveyard.

When Anders finished singing the chorus, one thing was apparent. They were a band to look out for. It all worked: their sound live, the song, and their stage presence, especially that of their lead singer. It seemed like LE had been blessed with a rare kind of aura. The atmosphere, once quiet in amazement, now buzzed with extreme excitement. Michael and Francisca knew it was going to be a one-of-a-kind show, not the first time LE had presented a new artist's debut, but the first from FFQ, one of the most popular agencies in the country.

Soon the running around the studio seemed to freeze. The audience got in order, and were very quiet, and the familiar background music of the talk show started to play. The boys had already been instructed on where they were going to sit after their music performance. Their seats were arranged in a row, adjacent to Michael and Francisca. Anders was going to be the first to the left, followed by Trance, Alphonso and then Twine. In front of them were the camera operators and other technicians, that those watching at home would not see. Then there was the audience that viewers at home would see.

Michael nodded toward the stage, where the boys stood, as an asking sign if they were ready. Twine nodded back as a response, and at the conclusion of LE's opening music,

"Good morning everyone and thanks for tuning in to Live in Entertainment. My name is Michael Chowa," he said an orotund voice.

"And I'm Francisca Opso," said a pleasant voice with a slight throaty sound.

"It's a beautiful day outside, and here in LE we are with the latest musical sensations in the country. They have yet to show us their musical talent, but they've already captured the hearts of many just by their charm and charisma."

"Yes, Michael, and we at LE are happy to be the first to show you their live performance of their debut music, "*Where Are You?*" Please welcome, For-Runners!"

The answering screams and applause were off-the-charts loud, but calmed down almost immediately. The audience was well prepared.

The cameras panned to the stage of Live in Entertainment, where Anders was holding onto the mike for dear life. He seemed to be struggling with getting control of his breath as his heart rate sped too quickly. But something happened. It was Twine's low voice and what he said. "You've got it, Bro."

That was all it took to get Anders in the zone. He took a now-familiar singing stance as the beat and melody of *Where Are You* began.

He was a sight to behold, young and talented, tall and daring. Anders lightened his grasp on the mike and sang the verse with feeling. One camera focused on him while another focused on all of them. He stood, pale with a wisp of pitch black hair moistened with nervous sweat, covering his left eye. He'd held part of his hair in a bun with a hairband, since it was an awkward length of hair that kept getting on his face, which he didn't like. He'd been dressed in a white, tight elbow-sleeved length graphic T-shirt and a black leather biker jacket. His dark jeans had been a struggle to put on as they were brand new, but walking around and sitting in them had helped expand them a bit. His favorite thing about his outfit was his boots. The tips and part of the heel were metal and the laces were red. He thought it looked rad.

The sound of cymbals made Twine the next focus. His talent for playing the drums was so apparent in the movement of the drumsticks and the pedal operated by his foot. Of course, the sound of the beats and how it accompanied Anders' voice showed that his skills were top-charted. He was dressed in a grey muscle Tee, with his jacket tied around his waist as he sat on the stool and focused on delivering good sounds. The camera focused on his arms a lot of times, biceps flexing, wrists moving fast. He was so absorbed in his playing, that his face took on the look of someone who wanted to prove something beyond imagination. He was in his zone and there was no denying it. But his haircut stood out, literally. Gelled away from his face and standing like a sharp spear, the stylist had made sure that the drummer wasn't going to have problems with his hair falling on his face because it was a pompadour hairstyle. It was a good call and was one less thing to worry about.

When the chorus was being sung by Anders, accompanied by Trance's backup vocals, Alphonso's bass guitar took the lead. His playful mannerism shone brightly. Jumping from place to place, he never missed a melody, and his wild side bangs went along with his movements. His biker jacket was so distressed that it could have been mistaken for an old one, but his gray cameo pants and clean riding boots, completed the look as 'intentionally unkempt.' He was in his music world, and gave the audience more than they'd expected from him, personality-wise.

Now Trance had a stage presence that was very surprising. This shy guitarist turned into a swoon-worthy performer when the music started. The way he handled his guitar would have been construed as suggestive, if one didn't know the kind of person he was. Then his voice, a voice that supported Anders' so well, was an added bonus for the band. He was dressed in a velvet navy blue jacket that seemed to reflect the light, and the blond tips in his hair also picked up the color. He looked every part the rocker without an inner shirt, and a bunch of dark and rose-gold colored chains around his neck. He wore black skinny-tailored pants, and were raised inches from his shoes to show a fun-colored polka dot pair of socks. He would become a fan-favorite, no doubt because it was hard not to notice and love him.

"Are you there? Noooo?" Anders sang the question with a smooth falsetto that made the hairs on the videographer's arms raise.

Utter silence, and then,

Thunderous clapping.

The applause and screams were so loud that the camera decided to pan past For-Runners and show how excited the audience was. Francisca took the time that the camera was away, to blot her eyes. Anders had tugged at her emotions, and even though she'd tried to hold it in, she just couldn't.

"Wow," Michael exclaimed as he stood up and walked toward For-Runners, as they made their way down the stage to take their seats.

He shook each of their hands and Francisca did as well, pausing long enough to say, "You're amazing," in Anders' ears.

"Thanks," he whispered back.

The clapping ended when they were all seated.

"Am I right when I say they were ah-ma-zing!?" Michael hollered at the audience.

"Yeeeeesssss!" the audience yelled.

"Look, Michael, look. I still have goosebumps," Francisca showed her arm to Michael.

"Yeah, that performance from For-Runners also gave me chills. For-Runners, before you introduce yourselves to our audience, please tell us a bit about your debut single, *Where Are You?*"

Eyes were on Anders, but he didn't make a move to answer the question so Alphonso took over. With a large smile on his face, he explained,

"*Where Are You* was written by Anders here," he said as he clapped and was joined by the audience. "Thanks, Bro. If you pay attention to the lyrics you'll hear pleading. It's a song pleading to be found, and to not be fearful of admitting vulnerability. We are new in this large music scene, and we are trying to find our place, and asking our fans to find us."

"Now, that is a way to open an interview, wow! You're Alphonso, right?" Michael asked.

"Yes."

"Thank you for that. And wonderful songwriting on your part," Michael pointed to Anders, who smiled.

"And here I thought it was about a lost love," Francisca said slyly.

Anders looked at the ground, Trance sniggered, Alphonso scratched his head and cleared his throat, Twine said, "It's open to interpretation."

The audience cheered.

"And with that, For-Runners please introduce yourselves," Michael said.

"I'm Anders," a slightly hoarse voice said.

"I'm Trance," a high tenor voice said.

"I'm Alphonso," a voice with an excited pitch said.

"Twine," said a low voice.

The audience clapped again and cheered.

"Wow," Michael said in excitement, taking in the reaction from the audience and marveling at the energy he felt. "Thank you," he said to them. "Phew! Anders, let's begin with you," Michael turned toward him. He didn't switch to English, but he was ready to translate because he knew that Anders understood the language, but still had some difficulties speaking it.

"You're the lead singer of For-Runners, only seventeen years old. When did you know you wanted to become a singer?"

Anders nodded, biting his lips as he thought of his answer. "I never planned on being a singer," he responded haltingly, trying to remember how to say some phrases, but nothing came to mind so he stopped talking.

The audience laughed, as well as the hosts and Trance.

"We heard you didn't have formal training prior to being an FFQ trainee?"

"No."

It was evident that Anders wasn't going to say more, so Francisca chipped in with some background information.

"You traveled here to become a model, and due to some mix-up, you ended up being a singer. Do you enjoy singing more than modeling?"

"I like them both," and then, he allowed a cheeky smile on his face when he heard Alphonso mutter, "jeez, Anders," under his breath.

There were squeals from the audience, undeniably teenage girls.

"I guess we can let Anders off the hook for his bad interview skills, because he compensates for it with that charming smile of his," said Francisca.

"And his voice," an audience member called out.

Giggles from the audience.

"Okay, Trance, you next," Michael said.

Trance seemed to have become smaller in his seat as he seemed to have deflated a bit.

"You gave off the impression of being quite shy, but the Trance I saw on stage was a different person."

Trance smiled.

"And you look so cool," Francisca said. "Don't you think he looks cool?" she asked the audience.

They responded with a resounding, "Yeessss!"

"You're just sixteen,"

"Aww" was heard in the audience and then laughter.

"Trance covered his face shyly.

Another "Aww" this time, louder.

"Let's not make him uncomfortable," Michael said.

Alphonso took Trance's hand away from his face to reveal a wide grin.

Laughter from the audience.

"You actually auditioned. It was said that you stunned the judges because when you walked in, it seemed like you struggled to speak, and then when you started singing and playing, I quote, 'we knew we had a rare find.' Being a shy person, what made you decide to audition?"

Trance, the moment he sat up, seemed to transform into a bold and cooler version of himself. The audience also noticed this as they 'ooooed.'

He cleared his throat. "I've always loved singing, but never liked to perform in front of people. It didn't have anything to do with stage fright. I didn't suffer from that. I just was never confident, and I'm a bit socially awkward, but I find that when I sing, I go somewhere else. It's like going to a world where I can be me and there's no judgment."

"You should give Anders some interviewing tutorials," Michael said.

Laughter.

"Did you audition to be a solo artist?" Francisca asked.

"No, I wanted to be in a group. My mom suggested that she thought I'd fare better and get out of my shell, if I was in a good group."

"So, are you in a good group?"

"Yes," Trance said with a wide smile.

"I think so, too. I look at your dynamics, how you all are so different and stand-out so much, but you seem to work perfectly together," Francisca said.

"Yeah, we didn't see it at first, but after practicing and making music together, we now see that we're stronger as a unit, and a better band with each of us in it."

"Thanks for adding that, Alphonso. Speaking of a better band, you and Twine were supposed to be a duo, until Trance was added and Anders later. By the way, Alphonso and Twine are both nineteen years old. How did the change feel, when you worked so hard with Twine, and thought you two were going to debut soon, only for others to be added to your duo group? Francisca asked.

Alphonso nodded and licked his lips, then said, "Honestly, it was hard to take in. Twine and I had done this together and we were sure we were ready. We even had an unofficial track and music video made. After getting good reviews we thought we were set."

Everyone waited quietly.

"Then we got summoned and on our way…" Twine started to chuckle silently, which made the audience join in. Alphonso also started to laugh. "Twine is laughing," he explained, "Because we'd done something the day before and thought we were being summoned for that. So we were so scared and sweating profusely."

"What did you two do?" Francisca asked.

"No comment," Twine answered quickly.

Laughter.

"All right, you'll tell us later," Michael said. "Go on," he said to Alphonso.

"Long story short," Alphonso continued, "We found out that there was a plan to add someone in our group and the third person was the winner of a singing competition and would be arriving in two weeks."

"That must have been a shock."

"It was. In fact, Twine said he would have preferred if we'd been called to be disciplined."

"Why you so unhappy, Twine?" asked Michael.

Twine nodded. He cleared his throat. "At that time I just felt that we'd been working hard for nothing."

"But we heard that you two were among the top five talented trainees and there was no doubt that you would debut with FFQ," Francisca said.

Twine laughed. "I learned from my seniors in the Agency that a trainee should never feel comfortable, because there is always someone else working harder for your spot. A trainee should only take a short break when the contract is signed, and then work twice as hard to show the world why the Agency chose him. So when I heard that we weren't going to be a duo anymore, I interpreted that as we were not good enough together." Then he quickly added. "I want to clarify that these were just my thoughts. FFQ never officially made Alphonso and me a duo. We just started working together and it became that way. Then people in the Agency started referring us as a duo."

"You are very good at this, Twine. You quickly cleared up what would have been a controversial statement. What do you think Michael, shouldn't he work with us?"

Laughter.

"So, what happened when you met Trance?"

"Twine didn't like me," Trance said.

"That's not true," Twine countered. "I just couldn't get two words out of him, and it was a bit irritating because I'd seen his stage performances and how cool he'd acted. So I wondered why he was acting shy. But I later realized that it was my fault, because I hadn't watch the long videos that showed behind-the-scenes to reveal the personality of the contestants. If I'd done that I would have known he was a shy person and given him a break."

Aww

"Trance, how did you feel when you thought Twine didn't like you?"

"I just hung out more with Alphonso," Trance responded.

"Good call," Michael said. "Did you notice when Twine warmed up to you and started to like you?"

Twine laughed. "I still don't like him that much," he said.

"You do now," Trance said. "And to answer your question, there is a fun story, but I don't know how much time we have."

"Tell us a concise version and we'll take a break after your story," Francisca said.

"Well, I was instructed to write a song on "heartbreak" and I was having a difficult time because I'd never been heartbroken before."

Alphonso laughed and said, "a heartbreak story at your age would be funny."

His statement made the audience laugh.

Trance covered his face for a moment and summoned up the confidence to continue. He cleared his throat. "So I went to talk to Mr. Rob to tell him that it was difficult. I wanted to remind him of my age because I was sure that I'd gotten the wrong task."

"For clarification, Mr. Rob is Mr. Ju Robert, CEO of FFQ," Francisca told the audience. "Go on."

"Well, Mr. Rob said I'd gotten the right assignment. He wanted to hear a song on that topic from someone my age. So I went back and tried, but was stuck. This assignment kept me awake. Then the next day in our dorm room, Twine was telling Alphonso a story about a breakup and I noticed something. He was telling it really loudly and repeating some parts a lot. I tried not to listen, but then I did listen. Then the way Alphonso was listening attentively and making some agreeable sounds, I knew he was faking. Then something dawned on me. Twine was actually helping me out with my task. Just like that, I had a song. I was writing non-stop. In fact, I had two versions of the song."

"I don't know what he's talking about," Twine said.

"I know you won't admit it, you know you helped me, Bro."

Aww

"You won't admit to helping him out?" Michael asked.

"I didn't," Twine said.

"Do you remember the story?" Francisca asked Alphonso.

"Well, Twine always tells stories about people who've broken up, and how they're behaving like the world was going to end."

Laughter.

"He didn't admit it when I told him that his story inspired my song and I thanked him. He said, 'I don't know what you're talking about,' and left."

"Whether you admit it or not, Twine, Trance is grateful," Francisca said. "We'll now take a short break and when we return, we'll talk about if the fourth person to join the group received a warm welcome, after the trio had gotten used to each other for almost a year."

There was a hand signal from the producer and then "cut."

The level of noise in the studio rose as Francisca stood, gesturing toward Miss bowl-cut. She ran up to where they all sat and Francisca pointed at the water jug. Miss bowl-cut took it and sped off. Meanwhile, Miss red-dye showed up with a small makeup bag and started touching up Francisca's face. Next, she blotted Michael's nose and powdered it a bit. In no time, she had quickly touched up the boys as the producers talked a bit with Francisca and Michael. The MC was busy with the audience, who were laughing out loud. The boys sat quietly and Trance was drinking some water that Miss bowl-cut had brought back.

"We'll continue the segment with a question to you, Anders. We stopped with how Alphonso and Twine reacted to having Trance join them. To continue smoothly, we'll ask how you were received by the boys when they found out that you were going to be the fourth member of the group," Francisca said.

Anders nodded.

"Remember, short and sweet answers are the best, but we also like good details. You've been coached well by your Agency so try not to feel pressured," Michael said.

"I know you have trouble with this, but don't worry, Twine will also weigh in. I intend to ask it like this, 'what was your first meeting with them like?'" Francisca said to Anders.

Anders took in a deep breath and nodded. "I'm ready," he said.

The producers alerted the MC that they were ready to roll so he could get the audience to prepare for filming.

Michael asked the boys if anyone needed a bathroom break and they said they were good.

Francisca took her seat and then the background music began.

"Before the break, we heard Trance describe how his group members helped him out with a songwriting assignment, which to him, was the moment he bonded with them. Now, we are itching to know if Anders was welcomed on the first day or if there's a bonding story, too. Tell us, Anders, how was your reception?"

Anders smiled a bit, as though recalling something favorable, and then he composed himself and said, "When I think about it now, it wasn't so bad."

"How so?" Michael asked.

He reached up and caught a strand of his hair, which he twisted as he thought of the best way to respond to Michael's question. "I'm not much of a talker, as you've already noticed," he shrugged. "I was in a new country and still trying to breathe the foreign air, so I wasn't in the mood to socialize. I met Trance first and was happy that he didn't say much. When I met Alphonso and Twine later, it bothered me at first that they didn't talk to me. But I got used to it."

"They didn't welcome you?" Francisca asked in an incredulous tone.

"I did," Alphonso offered in a high voice.

Laughter.

Anders nodded.

"And you, Twine?" Michael asked.

He exhaled loudly. "Um, I acknowledged he was there."

"Wow," Michael exclaimed. "You didn't like him from the get-go?"

"That's not the reason," Twine answered quickly. "It was the issue of making us a four-member group. I thought I'd gotten over it, but when he showed up, I had the same feelings again as when Trance arrived."

"Yes, that certainly must have been difficult. So, were you aware that he was going to be the lead singer?"

"No. That was later," Twine answered haltingly, and the hosts could tell that it was still a difficult topic, so they did what they did best, lightened the mood.

"Wow, Anders! You just showed up and took away their land didn't you?"

Laugher.

Anders smiled.

"But you know what, after a performance like that, we understand why you all were put in a group," Francisca said.

"I agree," Michael said. "You all have your different strengths, and in Alphonso's words earlier, you are stronger as a unit, and a better band together. For-Runners, everyone! Thank you for gracing Live in Entertainment with your presence.

"Thanks!"

"Thank you!!"

Chapter 11 (Bros)

"Happy birthday to you, happy birthday to you, happy birthday dear T-Boy, happy birthday to you!"

Mama Miso, as Twine's mother was popularly called, had shut down her restaurant for the day to celebrate her dear boy's birthday. She was a short, stout woman, whose presence did not need to be announced because she had a big personality. Wherever she went, she made sure people were fed, which wasn't a surprise since she owned *Nado*, a popular chain of noodle restaurants in the country, and it was well-known for its cone-shaped cakes. Twine had this specialty cake in front of him in the super-sized version of course. It was a very hot day but the restaurant was cool with ten guests that were Twine's close friends and family.

Twine shut his eyes and then opened them and blew out the flames of the candles on his midnight blue cone-shaped cake.

Everyone clapped in excitement, even the cute toddler who drooled as she looked excitedly at the cake. She was held back from pouncing on it by Twine's sister, Maya. Maya was the female version of Twine. Their faces were so alike that they could be mistaken for twins if they decided to dress identically. But since Twine's makeover, Maya was now easily differentiated. She had longer hair and wasn't as muscular as her brother. Her voice wasn't as deep as his either. Maya was a tomboy when they were much younger, and did get into fights with boys who thought she was Twine. She was older and stood her ground, defending her brother whenever she could. The fights always halted when they realized she was his sister. The siblings were very close.

Anders, Alphonso, Trance, a fellow agency mate from the band, *BOOM*, a friend from Twine's former neighborhood, and Benny were all in attendance.

There was so much food and non-alcoholic drinks, provided by the one and only Mama Miso.

Equipped with a knife, Twine cut the slick textured cake in triangular shapes. The first piece went to the toddler, who had started whining, but was giggling in no time. He fed her several bites until his mother scolded him about sharing the cake with everyone waiting. He was a bit red with embarrassment when he realized that everyone was looking at him. It was nice to see him lose his super-star persona for a minute.

He served a piece to Anders. "Thanks, Bro," Anders said.

Soon, a larger piece was falling onto Anders' plate and he looked up to see Mama Miso smiling at him.

"I'm fine, I don't need more," he protested.

"You need to eat. Your cheekbones are sticking out. You need to come to the restaurant more often and eat." She turned to Twine, "do you eat all the food I send to you alone? Why does your roommate look like he's starving? With all the money FFQ is making, how can this lovely boy be looking like this?"

Anders prayed for the ground to open up and swallow him as Alphonso and Trance started to laugh.

"It's his genes, Mama," Twine said. "Look at us?" he pointed to himself, Alphonso and Trance.

Mama Miso wasn't up for that explanation.

"Genes? What genes? Anyone who eats well shouldn't look like this." She took Anders' hands. "Make sure you come here more often and I'll make something you like. I'm sure it's hard to get used to food you didn't grow up with. Bring me the recipes and I'll make them for you, okay?"

Anders was dying to get the attention off his skinny bones, so he nodded quickly and asked Maya where he could get more ice for his drink.

"Sit down, Son, I'll get it for you," Mama Miso said as she walked away.

The laughter got louder and Maya mouthed, "sorry," with a shrug.

Anders took in a deep breath and tried to forget what had just happened.

Everyone was helping themselves to more food, the toddler was asleep on a portable crib, and Mama Miso called for their attention.

"I want to say something." Her eyes were noticeably swollen as though she'd been crying, but her face was alight with a big smile. "Twine's dad isn't here anymore and it is in these happy moments that I wish he'd been here to see his son." She exhaled audibly.

"When T-Boy told me he wanted to go into music, I wasn't happy about it. I wanted him to be educated and get a government job. I wanted him to make something of himself. I didn't want to deal with uncertainties, and worry about risks. But he was determined, and I had to grudgingly support him. You see, I had promised his dad to do my best to take care of our children. His dad had tried so hard for us, and worked until a horrific accident took him away. On his hospital bed, he kept reminding me that our Twine was like me and I should go easy on him."

She wiped her face, took in a deep breath and continued.

"When I realized that T-Boy was indeed serious about pursuing music, I knew I had to support him a hundred percent, and so, we all came up with ideas on what we could do best to make sure he succeeded. I researched, his big sister researched, and he also researched. It wasn't easy, but his drive and hard work convinced me that I was doing the right thing by letting him pursue his dream. He got accepted by FFQ and told us later. He'd done this part on his own. Now here we are. He is in a band with three other lovely boys who are equally as diligent and hard working. A group that has proven, within a year, that they are extraordinary. Sold-out venues, top-charted songs, and now preparing to go on tour next year. I knew my son would succeed, but I have to confess that I did not see this coming. I know his dad is proud of him, and I am proud of you, too, T-Boy. Continue to do well and remember to stay level-headed. Be humble, and give back. I love you."

Twine stood up with a tear-streaked face and went to hug his mother.

Others were wiping off tears, too.

"Sorry for my mushiness. I can't help being a proud mother," she laughed. "Please eat up, and I have go-to plates for anyone who wants to take some food with them." Then she looked at Anders. "I've packed some food for you so make sure you take it with you."

He nodded and sighed.

Since their debut last year, life had taken a turn for the best for all of them. For-Runners was in high demand in the music and entertainment industry, and was invited to perform in variety shows, governmental functions, and got numerous endorsements at home and abroad.

The album release day of their debut self-titled mini-album, *For-Runners*, was such a huge success that FFQ added to the boys' calendars more recording sessions. They were planning ahead for their first concert and having only six original songs wasn't going to cut it.

Anders' song, *Where Are You?*, jumped to number one on both domestic and international music charts. Fellow label mates and executives had already gotten ahead of themselves, congratulating For-Runners for music nominations that they were certain the boys would be nominated for.

It was a surprise that *Notice Me*, became an instant fan-favorite. Everyone now knew the back story of that song and some fans praised Everest for secretly taping him. While Anders was making a name within the band as a prolific songwriter, Twine was causing talk about possible fitness sponsorships. His physique hadn't gone unnoticed, and there were rumors that a giant corporation, *Protein Brothers*, was drafting a contract for him. Alphonso had already been voted in an online poll as choice actor for a TV show that was in the works, and baby-faced Trance, as he was now called, had already been approached by a couple of fashion designers, because they said his lanky stature and shy demeanor would work well with their fashion concept.

Where Are You? and *Notice Me* weren't the only hit songs in the mini-album. There was another song, the last minute addition, written by Anders and co-written by Trance that became their fastest, most downloaded track from the album, entitled, *Just Know*. *Just Know* was dubbed 'The Anthem' because of how fast it became popular, and even famous Pop-stars, home and abroad, started making their own versions of the song. In spite of its short time of release, it was ranked the fastest growing and most covered pop song online.

Just Know was a number one chart-topper for three consecutive weeks, until it dropped to top five, and still managed to stay in the top-twenty for months. This was a very rare occurrence for any band, not to mention a new, relatively unknown foreign group.

Anders wondered why people liked *Just Know*. He didn't undermine its potential, but he didn't understand the exact reason why it blew up so quickly.

"It's because of the two lines I added," Trance said, laughing.

When Anders had included Trance's name as a co-writer, Trance hadn't thought he deserved it, After all, Anders had already finished writing the song, but thought Trance's suggestions made it even better. Trance couldn't be happier now that the song was a huge hit.

Trance had walked in on Anders' singing the second verse and stopped to hear the whole song. He'd marveled at how easy songwriting seemed to be for Anders. Then he'd asked him what inspired the song, and Anders had said, "My six-year-old eyes." That had been the working title until they'd changed it before submitting it to Mr. Rob.

Now, a year later, just as was predicted, For-Runners had snagged rookie awards here and there because of their three stand-out songs. They had been nominated alongside veterans in the industry and won some. They had made a name for themselves as a band not to be trifled with. They were good musicians and people knew it. The band had managed to draw a wide range of fandom by people as young as seven years to as old as seventy years. This phenomenon had puzzled FFQ, but it was explained that the vibes spread by the band covered the cute demographic as well as the old- school demographic. The kid-cute groups were mostly Trance's and Alphonso's fans, the heavily teenage groups were mostly Twine's fans, and the older groups were mostly Ander's fans. It was no wonder that FFQ was puzzled, because the fan-base of each band member was a bit off with their personalities, although Twine and Anders were grateful for theirs.

One year later, the boys were very busy, seemed to have settled well with their various styles and public images, had a better living arrangement, and good looking bank accounts. One year later, they also seemed to have attracted a lot of crazies and were easily prone to rumors. The Agency was used to dealing with these issues, but the magnitude at which For-Runners was targeted was record-setting. The boys could not afford to be in any scandals and they were briefed on this daily.

They only had work and home phones, and only took in-coming calls from selected people including some family members. The Agency operated a group social media account that was controlled by managers and inspected by the executive assistant to the CEO. The boys were not allowed to make comments publicly, and were extensively prepared for all interviews. The boys were screened from head to toe before attending any public functions. They were not allowed to have girlfriends.

That last point didn't bode well with Alphonso and Twine.

"No girlfriends until what age?" Alphonso asked Benny.

"It's not about your ages. FFQ knows that some are more mature than others despite their ages so they go by fan-base mood."

"Fan-base mood. What is that?" Alphonso asked.

"Well, you guys are still new as a band to the public, and we can't afford to make the fans angry. Right now they see you all as 'theirs.' We want to keep it that way until they get used to you."

"For how long?" Twine asked.

"Based on the fan-base mood of course. We'll watch for the shift. This happens when they're settled and become your core followers, and then you'll have sympathizers who understand and support you when you start dating. Don't get me wrong, they may hate your girlfriends, but they won't hate the idea that you're in a relationship. They may even begin to 'ship' you with their favorite choice of a girlfriend for you."

"Urgh!" Alphonso exclaimed.

"All I know is if I find the love of my life tomorrow, I won't care about fan-base mood or whatever you call it."

Benny laughed. "You say that now, but wait until you see how crazy they can get, and then because of you, they may boycott your band and then...

"I get it," Alphonso retorted. "It's in our contract anyway."

"I'm glad you read it," Benny said, as he made his way out of their living room.

Twine and Anders were now rooming together and opposite their room was Alphonso's and Trance's room. They'd moved to B House over a month ago, an upgrade from F House. B House had Townhouse style apartments with more space and the boys couldn't be happier. For starters, they didn't have to deal with the noisiness of F House and the shared television and game rooms. Their apartment was usually cleaner, because the only person who made a mess was Alphonso, and not twenty-something other boys.

They usually hung out in their living room playing games and music. Their kitchen was the next best place as the refrigerator was usually stocked with food from Mama Miso, and the housekeeper was great at replacing finished items.

Twine was usually in the gym, Alphonso was usually playing games with Trance, and Anders was usually seated in the corner composing music. The boys had gotten close and also respected each other's space. The surprise of all was how close Twine and Anders had gotten, and it was all thanks to video chats and the room assignment.

"Mom, it's quite late so I have to log off now," Anders whispered.

"Speak louder," Everest said.

"Twine is asleep, Mom, so I can't talk loudly."

There were ruffling sounds coming from the bed across from Anders and the side table lamp came on. There was a yawn and then, "Anders, it's fine. Call me back when you're done."

"Hi, Mrs. Quigley," he said as he got up and took his blanket along with him.

"Hi, Twine," she responded.

Anders was a bit uneasy that he'd woken up Twine, but he was thankful that he had more time to chat with Everest. Feng was going to show up any moment if he waited a few minutes. He had gone out to buy some eggs.

"Did we wake Twine up?" she asked.

"Yes, but it's okay."

"Aww, I feel awful."

"He's fine with it, Mom. So you were saying that you and dad will visit me next month?"

"Yeah. I talked with Mr. Robert and he said the earlier the better because you all will soon start promoting your tour and you'll be very busy."

"Yes."

"Anders,"

"Mom?"

"Are you okay?"

Anders was taken aback by her question and frowned. "Yes. Why?"

"You look tired and I haven't seen any recent photos of you smiling. You always have that sad face, and the sexy one and…"

"Eww, Mom, come on, stop it."

She couldn't help laughing. "I'm just being real with you."

He made throw-up sounds. "Don't be real with me, it's weird."

"If you say so, Baby."

"I'm not a baby."

"You are my baby."

Anders shook his head. "Thank goodness Twine isn't here. I'm the leader for crying out loud. They'll stop respecting me if you keep calling me a baby."

"Okay, okay, Mr. Grown-up, I won't call you that in front of your friends."

"Ever."

"No deal. Just in front of your friends."

Urgh! He rubbed his eyes.

"You're sleepy. You should go to bed."

"I want to wait and say hi to Dad."

"Speak of the devil. Honey, come say bye to Anders, he needs to go to bed."

His father's face took up the whole screen, showing laugh lines around his eyes and mouth, and a strand of grey hair that was certainly new."

"Hey, Dad,"

"Hey, Pop-star. How are you?"

"Doing well. And you?"

"Still kneading the flour like the pro I am. We watched the award ceremony and tried to call you, but the lines weren't going through. Congratulations, Buddy. You and your group members are making us proud."

Anders smiled. "Thanks, Dad."

"Has mom mentioned to you that we'll be seeing you soon?"

He nodded.

"Good. Can't wait."

"Me, too."

"Now take care and get some sleep."

"Will do. Bye, Dad."

"Bye!"

"Bye, Sweetie," Everest said behind Feng and the call ended.

Anders sighed, feeling happy after seeing his parents. He shut the tablet and remembered Twine had left the room to give him some privacy. He went to get him to return.

"It was your job to negotiate the license and you're telling me we don't have it?"

Mr. Rob's face was even more pale than usual as he stared at the copyright officer with a face that looked worse than death. He had just been informed that two songs, which were supposed to be part of the lineup for For-Runners' upcoming tour, were already licensed to a competing agency with a tour around the same time. Tours are the most successful when the attendees can sing-along to popular songs; songs that have been around for ages and have special places in some people's hearts. There are some older bands that have classics that people love. For-Runners was supposed to include two classic songs by all-time favorite artists, but had lost on them since their competitor had already gotten the exclusive rights to those songs for six months. No one could dispute the fact that Mr. Rob was extremely angry.

Anders was a bit disappointed because he'd looked forward to singing one of the songs, which was a worldwide favorite and an anthem love song. But there were other songs that could replace it. He didn't think that should have made Mr. Rob so angry, but he knew that people with pride didn't like losing to their competitors. He nodded quietly when Mr. Rob said they'd get back to the group with two replacement songs.

Anders left the meeting with a sigh of relief. The auditorium had become too stuffy and it had seemed difficult to breathe in there. This was the part of being the leader that the others didn't envy. The meetings were always tense, and everyone except Mr. Rob, always came out sweating even though the room temperature was kept low.

As he walked into the apartment, "Booooo!"

He fell backward, landing on his derriere.

The laughter from Trance was thunderous. He had succeeded in making Anders flinch after numerous failed attempts.

Anders was wincing because his butt really hurt and he wasn't a happy camper in that moment. His tailbone felt broken and he didn't think he could stand up.

"Sorry, Man, here, give me your hands."

Anders swatted away Trance's attempt to help him up.

Trance noticed Anders' facial expression and all humor vanished from his face.

"Are you okay, Bro?" he took both of Anders' hands, even though he'd protested, and pulled him up. Anders groaned in pain as shots of electric-like sparks moved from his tailbone to his thighs.

"Oh no," Trance said in worry. "Let's walk slowly to the couch."

They both moved, getting only a fleeting glance from Alphonso, who looked like he wanted to kill someone. He was muttering curses under his breath as he read something from the laptop.

Trance set some throw pillows around the couch and helped Anders settle on it. It took Anders several minutes to find a comfortable position and then he let out a loud breath.

"I'm so sorry, Bro," Trance apologized for the umpteenth time.

"It's okay." Then he looked around. "Where is Twine? Check the room and call him out for a briefing."

Trance nodded and left.

"Hey, Alphonso, head over here, Man, for a briefing."

Alphonso snapped the laptop shut, took a deep breath and made his way toward the couch.

"What's wrong?" Anders asked him.

"Internet trolls."

"I've told you to stop reading those comments."

"I know, but we have to know what the fans are saying and what they expect to see on our tour."

"Benny tells us that."

"Benny doesn't do a thorough job. He didn't know about the song requests. He didn't know about the unofficial fan gathering. He didn't know about the merchandise."

"Okay, got it. Then tread carefully, how about that? Remember we can't please everyone, so stop letting them get to you."

"Do you know the rumor out there about you?"

"Don't want to know, thanks."

"I think you'd like to know if you ever want to get a girlfr…"

"Hey, Man, you okay?" Twine's muscly structure stumped in.

"Trance decided to get rid of my behind."

Twine frowned.

"I said I'm sorry, Man. Should I get ice?"

Alphonso laughed out loud.

Anders gestured for both of them to take a seat. *My Destiny* and *Champions* are out. We have to figure out other classics for the tour."

"What?" they all exclaimed in unison.

"I thought Mr. Rob approved them." Twine said.

"Yeah, but *Caesar Entertainment* has exclusive rights to the songs for six months."

"Seriously? Both songs? You guys think I'm crazy when I say they're out to get us. You know I've been saying that one of those internet trolls is from *Caesar*. He or she always knows inside gist," Alphonso said.

"Well, we've got three days to come up with five song choices and then they'll let us know which two that we're going to add to the list."

"That shouldn't be a problem," Twine said.

Anders agreed. It wasn't a hard task to come up with classic hits that people loved to sing. The issue was if the Agency would be granted permission to use them by their owners or their estates.

"That reminds me. Trance, Mr. Rob said he'd like to take a look at *Bleeding Heart* as a possibility for one of the songs we'll perform, so he wants you to fix the bridge and present it to him in our next meeting."

Trance's eyes grew wide.

"Trance, did you hear me?"

"Ye—sss" he stuttered.

"What's the problem?" Anders asked, noticing that the other two members looked uncomfortable.

"Do you know Charlie Whey, who was once an FFQ trainee but signed with *Caesar Entertainment?*"

"Yes."

"I wrote that song with him or I should say I wrote most of the song and he contributed the bridge."

"Okay? So what is the issue?"

He recorded the song without permission from FFQ when he went to *Caesar* and there was a lawsuit as a result because it was a property of FFQ.

"Oh."

"Yes. So a few people already know the song as Charlie's and if they hear us sing it –" his voice trailed.

Anders scratched his head. "I hate this rivalry issue. It's so annoying."

"I'm positive that this will cause problems," Twine said.

"Problems for *Caesar* because people will ask questions, and then they'll find out that it is your song."

"But I don't want problems. Charlie didn't do it to cause problems. He just recorded it for fun and uploaded it to his personal page. He never said *Caesar* claimed it. I don't know how it got out of hand," Trance said.

"That's what this business is," Alphonso said. "Mr. Rob has a plan, Bro, so you better fix the bridge and present the song to him on time."

Trance sighed heavily.

That evening, Benny brought some heating pads for Anders' sore tailbone. Anders had been lying on the couch in the living room all day, dodging quirky comments from the boys about massaging his butt, or the favorite, Alphonso's volunteering to see if the tailbone had moved so he could place it back in its original place.

Anders knew it wasn't too bad, but he didn't want to sit on it while it was still tender. When Benny left, he got up slowly and sat down on one side of his butt cheek. He looked around to make sure he was the only one in the living room. He wanted to avoid the annoying comments from the boys. Where did they all go? He wondered.

He opened one of the packs, pulled down his pants and plastered on the heating pad. It felt good. He sat down carefully and it wasn't as bad as he'd imagined it would be. He then sat low on the couch as he relaxed a bit. The next time he opened his eyes, it was dark outside.

The apartment was unusually quiet, which made him wonder where they all were. Had they had dinner yet? Maybe they hadn't wanted to wake him up. He looked around and noticed that the apartment phone was missing. Someone was still around.

He groaned as he stood up, but noticed that the pain had diminished. This gave him more confidence to stand erect, which he did without difficulty. He took out the heating pad and decided he'd replace it before bed. He went to the kitchen to dispose it, and just as he was about to switch on the light, he heard someone talking.

"Mama, please, no matter how bad it is, don't keep it from me. She is my kid. I wasn't happy when I heard it from Maya. I know you don't want me to worry and I trust you to take care of her, but just imagine how I felt. It was a fever, Mama, and I didn't know about it."

Silence.

"I know, I know, but I'll prefer to know. I won't run down there like I used to. I trust you. But I always want to know."

Silence.

"Please put her on the phone." His voice immediately changed to a tiny sound filled with so much affection that Anders soon understood what was going on.

"Elvira baby, how are you? Good, good? Did Mama give you a lollipop? Yes, yes. Did you like your new plushie?" He laughed heartily. "Girls, and never being satisfied. Okay, I'll buy you the white one. Be a good girl, okay, and stop spitting out your peas. Mama told me, Love. I love you. Me, too."

Then he made a kiss sound.

Anders was in shock. *Who is Elvira?*

He didn't get the chance to walk out of the kitchen before the door to the balcony opened and closed and the lights came on. At first, Twine looked at him fleetingly, but his eyes returned to Anders' face. He knew. He sighed heavily and his shoulders slumped.

Anders couldn't get his eyes off Twine. Was he a father? Him? He couldn't be.

Twine stood where he was and lowered his eyes to the ground. Then he stood as straight as he usually did, looked Anders straight in eyes, and said, "The others aren't aware." Even though he tried his best to look confident, his eyes gave him away. There was worry there, and his constant swallowing showed he was afraid.

"Aren't aware of what?" Anders managed to ask.

Chapter 12 (Seventeen)

"I named her Elvira, after my grandmother, and the only people who know she's my child are her mother, my mother, and my sister. And now, you, too. Everyone else thinks she's my little cousin. I hope I can keep it that way for a long time."

"Don't worry, Bro. No one is going to hear it from me," Anders said.

Twine was evidently struggling with the fact that this secret was out. He suddenly looked like he had aged to twice his age, and the line between his eyebrows etched deep. "I really liked her mom," he said, smiling bitterly, "Sha is her name. She, she…hmm."

"Another time, Bro. You don't have to tell me now."

"There really isn't much to tell. I'd seen her around, followed her around for some time, got her to talk to me, slept with her. She found out she was pregnant, and I found out she was actually married and was just here for university."

Anders held his breath, knowing that he couldn't make the sound he wanted to without making Twine uncomfortable. There was definitely much to tell – but he said nothing.

"So she lied to her husband and told him that she couldn't return home anytime soon, because of some sort of school requirement and extra classes she needed to take. She stayed with my mom throughout the pregnancy and barely stepped outside the house.

"I was here at the Agency. It was messed up. I tried my best to focus, and on days that I couldn't, I went home to see her. Soon, I couldn't take breaks like I wanted to, and didn't see her for weeks at a time. My mother called to let me know that she'd gone into labor, but I couldn't leave. She gave birth and I wasn't there. Then four days later, my mother called and said Sha was gone. I was supposed to get a break that weekend, but I'd missed her by one day.

"I still remember how horrible I felt. I know she didn't love me, but I would have loved to say goodbye. She was conflicted about leaving the baby, but my mom was able to convince her to leave it. We never talked about what would happen after she gave birth, but I was sure she'd leave. I just didn't think it would be when the baby was only a few days old.

"I didn't wait until the weekend to go home after my mom called. I left immediately. When I arrived home, I saw Maya holding the baby who was fast asleep. I remember how quiet the house was and how I could hear her breathe softly. You know, I was happy she hadn't taken Elvira along with her."

Anders didn't say a word, but listened. He'd noticed a new side of Twine. He had to admit that he was amazed. He'd never heard him speak so deeply about anything, which made him seem so grown up.

"When my mother came home and saw me with Elvira, she tried to defend Sha. She said, 'she was a confused girl who wasn't ready for this. Don't hold any grudges against her. Don't hold on to her. This is your gift from her. Keep her safe.' I started to cry," he laughed as he recollected his mother's words.

"Anyway, my mother told me to think about how we were going to raise Elvira, and we decided that the only way I could succeed at FFQ was to keep this fact hidden." He looked up at Anders.

Anders nodded. "Can I ask something?"

"Sure."

"Has Sha reached out to you?"

"I haven't heard from her since then."

Anders was a bit surprised, but he quickly masked his facial expression. "What if she reaches out now...I mean now that you're on TV?"

Twine shrugged. "Well, I'll let her see Elvira, but I can't have anything to do with her. I don't feel the same way about her that I did when I was seventeen."

Chapter 13 (Bye Bye)

"Hey, T, here, I think this one is meant for you. My mom must have made a mistake when she labeled them." Anders handed a T-shirt to Twine that he'd brought out from his suitcase. When Everest and Feng had visited Anders a couple of months ago, they'd brought some gifts for the band members. Everest had started teaching a younger group of students, and she talked so much about her Pop-star son that her students decided to design T-shirts for For-Runners. Anders had just unfolded the T-shirt and noticed Twine's face all over it.

Twine took it and laughed aloud as he saw the different facial expressions of his face. They were a collage of pictures with texts around them that explained the different emotions. The back of the T-shirt had a huge, "We Love For-Runners" in bold font.

Speaking of Everest and Feng, their visit had felt brief to Anders, but he'd been happy they'd come. They'd gotten to see him perform with the group on a televised fan meeting and they were introduced. To his horror, Everest blew a kiss to him, and he couldn't ignore her as the camera was focused on both of them. He'd used the chance to say, "Happy Birthday, Mom," even though she'd warned him several times not to mention it. The crowd cheered and started to sing the "Happy Birthday" song, and Everest looked like she'd prefer to be swallowed by hot larva from a newly-erupted volcano.

Maya was also in attendance and Trance's younger brother, Togo, also came to the event. Alphonso's parents had visited him earlier in the week because the fan meeting coincided with a previous engagement that they couldn't miss.

Mama Miso had sent a meal truck with a For-Runners banner on it, and this had left such an awed impression on Feng that he couldn't stop talking about it. He'd toyed with the idea of a business where he could rent food trucks to fans to support their favorite bands for affordable prices. Anders had been over the moon throughout their visit.

Then he'd read the hate comments just three days ago and hadn't been feeling well ever since. Even Everest could tell that something was wrong when she spoke with him on the phone the day before. But he'd lied, and said he was a bit stressed and nervous because their first-ever performance for the tour was in three days.

The haters had posted comments with doubts about Anders' true parentage. It was no argument that he didn't look like his parents, but what got him angry was how the internet trolls wrote about it as though they were experts in the field of biology. They went so far as labeling his parent's faces side by side with his, and showing how the only identical feature he had in common with his father was his facial structure.

Then, there were those who still took offense that 'the foreigner' was the leader of the group and found all sorts of faults in his vocals. That wasn't the end of it. They already predicted that the tour was going to be a bust since they hadn't sold out their largest venue yet.

So Anders was feeling down, but he tried his best to give a hundred percent during their practices. They'd just returned from practicing in the venue and he was definitely satisfied with the result. Today everyone was on time. Their choreography with the backup dancers went well. The stage design was in its final stages as some of the lights needed to be changed, and the movable parts of the stage needed some reconstruction. All this was going to be done before the big day, which was just three days away, the engineers assured. The only part of the show that was left to be smoothed out by the band members and producers, was their exiting choreography. The stage managers and producers were still deciding if the group should all leave through a lowering stage design, or if they should leave through a back door that would be constructed behind the stairs. That would be decided the next day at practice.

The boys were given a suite in the hotel and it was massive. Alphonso and Trance were playing pool, trying to loosen up after the tense practice. Twine was looking at his wallet and judging from his expression, Anders guessed he was looking at Elvira's picture.

"Guys, gather round," Anders called out. Benny wants us to go through all the lyrics again and see if the fan chants are right, so that he can send it to the producers for publication on the official fan site tonight."

FFQ was known for getting their fans heavily involved in their concerts. They encouraged the fans to buy tour packages for uniformity purposes. It looked great in film. The merchandise was specially produced for specific tours and they had a special color theme for the concerts. This way, the concert halls always looked bright because the color stood out. For-Runners' color theme for their tour was orange and their official fan-base was named 'Forever.' Forever stuck as the For-Runners fan group name when Trance was quoted saying, "I wish this were something we could do forever, just because I'd like the fans to go with us forever." Mr. Rob approved the fan group name.

For their "Forever Tour," the Set-list was complete. For the first half of the show, the show opener was a fan-favorite upbeat song, then six songs would be performed during the main show, and a special guest performance would follow. Then there would be a short break with a mini-movie about how For-Runners had been formed and how they'd won the hearts of the fans. For the second half of the show, they were going to perform two songs and then two show closers.

FFQ had decided to add an encore performance recently, which they were still trying to tie in with how the boys were going to depart from the stage. In the meantime, their task was to cross-check the lyrical chants, approve them, and send them to Benny. Lyrical chants were very exciting. They were the parts of the music where the fans got to participate when their favorite bands were performing. When the band sings, the fans can sing along to a part of a verse or chorus. This heightens the emotion of the music and gives the singer a chance to breathe. For the song, *Just Know*, there is a part where the fans chant, "I want you to know," and then Anders sings, "because you should know," right before the bridge. It always got him a bit emotional, and also got more air into his lungs, so that when he began the bridge, it came off more powerfully. He liked it.

"Alphonso and Trance dropped their pool cues and headed toward Anders, who was slumped on a love seat. Twine already sat on the couch nearest to Anders.

"You feeling better?" Trance asked as he sat on the arm of the couch beside Twine.

Anders nodded.

"You should know better, Bro. You were the one who always scolded me against reading those comments."

"Hmm," Anders exclaimed. He sat up and placed the laptop on the coffee table and told everyone to draw closer.

It was difficult to move the couch so they pulled the cushions to the floor and sat down, huddling around the coffee table.

The screen lit with the lyrical videos of the Set-list with accompanying fan chants that Benny had sent them. Anders started off with, *Where Are You?* They listened, read the lyrics and paid attention to how the chanted parts flowed. There was a collective sigh when the song ended.

"What do you all think? Good?" He asked.

"Good," Alphonso said.

"Me like!" That from Trance.

"I approve," said Twine.

Anders nodded. "I agree. One down, nine more to go."

They all sighed. "This is getting surreal," Trance said.

Anders was noticeably jittery and it had nothing to do with caffeine. In fact, he wasn't into any fancy drinks and stuck to water, but near concert time, he only took sips of water to soothe his throat, and wanted to avoid needing the bathroom at all costs.

But something was different with him. It wasn't nervousness per se. This was much worse.

"Are you okay?" one of the ladies who was touching up their makeup asked him, as she skillfully patted dry sweat from his forehead. "Your eyes are bloodshot," she said.

Anders knew he wasn't sick and couldn't explain what was going on with him. He had stumbled twice already, once on his way out of the dressing room, and the second time when they did a quick practice of their dance choreography at the back near the private garage of the concert hall.

It was after that second time, that his heart rate had increased so high that he thought he was going to faint. Twine had pulled him up and held him until he was sure he could stand without staggering. He'd eaten and had a good amount of sleep. He didn't feel too cold or too hot. His head wasn't pounding. There was no pain and nothing seemed out of the ordinary, but his heart wouldn't stop beating fast. And his hands were shaky.

Twine brushed it off as nervousness and told him to remember that they were all going to be there with him. Alphonso massaged his shoulders a bit, and Trance offered him some water, which he refused.

They were going to be rising onto the stage soon, and Anders was praying silently not to pass out. "I'm okay," he chanted. "I know I'm okay."

He glanced at the projector and saw the crowd, orange, as they held orange banners, wore orange shirts, and waved orange glow sticks. He still couldn't believe the turnout. He couldn't believe they'd become so popular that people filled up the arena to see For-Runners. Meanwhile, around him, people were running helter-skelter, trying to finish up with last minute preparations. They were in the ground level in an extension building of the concert hall, a location built so that performers and their crew were out-of-sight of the attendees in the hall. The extension had various entrances to the stage and floor of the concert hall. The boys were going to access the hall with the lift that would take them up to the stage. They'd practiced their entrance and exits earlier in the day and both had worked out perfectly and timely.

"It's time, guys," Anders heard a voice say. It took him some time to connect the voice to the owner, Benny. "Anders, Anders…"

"Yeah," he responded, but his voice sounded far away. *What's going on?*

"Are you okay? You're sweating so much."

He took in a deep breath, rubbed his eyes and opened them wide. "I'm fine," he said as he stood up. This time, he didn't need any help and he seemed okay, but he was a bit off. He seemed to be living outside his body, well, that's how it felt. He didn't know if he was awake or dreaming. He could see himself get up and put on an assuring smile as he took a paper napkin from the table and blotted out the sweat sprinkled on his forehead and neck.

He could see the worried looks on those who were looking at him.

"I'm fine, everyone," he heard himself say and felt the forced smile on his face. He heard himself clear his throat and tried again with the smile. *That's better.*

"Gather round everyone," he said again, still sounding far away, but a bit better than he'd felt earlier when he'd woken up. He could manage this, he thought.

They all held hands: the band members, the crew members, and everyone that was around.

"We are here to perform. We don't have anything to prove except to give and have a good time. We are prepared. We are ready. Am I right?"

"Yes, you are!"

"For-Runners, here?" Anders yelled.

"For-Runners, now!" Everyone responded.

At the time when the boys were thinking of hype-words to help them get into the spirit of a performance, everything they'd come up with sounded so cliché and funny. They knew they needed something at the beginning and the end of every practice. They needed to get hyped before their performance.

Anders tried out some phrases, which could have worked, but didn't feel natural to him. Then one evening he overheard one of the choreographers helping out another dancer, who was finding it difficult to catch on with the timing of a back flip. The dancer had gotten the moves days before, but on this particular day, she was finding it difficult to execute it. So the lead choreographer was encouraging her and Anders picked up the phrase, "The only difference between the You, here and now, from the You, a couple of days ago is growth and experience. Show it to me."

It stuck. Anders kept the words, Here and Now.

Even with earplugs, the screams were loud. He was amazed. The sense of being away from his body hadn't left him, and by this time he knew it wasn't a dream. He'd never heard of this phenomenon before, and didn't understand what was happening to him, but he was determined to perform the best he could even though he didn't feel like himself.

The accompanying band on the stage had already started with their intro tune before they rose up to the stage. The lights from the top were supposed to appear in different lines and then combine as one and focus on the boys, who were in their different spots on the stage.

It did that, and turned from blue to orange, and then a clear bright stage light. At a point in the music where the strings took over, Twine went to his drum- set and took up his drumsticks. Alphonso and Trance both turned around to pick up their bass and electric guitars on the stands behind them. Anders took a few steps to the left and lifted the microphone stand to his spot. All worries left him the moment he heard his voice. He didn't miss the pitch. He was right on cue. The only problem was that he sounded far away, but he was determined not to let that bother him. He was there to perform. They were there to give and have a good time.

The boys were still buzzed from the energy of the crowd as the wardrobe team helped them undress and change their outfits for the second half of the show. Alphonso couldn't shut up because he was so excited. He couldn't be blamed. The show had gone on so smoothly, that when the last song from the first half of the show ended, they weren't ready to leave just yet. But they'd practiced their exit and were on time on the lift section of the stage that descended into the ground level.

Their special guest, Minor K, was on the stage now, singing and dancing to the cheering crowd.

"Alphonso was chatting with Twine about the cool drumming solo he'd had after their third song."

The makeup team was fidgeting around as they waited for wardrobe to conclude their tasks.

"Get me a pair of scissors," one lady shouted.

The hair team already started with Trance's hair as wardrobe took care of lacing his shoes.

In all this chaos, Anders sat quietly, looking at his reflection in the mirror as he wondered what was going on. He saw his reflection clearly, but he didn't think he was looking at it with his eyes. Something was profoundly wrong, but he was going to wait until the show ended, to worry about it. He'd successfully done the first half, and hoped that the second half was going to go as smoothly.

Twine passed him a cup, "warm water with honey," he said.

"Thanks," he whispered and took a sip. Then he drank more. His throat needed it.

One of the stage managers peeped through the door of the dressing room and said, "This is a good time for a bathroom break guys, and then we have to go backstage. We're using the backdoor for your second stage entrance."

"Already used the bathroom," Alphonso said.

"Just a moment," the lady fixing Trance's buttons said to him as he was about to run off.

He heard something. "What was that?" Anders asked Twine, who'd come around to where he sat.

"I was asking if you're good," he said.

Anders nodded.

Twine wasn't convinced; his expression said it all, but he wasn't going to push. Not now. They had a show to focus on, and he just hoped Anders was okay enough to pull through. The first half had gone very well, but he'd noticed Anders stagger twice. He couldn't see Anders' face to know if it was intentional, since he played the drums behind him, but he thought something was wrong.

And as Anders sat quietly now, the way his face looked pallid as chalk and expressionless, was a bit worrisome. But his voice had been great, so that wasn't the problem. Was he sick?

One of the makeup ladies came beside them and took a look at Anders. She frowned and muttered something under her breath. She opened her fanny pack and fetched some powder and brush.

"Just a bit of color," she said, as she brushed his face. Then she looked at him with her head slanted to the side and her frown returned. Her hand went up to feel his forehead, and she immediately took it away and apologized when she saw his eyes widen. She had a nervous smile on her face as she said, "sorry, I thought you weren't feeling well, but your head is cool. Your coloring is just a bit..." she paused, "off."

"I'm fine," Anders said.

"Ready For-Runners?" a man yelled from the door.

"Let's go," Twine said.

Anders stood up slowly, making sure he had his balance, because the last thing he wanted was to alarm everybody. He had control of his feet and walked steadily out of the room.

Now they were gathered behind the stage, waiting for the tune that prompted them to run out to the stage. It started, and right on the cue, the boys ran out to their spots, and the crowd exploded in screams as they saw their favorite act of the night return to the stage.

It was getting blurry. At first, he didn't notice as the stage light was doing its dance with different colors of lights taking different shapes. But then, he really felt like he was losing the thin thread that held his inner body with the outer body, and he wasn't in control of his senses. His voice was getting farther and farther away from his lips; his sight was getting blurrier and dimmer, and his limbs were getting heavier to move.

Please, please, please, he started to say in his head. *We're almost done, please.*

He decided to improvise. He knew if he tried to dance the choreography, something was definitely going to go wrong. He stood where he was and focused on singing. The group danced and with his peripheral he saw that they didn't act as though something was amiss. *Good job, guys.*

It was nearly the end of the encore performance and his heart started to race unnaturally again, *Why now?*

He belted the last note. He'd done it. Small problem, he couldn't move. Good thing the lights went out in that moment. But they were supposed to exit through the back of the stage and he couldn't get himself to move. Then he inhaled deeply and tried again, but something hit him with a force so hard on his chest, that the pain made his breath cut short. He gasped, struggling to pull air in, but his chest had gotten tight. He grasped at his chest, his nails clawing through his shirt; the pain inflicted by his nails was no a match for the sharp and unbearable one deep in his chest. Was he having a heart attack? he wondered, just as he tightened his eyes in involuntary response to the pain, and then he saw nothing.

There was a beeping sound. He knew where he was, because he'd watched enough TV to recognize that sound anywhere. What he didn't know was why he was there.

It returned to him. Something had happened to him just before he'd managed to leave the stage after the encore. What perfect timing, he mused. Then a tiny recollection returned to him of how he'd felt before losing consciousness, and his stomach recoiled like he was going to vomit. The pain had been intense.

He opened his eyes slowly and confirmed where he was: a hospital, in a private room.

It was quite dark and there was no one around.

He had an oxygen mask on his face. He removed it to the disagreement of the machine it was attached to, which started to beep crazily. In no time, a nurse rushed into the room, and immediately looked relieved to see wide eyes looking back at her.

She smiled, "You're awake."

He smiled back and winced. His lip was so chapped that it cut when he smiled. He licked it and regretted it instantly. It was bitter and a bit metallic from bleeding. The nurse busied herself as she looked at her chart and unplugged a couple of things here and there. She didn't remove the needle that was stuck in his arm from a dripping bag.

"Here, drink some water," she said, adjusting the bed with a remote to help him sit up, and handed him a cup of water. "I'll call another nurse to check your vitals, and I'll let your guardian know that you're awake."

He nodded as he sipped. She took the cup from him when he was done, placed it on the side table, and asked if he wanted the bed lowered.

He shook his head.

She picked up her chart and said, just before she turned to leave, "Someone will be here soon."

"Sorry, how long have I been here?"

She frowned a bit and then said, "Two days, I believe."

Say what?

Everest and Feng had promised to video-chat with Anders on the day of his big concert despite the time difference. The day before, a baking emergency arose and Feng needed to rescue a wedding reception from a catering disaster. Everest was naturally enlisted to help, and they drove a few hours away to solve the problem. Due to this unforeseen circumstance, their plan of video-chatting from the warmth of their home was foiled, as the venue had bad phone reception and the video kept freezing.

Feng sent Anders an email explaining the problem, and letting him know that they'll chat after his concert. It would be nice to hear how it went, and Everest sent her love.

Tired and looking forward to some rest, Everest and Feng were driving back to the city very early in the morning. They both would have loved to take a day off from work, but their jobs needed almost a perfect attendance due to horrible repercussions if they missed a day. A sick day for a teacher affected the students badly. A closed bakery was hard on the company's bottom line. In short, Everest and Feng had to be at work the next day. So they planned to get home, take showers and catch a few hours of sleep, and then head to work. They were going to meet up around lunch time to contact Anders, late at night in Anders part of the world, but he was going to stay awake for them.

Suddenly, a charter bus overtook them and was so close to them that Feng had to swerve a bit to his right to leave a few inches of space between the vehicles. But there was a problem with that move. Because Feng hadn't used his indicator and had moved largely out of his lane, another car that was trying to overtake him on the right collided with him. The impact wouldn't have been so deadly, if Feng's vehicle hadn't spun to the left lane in front of an approaching speeding truck.

It happened as fast as a spinning figure skater on ice, but Everest saw it as slowly as a Ferris wheel. She'd screamed from the beginning, when the car swerved leaving loud screeches in its wake. In the end, the car sounded like it was being squeezed and crushed in a junkyard, as it landed harshly on jagged rock formations.

Everest knew that it was pointless trying to move. She was unnaturally contorted, and the vehicle whined with every tiny movement. She could only open one eye, and with that tried to look toward her left to check on Feng. That was impossible because she couldn't move her neck. She tried to speak, only to hear gurgling sounds, but no voice. Then she heard strained breathing sounds, which weren't coming from her. Everest didn't delude herself on the reality of their unfortunate circumstances, and she stayed stuck in stickiness that she guessed was blood and probably engine oil because she'd lost her sense of smell. Only one part of her body still had its full functionality in that moment and that was her head. She could feel it. It throbbed unimaginably, and hot liquid trickled down the back of it. She wanted to say something to Feng very badly, but it was pointless. No voice, no movements, no way to convey her words.

Feng knew he'd made a fatal mistake, when his feet pressed hard on the breaks, and the car spun from being struck on the passenger side. Now he tried to gather his thoughts, as he felt heat, spills, and a shattered airbag engulf him like a sandwich made of goo, scraps and metal. He couldn't move any part of his body. He suspected his jaw was broken because he couldn't feel it. His nose was surprisingly clear, and all he could do was slowly and painfully take in and release air. "Everest," he wanted to call out. "Everest," he yearned to touch her. But it was fruitless, because he knew she was gone. Everest, his dear wife, didn't need to say a word when she was near, because he could feel her presence in the air. But the air was cold now, too cold. There was no life in it. And then he thought, "don't go far, my dear Everest. I'm close on your heels. Wait a bit for me to say bye, bye to Anders.

Chapter 14 (Barely Living)

For a few months now, Anders had been the number one topic in boyband hemisphere. It all started after the news of his parent's painful exit. He'd just left the hospital, a quiet chauffeur whom he'd never met before, showed up with the doctor and a nurse, and a message from Mr. Rob saying that he should be brought straight to his home from the hospital. That was strange. Mr. Ju Robert never invited anyone to his home. Everything was always business; and meetings of all kinds, both formal and informal, took place at the Agency headquarters or at restaurants.

Anders followed quietly, clutching the copy of doctor's report that he was supposed to give to Mr. Rob. His head still rang with the words of the doctor, "your tests are inconclusive as we are unable to determine the cause of your symptoms. But there is nothing alarming for you to concern yourself with."

He stood in awe at the mansion that rose in front of him. This was the kind of house that he'd always wondered why people built when they didn't have many children. He didn't know if he was supposed to press a doorbell or if he was going to be approached by someone. The chauffeur had dropped him off, reversed, and driven off without saying anything to him. Anders walked closer to the gate, which was a golden and black metallic structure, with tiny rectangular openings that showed what the mansion inside looked like. The gate looked almost like a crest with both ends extended and attached to the stone fence. It reminded him of a wrestler's belt.

He looked carefully from one end of the gate to the other, but didn't see any doorbell button. So he walked back to the front of the gate and pulled the handle. It was open. Weird, he thought. He looked behind him and only saw the deserted street, and the neighboring house with an equally stern-looking gate. He pulled the handle and opened the gate wider, letting himself in, and closing it behind him.

"Hi," he heard a tiny voice that made him jump.

To his right was a little boy, about five years old, who was painting on an easel as tall as he was. This was a bit unsettling because the boy seemed too young for the kind of composure he had, brush in mid-air, and curious eyes surveying Anders. Anders sneaked a peek at what the boy was painting on the canvas and almost exclaimed out loud.

It was a replica of the mansion, from a sideways point of view. *No way.*

"Hey, er, I'm here to see Mr. Rob," he said to the boy, who was now studying his painting with his head slanted and his eyes narrowed.

"He's in there," the boy responded, with his chin directed to the front door.

"Thanks," Anders said, but stopped and said, "Nice painting."

The boy nodded, not looking at Anders and as though saying, "I know."

Anders smiled, knowing whose son he was.

The door was slightly opened a crack and Anders pushed it in, slowly. Just as the little boy had said, Mr. Rob was in there. The colorful candy land that was Mr. Rob's living room was shocking. This wasn't expected at all. Anders stood where he was, looking around the room and forgetting his manners. The TV was on and a popular variety show was playing. A few lights were on, even though it was bright outside, and the colors in the living room already brightened up the place. The furniture was a bright mixture of primary colors, and most shocking of all, it was warm. Everything he'd just noticed was in contrast to the CEO he'd come to know. Then Anders looked at Mr. Rob, who was looking at him, and noticed that all the color around them did nothing to soften his grey and pallid coloring.

"Sorry," he said nervously. "Hello, Mr. Rob."

Mr. Rob nodded and beckoned to him with the wave of his palm. He was sitting at a desk behind a large couch, where there was a setting for a makeshift office. Mr. Rob proved to be a workaholic even in the comfort of his nice home.

"My wife doesn't want me to turn the game room into a home office so she settled for this," he said as he indicated the seat opposite him for Anders to sit down.

"Thanks," Anders said with a smile.

Mr. Rob had a different air about him in his home. He seemed more human. And there was another noticeable difference. His voice sounded softer. This made Anders shift in his seat. Was there something that the doctor had left out of the report that only Mr. Rob knew about? He wondered.

He handed the envelope with the doctor's report to Mr. Rob.

He took it and placed it on the table without opening it to look at the contents. Then he closed the book that he'd been reading and crossed his hands on the desk. "How are you?" he asked Anders.

Was that a confirmation of his fears? Anders wondered. "I'm okay."

Mr. Rob nodded. His eyes went to his folded hands for a few minutes and then with a sigh he said, "Anders, your parents had an accident and they didn't make it out alive."

He must have heard wrong, he thought. Did Mr. Rob just say, parents?

Mr. Rob told Anders that he'd been alerted to the tragedy when he was on his way to see him at the hospital. He thought that Anders didn't need to know the gory details until he was able to take in the news. It was shocking, he knew, and he was sorry for Anders' loss. Plans would be made for Anders to go home and meet with his aunt, who was his closest surviving relative in the family. His aunt has already started planning the funeral. The band members would not attend, unfortunately, but Anders had their support, and the tour would be halted because they wanted to wait for him and be able to perform together.

In the following minutes, Anders only heard the words, "shocking," "sorry," "home," "aunt," "funeral," "band" – and then all went dark.

He would have preferred not to have woken up, he thought for the thousandth time. The doctors had said they hadn't found anything, and even after he'd explained the symptoms he'd had before the incident, they still hadn't been able to say what had been the problem. That's because the problem wasn't physical.

While Anders was going through his unexplainable experience, his parents had been bleeding to death in a deep ravine. They'd been in a ghastly accident, and before the EMTs could extract them, it was too late. They'd been driving in the wee hours of the morning, and the car, after getting hit by a truck, had spun off the road and somersaulted deep into a rugged-terrain ravine. It was known as a death trap for inexperienced hikers, but popular among crazy mountain climbers. Anders couldn't and wouldn't comprehend what had happened. He believed he was having a lengthy nightmare.

Rumors were everywhere that the frontman of For-Runners was suffering from a deadly disease. That was the only explanation for his being hospitalized back to back, with leaked photos of his looking paler than he already was, and somewhat lifeless.

FFQ had to hold press conferences to refute the rumors, and explain the circumstances that had occurred, without giving away too much information. "Anders had been extremely dehydrated during the concert," their publicist explained, telling a white lie to stop fans from fretting. The second hospitalization reason was the truth. "Anders had gotten the upsetting news about his parents. Please be kind and respectful at this time, as he tries to come to terms with this personal tragedy and grief. Thank you," she'd said with a shaky voice and walked away from the room filled with reporters and photographers.

Now he understood the phrase, "barely living," in terms of just existing. The symptoms he'd had on concert day had returned, but this time he didn't care. He stumbled a lot, made incomprehensible statements, didn't have an appetite, and blanked out frequently.

This behavior was so alarming to his bandmates and everyone who came in contact with him, that the Agency put him on bed rest, and conducted psych evaluations on him. The results were what they'd expected. He was reacting to the extreme grief that hadn't yet been resolved. What they couldn't explain, was why this behavior had appeared before he'd heard the bad news about his parents. The speculation was that suppressed guilt can be a strong link in a very close family. There was a possibility that Anders was feeling guilty about leaving his parents, and that link intensified when they'd died, causing the adverse reaction that was manifested physically. Of course, there were no clinical studies out there to support this claim, but this was the only explanation they had and could accept.

Anders had to be pushed in a wheelchair at the airport where he would board a plane home. He'd been masked, and garbed to cover his whole body except his eyes, but the mask didn't do anything to hide how bony-faced he'd become. His protruding shoulders could be seen even though he'd been wrapped in blankets. There was a crowd of fans, and the paparazzi were all clicking away at an unresponsive Anders. Security pushed, fans screamed, the flashing lights were endless.

The bodyguards and security managed to get him to a VIP lounge as quickly as possible, to minimize prying eyes and get him on the plane with a different boarding entrance.

The internet blew up with photos of his current state. His waif-looking body was the topic of numerous threads, and the rumors only got worse. Some sites wrote that it'd been confirmed that he was really sick, and his parent's tragedy only made him worse. Some news outlets dug deeper to find the story that his parents were supposed to be home, streaming his concert live, but a last minute change in plans resulted in the car accident. Some said his parents were speeding home in order to video-chat with him before he went to bed. Of course, considering the time difference, this was false, but no one seemed to pay attention to that.

His home was no exception to the badgering of reporters and fans. If Anders were in his right mind, he would have been surprised how popular For-Runners had become internationally. This would have been a great opportunity to conduct fan-meets, but the timing was too tragic. FFQ prided itself on taking care of their own, and they wouldn't stoop so low as to use such an ill-fated situation to their benefit.

Veronica Atelier, Anders' aunt, was always within arm's reach. Since he'd come home, and after her ear-splitting scream due to his appearance, she'd tasked herself with getting him back to normal, with normal meaning his looking like a human being once again.

He'd managed to stand without aid during the funeral of his parents. Tears had flowed down his face, but that was the only indication that he wasn't a statue. His scary appearance, though still worrisome, became much better after constant prodding from his aunt, and her shoving food in his face. The dark shadows under his eyes had worsened, and unfortunately, there were no makeup artists around to conceal them. Even with the continuous flow of tears, he knew he wasn't really crying. Crying should create some lightness and relief, but all that happened was his giving way to tears when he heard his mother's former students call her name.

Numerous friends attended even though they'd had to travel from far away. Everest and Feng had still considered themselves new to the area even after a couple of years had passed, but the number of people who attended the funeral said otherwise. They were clearly loved.

He wiped his face and walked in between the coffins and placed his palms on both of them. "I can't make sense of this, Mom, Dad" he murmured, his breath hitching. "Maybe one day I will, but not today. This cruel world just took you away. I didn't even get the chance to tell you how well our first show went," he sighed. He was well aware of the eyes digging holes in his back. He didn't feel anything and couldn't cry out. He was sorry for those who were expecting this reaction, but all he wanted to do was sleep, sleep for a very long time.

They started to lower the coffins. He watched. He felt his heart was being stabbed, but he couldn't react. He stood where he was, looking as if he were nailed to the ground.

There was wailing and murmuring, there was sniffling and coughing. He couldn't believe that he wouldn't hear his parents' voices again. He wouldn't hear his mom's laughter and playful scolding. He wouldn't smell his dad's fresh bread and hear his off-tune whistling. He wouldn't hear them argue, and try to ask him who was at fault. He wouldn't be teased by his mom who wished he'd been a girl. His dad wouldn't play pretend rock star with the rolling pin. It didn't make sense.

They all walked up to him, one after the other and in pairs, to pay their respects. Their voices were muffled, but he knew that they'd give him a break if he didn't nod, and so he didn't bother straining to hear them. Then a hand shook his shoulder to alert him. "Everyone is almost gone," his aunt said. "I think we should head home now." He didn't look at her. It was freaky how people said that sometimes one sounds like a sibling. Veronica sounded like Everest as she spoke softly. He swallowed and nodded, walking slowly behind her, not daring to look up and find out if it were really Everest, and all this had been a cruel joke.

Chapter 15 (The No Scandal Clause)

Veronica held his hands and stood on her tiptoes, peering into his eyes. He was forced to look back at her, feeling thankful that she had different colored eyes than Everest. It had been hard when he'd seen familiar mannerisms, and reminded himself that she wasn't his mother.

"You look better, so I don't feel too scared to be sending you back."

"I'm fine."

"But I'm not a hundred percent convinced. I'm only agreeing to this because you suggested it would help you take your mind off things, and everything here reminds you of them. I know the feeling, so I understand. But Anders, listen carefully, the moment you feel overwhelmed, come back home. It's you first, before anything else, okay?"

He nodded, happy that she had done this in the privacy of the exclusive lounge in the airport. He wouldn't have been able to stand the stares. Two weeks here had been a mess, but also a chance for him to face the fact that he was never going to see his parents again. His aunt had been by his side day and night, which had made him a bit claustrophobic, but he couldn't have been more thankful that she had been there when he'd waked up at night with nightmares.

She said she saw improvements in his appearance and appetite. He knew he had improved as well. All he had to do was listen to her, and repeat: Eat. Take a shower. Let's go for a walk. Eat. Relax. Listen to music. Eat. Go get some sun. It became routine and it helped him outwardly. Inwardly? He had no answer for that.

He'd had a chance to chat with the group when Veronica finally agreed to put them through to him. She'd been very watchful of him, and made sure he didn't speak to anyone or use the computer. If she'd known that he wasn't interested in doing any of those things, she would have relaxed.

They all looked genuinely happy to see him. Trance smiled so widely that Anders feared for the elasticity of his mouth.

He told them that he felt better and was ready to continue the tour. He just had to convince his aunt, and he urged them to continue to practice because he was.

"No slacking off here, Bro," Alphonso said.

"Just focus on your health and we'll see you when we see you," Twine said.

Now he would see them in a few hours' time. His flight was smooth, and he had on his eye mask the whole journey, only taking it off twice to eat something, and when he had to use the bathroom.

His return was very quiet. He'd exited through the back of the plane and was escorted by airport security, who took him through a different gate. Benny was there to meet him and smiled happily when he saw him approaching. Anders smiled back.

"I'm glad you're back," he said. "Have you eaten? The others are at Mama Miso's restaurant."

They all looked like they were treading on eggshells around him, taking care not to say the wrong thing lest he break. He wondered how many times he would have to assure them that he was fine and he didn't want to be treated differently. There was a moment when he had to take a break to go and look at himself in the mirror, because it seemed as though there had to be something that was making them act so cautiously around him, maybe he had something on his face that they were embarrassed to mention. Lo and behold, his face was as pale as it had always been since he'd taken notice of how he looked.

Mr. Rob checked up on him a few times within the week which was odd, but Anders could care less. Days after his return, Mr. Rob called for a meeting with For-Runners and the tour managers to talk about continuing the tour. They'd canceled two concerts and still had seven more to go. They needed to announce Anders' return, but in a way that an uproar wouldn't ensue, and that the fans wouldn't think that he was rushed back to work. Anders suggested that a video thanking everyone for their well-wishes, and letting them know that he wanted to return, would help. Also, he was going to stress the fact that his parents had been very supportive of his leaving home and joining the band, so they'd be happy that he was continuing the tour.

It was difficult to ignore the celebrity news sites, but he tried his best. It was difficult to be present the whole time, but he shook himself alert when he felt that he was slipping into somewhere dark. Being around his group was helpful, and playing their songs with the fan chants, he found, was the best medicine for him. He encouraged himself to focus on finishing the tour, even if he didn't enjoy it as he should have. He would finish it for his bandmates and for his parents. He'd deal with whatever came later.

It was no surprise that he was back to being the topic in the world of celebs. He heard how the news about their continuing the tour with him was a surprise. As they'd suspected, there was uproar targeting FFQ, and calling it inhumane for subjecting Anders to work after such a horrible tragedy. Anders' video was a good call, even though it didn't quench the heat entirely.

When Anders left the studio after practice, he overheard someone say that it seemed like news sites enjoyed making up rumors about him. Anders knew not to go online and check. He didn't need to know what the rumors were about. All he cared about was completing the tour successfully.

And he got his wish because his return to the stage was epic. The venue overflowed. The fans were beyond enthusiastic, and this time he was in control of himself. He sang with as much feeling as he could muster without going over the edge. When his heart pained, and he felt he was going to weep, all he had to do was look up at the flickering lights, which hurt his eyes a bit, and made him lose the sad feeling for a moment. He'd read somewhere about artists who used that method when they got too emotional while performing on stage. It worked. He was able to hold it all in until the end.

The last performance of the tour was supposed to be special. The venue was known as The Arena. It was an old, yet magnificent-looking, structure with so many stories to tell. If any artist or band managed to fill up all its seats, the band had officially made it. While it was a worry to perform there at the beginning of their touring, with that huge uncertainty that loomed over their heads, they were overjoyed when they heard the "sold out" bell on the news. They had sold out The Arena. They were shocked.

Mr. Rob acted like he'd known it would happen all along, or he wouldn't have allowed the venue to be added to their line-up when they planned the tour. The popular stars sold that venue in days. Once, it took just hours for the ballad king, Josh Craig, to fill it up. But For-Runners, after a month, finally did it.

As the fans chanted, the structure threatened to collapse. Artists, who'd performed at The Arena, usually said that this special effect of the venue even made their performance more ethereal. The ground seemed to vibrate. The voices seemed to echo. The air was a mixture of natural musk and fragrance that was pleasant to the senses. It was like being surrounded by angels while simmering in beautiful sounds. The Arena experience was always a thrill for the performers and the attendees as well. Anders agreed with everything they'd said as he was experiencing it himself in high intensity.

It was a night to remember. Singing the second classic song on their Set-list as part of their closing act was beyond amazing, so much so that he forgot his troubles. When they all bowed and the lights went off, he had to hold back the tears that were almost on the surface of his eyelids. "Not now," he murmured and swallowed hard.

"They can turn against you in a snap of the finger. They don't deserve to be called my fans."

"Shut up, Anders! It's stuff like this that made them turn against you in the first place. What's happening to you, Bro?"

He gazed lazily at Alphonso, who seemed to have multiplied. He shut his eyes again and placed the pillow on his face. Alphonso knew it was time to leave the room.

This was now Anders' way of ending a conversation.

Did he just ask what's happening to me? Anders thought, as he heard Alphonso's footsteps exit the room. Their tour had been deemed extremely successful for a relatively new band. The buzz wasn't over even after the tour had been ended for weeks. The boys got increasingly busy, but the board of directors agreed that Anders should be given a break. It was in one of his quiet moments that he thought it happened. Because he'd been okay all along, but in one moment, his mind acted strangely and his body followed suit.

He began to get irritated over every little thing, but he couldn't be seen lashing out so he held it in. He began to get tired easily, and found it very hard to get out of bed in the morning. He wasn't interested in food, and had to be reminded and sometimes forced to eat. But the greatest indicator of all was when he didn't want to pick up a pen to write music or even think of going to the studio. Something was very wrong with Anders, and he couldn't deny it, but ignored it purposefully. If others in the Agency noticed as well, which he suspected they did, they just let him be.

But his odd behavior was not going unnoticed to the public. His tantrum when he shoved past a paparazzi that had appeared from nowhere, was videoed and circulated online. When he murmured, "f you," under his breath to a fashion critic who called him "gender-bender wanna-be," that also didn't go unnoticed. People who called themselves behavioral experts were already diagnosing his recent outbursts as a mental problem, while others were saying that fame had gone to his head so he'd forgotten how to be humble. His fans, well, some were sympathetic, reminding everyone that he'd just lost his parents, while some so-called fans teased that puberty was finally catching up with him.

He found himself getting angrier by the day, and didn't know exactly why. Sure, he was still dealing with the grief of losing his parents and there was some anger, but this type of anger wasn't directed at the world; it was directed at himself, and he didn't know what to do about it. FFQ was still in search of the right therapist for him. He'd agreed to it as part of his healing process and quiet break time. He knew that deep down he wanted help, but at the same time a troublesome sense within him, which had never existed before, was brewing and refusing to work on the problem. He didn't talk to anyone about it, and tried to do what he knew best, keep it all in, but this was proving destructive to his health.

In order to avoid causing more trouble, he confined himself to his bed, and stewed in hot anger when he heard the latest rumor about him. Apparently, he was planning on leaving For-Runners. Fans that used to adore him didn't anymore. He was going to break up a perfect group and they were out to get him. This rumor was fueled by his absence from the public eye and only the other three members were being spotted.

FFQ quickly denied this, and explained that Anders was taking needed time off to sort out family matters, and urged that his privacy be respected at this time. Some fans were relieved to hear this and reposted the Agency's statement online. Others still speculated, and said they wanted to hear it from Anders himself. Anders? He just wanted to be left alone, and so his bandmates did, until Twine got tired of it. It was on one afternoon when Anders had just walked into the room after a stop in the bathroom. He saw Twine sitting on his bed.

"Move."

Twine didn't budge.

"Didn't you hear me?"

Twine slowly looked up at the lanky figure scowling above him. "I did." But he made no effort to move.

Anders grabbed his hand and pulled him away from the bed, but this was fruitless. In fact, it was pitiful, because there was no strength in him to be able to pull Twine. Twine was a bit surprised by this, and a deep frown etched his forehead. Then, in anger, he kicked Twine's shin. Twine, shocked by this outburst of violence from Anders, roared in pain, and at the same time, lunged at Anders, grabbed him by the collar of his shirt, and looked fiercely into his eyes. He didn't need to say the words because Anders understood that it meant, "Don't try me."

Shame was written all over Anders' face, and his eyes dropped along with his slumping shoulders. Twine noticed this immediate loss of air and dropped his hands from his collar. He cleared his throat and rearranged his stance, moving aside so Anders could get on his bed.

"You know, if you don't say anything, then we won't know how to help."

Anders still stood where he was with his head bowed.

"Mr. Rob wants to see you. He's in his office."

Anders looked up now. "What for?"

Twine shrugged and was about to leave, but stopped. "I'll see you when you get back. My mom will be here this evening."

All the way to Mr. Rob's office, Anders made it a point to walk with his head raised up. He didn't make eye contact with anyone, but his peripheral vision spotted eyeballs on him. No one said anything to him, but he heard his name come up in hushed tones as people saw him walk by. He didn't care.

Mr. Rob was on the phone, but Jiju said he could go into the office and have a seat. This was the first time that Anders had no particular reaction to her red mane or large green eyes; another tell-tale that he wasn't okay.

Mr. Rob dropped the phone. "Good to see you, Anders. I just wanted to discuss a few things with you in person." He paused and surveyed Anders' face, but he was expressionless, and Anders wondered what he was thinking. He evidently decided not to say it and continued with why he had invited Anders to his office.

"I've pushed aside this important matter for some time in order not to upset you." He opened the folder in front of him and picked up the stapled pages, which he passed to Anders. "It is a case of your transfer of guardianship." He didn't say more, which was a cue for Anders to read the papers.

He flipped to the second page and started reading. The office was eerily quiet, only interrupted by the sound of the flipping pages. Even the refrigerator which usually let out a buzzing sound, was soundless. Anders didn't want to look up to see Mr. Rob's hollow eyes on him because he could feel them. He skimmed some lines, the ones with heavy legal wordings, but he understood the gist of all the paragraphs. It was a legal issue that was to be answered with haste because although the terms of his contracts hadn't changed, his legal guardian had.

Anders nodded, closed the pages and looked up, handing them to Mr. Rob.

"I just wanted you to know that we'll keep closely in touch with your aunt, Veronica Atelier, as she is now your new guardian. Here is a letter you should read," he passed a different two-page sheet to Anders.

It was a letter that granted the CEO of FFQ, Mr. Ju Roberts, partial guardianship, in the event that matters needed immediate attention, and the long-distance would prevent Veronica's immediate action.

Anders read that also and didn't care. He returned it to Mr. Rob after he was done reading it to the end where she had signed. However, he noticed the signature line for Mr. Rob was blank.

"This is the main reason why I called you here," Mr. Rob said. "I want to make sure it is okay with you before I sign this."

"Sure," Anders said without missing a beat.

Mr. Rob was about to say something, but stopped. Then he nodded, picked up a pen from a stationery cup and signed the letter. "This will be mailed to the attorney of your parents' estates this evening."

Anders sat there as though Mr. Rob was talking to someone else.

There was silence between them until Mr. Rob broke it. "You will begin therapy tomorrow. Benny will pick you up in the morning at eight."

Anders didn't say a word.

"You may go now."

Standing up from the chair wasn't as easy a feat as it usually was for him or any young person. He did it with a second try as he held both seat arms for aid. This didn't go unnoticed to Mr. Rob.

Twine shook him awake. "What?" he asked tiredly.

"My mom is here and she wants to see you."

It took Anders too much effort to move both legs to the floor to stand up. It took him another moment to change his shirt and fetch a hat.

Anders could hear sounds coming from their living room. Twine stood aside, waiting for him, as though the distance they had to walk to meet his mom were far away. They made their way eventually to the living room. The doors were opened wide and they entered. There was a mixture of sweet and spicy aromas, and Anders couldn't stop his stomach from growling. This made Twine smile even though he didn't look at Anders. They were greeted by many different dishes lined up on a long rectangular table. Trance and Alphonso were already there helping themselves, and a few people that Anders didn't care to pay attention to.

"You're awake," Alphonso said enthusiastically.

Then there was a small shriek of horror. It was Mama Miso looking at Anders. She turned to Twine with a scowl and said, "You have not been sharing the food I send, you silly glutton!"

He could vaguely make out what was happening around him. He knew there was a crowd. He knew they were focused on him. He knew he was saying something to them, all-be-it too loud, but he thought their reaction to what he was saying was odd. They were supposed to agree with him, but they were jeering. Some had their fists in the air, but it wasn't done in his support. They looked angry.

Suddenly, two people got hold of his arms and started to drag him away from the crowd, which seemed to continue to grow. He was struggling, but he didn't have enough energy to break free from the hold. He kicked and buckled, but their grip was so tight that he finally gave up.

Soon he found himself in familiar territory, his room, and they dropped him on his bed. It took him a while to place himself in a more comfortable position. The room seemed to be spinning and his bed looked uneven like waves. The people who stood above him were talking to each other. They didn't sound happy. He decided to shut his eyes when everything seemed unsteady and shaky. He felt like he might throw up.

"Bring Anders here this minute!" Mr. Rob bellowed with a voice that would never have been associated with him. The nasal sound had all but disappeared, and a very grainy angry voice was heard. "He seems to have forgotten about the terms of his contract." Mr. Rob shrilled, looking formidably deadly and ready to bite off the head of the perpetrator.

"I'm sorry, Mr. Rob, he has passed out."

The next thing he knew, he opened his eyes to a dark room, splitting headache, and uncomfortable stomach ache. It took him a few minutes to place his location and another few to recall what had happened. The lights turned on and a dismayed-looking Trance peered at him and said, "Mr. Rob would like you to see him in his office tomorrow at seven in the morning."

Anders had started seeing a therapist and the situation happened on his third visit. The first session had been more to test the waters. The therapist had introduced herself, explaining what she specialized in, and the results she hoped her patients would have at the conclusion of their final session. Of course, each patient had his own pace and the end focus was healing. She went ahead to tell him stories that he thought had nothing to do with therapy, but he listened attentively. When she asked him questions, he didn't respond. She decided to read a report on what she knew about him, and said that he was free to correct her if anything was wrong.

He did not say anything until she was done. She read two incorrect things, maybe on purpose, but he didn't correct her. One was his date of birth and the other was he didn't like chicken. It was a session spent quietly, but he wasn't released until his time was over.

"I'll see you in three days," she said.

He got up from the chair without a word, bowed his head a bit and walked out of the room.

He learned that the therapist, Dr. Sandra Kim, was the exclusive FFQ therapist. She had her office in the health and wellness section of the headquarters. He wondered how many people's secrets she had in that brain of hers. As he walked down the hallway, he could hear someone moan in pain, coming from one of the physical therapy rooms. He located the stairs and decided to take them. He didn't want to have to chat with anyone in the elevator.

On his second visit, Dr. Kim spent her time trying to get Anders to open up. She acknowledged the fact that everything had its' time, but she needed some responses from him and not just a blank stare. She got a reaction finally. It was when she read from her note she'd entitled, Anders, before and after, that he said something. At first, Dr. Kim had mentioned what she'd found out about how Anders' behavior used to be. She also said people around him widely believed that he'd changed after the news of the untimely death of his parents. But when she said she believed people never changed, and Anders was probably letting his real character manifest, she got a reaction. Then she said, he hadn't been in the group for a long time so people hadn't really known his true colors. He reacted all right.

It became a heated session and was actually cut short in mid-sentence when the time was over. He didn't get up. He wanted to finish the point he was making and Dr. Kim let him. When he got up, bowed and turned to leave, he swore he saw a flicker of a smile on her face.

Session three was the cause of the trouble. Session three had left him hollow, and while he'd tried not to show it during the session, he'd found himself trying not to cry out in anger when he left her office, and was standing glued in the stairwell breathing heavily. *Why did she have to go there?* Dr. Kim had revisited the day of his parents' accident, drawing a parallel between what had been happening to them and him at the same time. She wanted to break the belief that somehow there was a link. She told Anders that it was not scientifically proven, so the theory didn't hold. That it could have been just a coincidence. Then she said the word, guilt, and he stopped listening.

He'd left the session in a haze and instead of walking back to B House he'd gone to F House instead. He didn't pay attention to the surprised looks he got. He just made his way straight to the TV room and to a small cabinet at the back where he'd once seen half a bottle of Scotch. It was still there. He took it, found a loveseat, sat down, opened the bottle, and downed it.

Now he'd just heard that he has to meet with Mr. Rob in the morning. He didn't know what the time was, but he knew it wasn't too late if Trance was still awake, and Twine's bed was empty. He was going to vomit, he was sure.

He was there before seven. He sat in the reception room, trying to ignore Jiju's loud yawns.

"I'm going to quickly make some coffee. Do you want a cup?" she asked, her usually bright large eyes still in slits, with

145

emphasis on their unique moon shape. He was taken aback for a bit, and then snapped himself awake and said, "No, thanks."

She pushed the slightly hidden door and disappeared for a few minutes.

That was fast, Anders thought when she came out with a paper cup with steam rising from its brim. She took a sip as she went to her desk. "Arr," she sighed in satisfaction.

She typed something on the computer and then got up, took a bunch of keys and went into Mr. Rob's office. She unlocked it and went inside. She was out in no time with a tray of mugs and locked the door behind her. She went back into the room where she'd gone to get coffee. Then she was out again with another set of mugs on another tray and opened up Mr. Rob's office.

Anders watched her work because he'd come empty-handed and was bored. He knew not to bring along his iPod because he didn't want to look disrespectful, with earphones in his ears when Mr. Rob showed up. No one needed to tell him that he was in trouble and was expected to look remorseful.

Jiju returned to her desk, took a sip of coffee and began to work on her computer. It seemed like with every sip, her eyes got brighter. He looked away because he didn't want to get caught staring, and he then noticed that she'd stopped typing. He looked up at her and she was staring dead straight at him. He didn't look away, not because of her mesmerizing eyes, but because he didn't want to seem shy or look guilty for any reason.

She sighed, still keeping her gaze on him. "I know it's not my place," she said, "but I just want to say something to you. First of all, I am sorry for your loss," she swallowed and looked away, her eyes darting here and there as though thinking about how to word what she was going to say next. Then she looked at him again. "I'm a fan – of yours especially. No one in this Agency can argue that you're really talented. I just wanted to let you know that so many people are here for you, so please don't throw away this opportunity. Even Mr. Rob is a fan – I mean, I've never seen him talk about any of his artists with a smile." She laughed. "It's scary when he smiles, have you seen it?"

Anders didn't hear her question because the laugh had distracted him. The sound of it was unexpected, let alone the way her eyes disappeared, leaving a curve in its wake. She is so beautiful, he thought and –

Mr. Rob walked in, suitcase in tow, wearing formal attire of a sharply pressed grey suit. Without glancing at Anders, "come into my office," he said. He nodded to Jiju's greeting without glancing at her either.

Anders followed behind and closed the door when he entered.

Mr. Rob placed the suitcase on his desk and went to pick up a bottle of water from the refrigerator. Anders stood awkwardly by the door.

Walking behind his desk with the bottle of water, he used his spare hand to gesture to Anders to take a seat. He sat down as well. To Anders, Mr. Rob didn't look angry, but he was a master at hiding his emotions anyway. But Anders was glad that Mr. Rob had had some time to cool off. It would have been worse if he'd been here yesterday.

"What happened yesterday?" He went straight to the point.

Anders scratched his head, not knowing where to begin or if he could even tell the beginning. "To be honest, I don't remember," he said.

Mr. Rob didn't react to his response, but his cool words put Anders on edge. "Let me help you remember," he said. With that, he fetched his cell phone, unlocked it and found what he was looking for. He pressed a button, placed it on the table and pushed it to Anders' view.

The volume was so loud that Anders cringed at hearing his slurred speech. He watched the video and it dawned on him that the things he thought had happened, had not happened the way he remembered it. He had been venting out of anger at the therapist's audacity of inferring that he had never been a good person. He called his fellow group members pretenders, and that they only cared about his talent for writing good songs. Where were they now that he was sad about his parent's death? Where were they?

Anders closed his eyes as he heard that. Then just before he was dragged off, he'd said, "Leave me alone! I want my mom!"

"Anders, I have to admit that your recent behavior baffles me. I'm a good judge of character. I would have bet that you could have handled this tragedy, no matter the magnitude, better than this."

Anders now looked up to meet Mr. Rob's gaze. He was holding in the anger that was rising in him. *What does he mean by that? How is someone supposed to guess how a person can handle losing both parents at once in a horrible accident?*

Mr. Rob may have sensed Anders' rising anger and said, "I also have to admit that I haven't known anyone who lost both parents in a night that should have been a night of celebration. I'm sorry, but I have to remind you that life goes on. I have to remind you that people are depending on you. I have to remind you that you have important work to do. I have to remind you that you signed a contract. Do you want me to provide a copy so you can reacquaint yourself with the section concerning scandals? Because your actions could cost us. Don't forget that your group is still in its delicate growth stage, and the other members need you all to succeed. You are the leader, Anders, act like one!"

The other members, he thought. Even though he was going through a personal tragedy of this magnitude, he had to think of the other members. He had to do what was right for all of them and not just focus on himself. He sighed loudly.

"We managed to contain this video before it was posted online. I'm giving you a warning. You may leave."

Chapter 16 (Suspension)

"What's this?" he asked, as the waiter offered him the glass. "It is a traditional fermented drink."

"Then I shouldn't drink it."

"We're serving it to everyone here and you can just take a sip after the toast as a sign of respect."

"Okay."

Anders took a sip of the drink. Then the only other drink he had was the cranberry punch. They'd substituted it for those who were underage. But something was wrong. He'd been lightheaded afterward, and asked to be accompanied to the gardens so he could get some air. A server had escorted him. He'd remembered walking a bit and then sitting on a bench.

He'd remember hearing sounds of laughter and cheers coming from the ballroom.

FFQ was having its annual Agency celebration, which coincided with Mr. Rob's birthday. It was a massive celebration taking place in one of the grandest hotels in the city. The crème de la crème of the music industry were invited. Government officials were in attendance. Fellow Agency-mates were there. Even a few competitors of FFQ showed up. It was a big deal, and a chance for investors to look around the ballroom and see the 'money people' and accomplished individuals in attendance.

Then he heard siren sounds, saw colored and flashing lights. He heard chaos in form of voices and a honking vehicle. He was horizontal and he felt feverish.

He'd blown it. There was no way they'd let this go. When he walked into the room and saw their grim faces, he knew what would come next. To his surprise, Mr. Rob didn't start screaming at him, no, he just had a smirk that looked wicked and then handed him a red folder.

"Sign it," he said. "I think you need some time for self-reflection."

"I just –" Anders started to say.

"No need for that. You will be given a chance to apologize. Sign the document and leave. You are interrupting an important meeting at this moment."

Someone sighed, which made him realize where he was and all the people who were there. It was a board meeting and Mr. Rob had instructed Jiju to let him in whenever he showed up, even in the middle of a meeting. This was serious. Anders opened the folder, which already had a pen stuck to the jacket. He took the pen and didn't bother reading what was on the sheet of paper. He saw the bolded word, "Suspension," and that was all he needed to see. Deep down he was relieved. Why? It hadn't said, "Termination." That was the word he wanted to avoid. He could tell he'd avoided that word when Mr. Rob said he thought he needed some time for self-reflection. But the confirmation was what he needed to see and he almost cried in thanks. He held his tears in, though, and waited until he'd walked out of the office. Both hands covered his face and he let himself cry. For the first time in weeks, he felt ashamed. He felt sorry, and that was a huge turn of events. Maybe he was going to be okay after all.

It was another drunken incident. If only he was a quiet drunk. If only. Anders had been given a spiked punch drink at the Agency annual party. It still wasn't clear how his drink got spiked, but it had also contained substances that were meant to make a person relax, but had an adverse reaction on Anders' behavior. An investigation was still on-going concerning the issue, but the backlash, due to his outburst, was huge.

The incident had been filmed and due to the fact that it had been in a public place, the Agency wasn't able to contain the fast spread of the video. It showed Anders sitting on a bench with his head between his knees. Someone had asked him, "Are you okay?"

He didn't respond at first. Then there was a hand that patted his shoulder. So he raised his head slowly and looked at the person who'd patted him. "I'm fine," he responded, his speech slurred.

Then he caught wind of another person and looked in that direction. It was this person that was filming. The video showed Anders looking confused, eyes bloodshot, face pale and sweaty with protruding cheekbones. He looked skeletal and a bit demented. It took him a while to realize that he was being filmed as he just kept looking in the direction of the video. The first person who'd asked if he was okay could be heard telling the person filming to "stop videoing."

Then Anders could be seen struggling to get on his feet. He staggered badly and at one point had to grip tightly on the bench to be able to stand up. When he was able to stand more firmly, he turned toward the direction of the person filming and could be heard using profanities and threatening to "break that effing thing!"

Soon there was a scuffle and a cry and it wasn't Anders' voice. Then the person screamed saying he would sue Anders. Anders could be heard laughing as he urged the person to go on and this is where the video ended. No one could explain how Anders' had gotten a swollen split lip, a slash on his shoulder and two bruised fingers. He was found passed out and bleeding on the garden grounds and the police were called.

Not long after, the video was circulating online and one person who was questioned only saw when Anders supposedly assaulted the person who was videoing. When he awoke in the hospital, he knew he was in big trouble. The evidence was that Veronica was napping in a chair beside his bed, and the expression on her face wasn't sadness, but the same expression Everest always had when Anders had gotten on her nerves.

Now he'd seen the full extent of his actions and the nation-wide uproar. He was truly frightened for the first time since he left home, but the worst feeling was the guilt he felt for letting his group members down. He spoke to the police before he was discharged from the hospital. He found out that his toxicology report showed that there were other questionable substances along with the cranberry juice in his system. They took his statement and alerted him to the fact that he was being investigated. Then he was told about a fine that he was supposed to pay. The person he'd assaulted had settled and the charges had been dropped. Since it was his first offense, and since some foul play was involved, he was going to get community service as punishment.

The ride home with Veronica sitting quietly beside him was intense. He wished she would say something, but she didn't utter a word. The only thing she'd said when she woke up and saw him looking at her was, "good, you're awake. Did the doctor come already?"

Then when they reached B House, Alphonso, who'd been playing a game, acknowledged Veronica with greetings, but didn't look Anders' way. He went to the bedroom, with Veronica following behind. He knocked to let Twine know that he was coming in with his aunt, and when Twine didn't respond, he opened the door to find that he wasn't there.

She'd already been in his room. He saw a suitcase and her purse on his bed. He became very tired all of a sudden and climbed into the bed and lay down.

She pulled a chair close to him, took a seat and then began to study her fingers. Soon she stopped, took in a deep breath and said, "Do you want to come home? The ball is in your court."

Anders looked at her. He didn't answer immediately because he was actually considering her question. *Did he?*

He could go home and start all over. He could forget this as a small life flaw. But did he? "No," he responded finally.

She nodded. "It's not easy to be so young and lose your parents. But you should be thankful for the time and memories you had with them. You had their love and still do. Now what matters is how you decide to spend every minute being the good kid they had. The world won't pity you or give you a break. It will dish out whatever it pleases. You will have to decide to either eat it or forego it." She sighed. "I don't know what to say, Anders. I don't know if someone did this to you on purpose or you got careless, I don't know."

"I thought it was only cranberry juice," he said.

"But it wasn't!" She raised her voice. "I'm sorry," she apologized. "I'm a bit stressed. When they called me and said you'd had another episode, I just.... I just started wishing Everest were alive."

Anders sat up. "Episode, what episode?"

She made a sound that was almost like laughter, but it wasn't a happy one. "Apparently you're the kind they call an imprudent drunk and this is not the first time."

He couldn't argue with that.

The door opened and it was Twine. He smiled when he said hi to Veronica, and said he just wanted to pick up something from his dresser.

"Please ignore me and take your time," she said to him.

He went about his business and in no time was gone out of the room. Anders didn't fail to notice that he wasn't acknowledged. He deserved that, he thought.

"I'm sorry," he said quietly to Veronica. "I'll be more careful in the future."

Now she chuckled. He was taken aback. She explained, "Well you have to hope there is a future after you talk to your boss."

"You mean the CEO."

"Sure."

He sighed. "What day is today?"

He cried again when he got back to B House. Veronica was taking a nap on the couch, but otherwise, the apartment was empty. He went into the bedroom and opened the envelope that Jiju had given him. She'd been horrified to see him crying and didn't know what to do. So she'd just murmured something and given him the envelope. He'd wiped his tears, swallowed hard and left.

He sat down on the bed and opened the envelope. It contained copies of documents that he needed to keep: the incident that was reported to the police, his own statement, and information on his community service details. There was another document that was entitled, "How to write an effective letter of apology." There was a post-it note on the document that said, "Contact Benny concerning this."

It looked like they were filming a scene in a low budget movie. He was seated in a small room in the FFQ building. Depending on the day of the week, that room served as storage space. He'd seen some trainees store their musical instruments here on the weekends. It was a sad scene, with him looking as though he'd been demoted from a higher position and moved to a lower level in disgrace .

No one cared that the apology video ought to look nice. No hair and makeup personnel at his disposal. He looked pitiful and believed it was done on purpose. All he had to focus on was to properly execute a perfectly heartfelt apology, -- look the part, say the right things and present it to the perfect group. This letter of apology had been written three times before it was approved by the managers. Don't give unnecessary excuses, and explain how you plan on taking responsibility for your actions, they'd said. The public opinion of you is very bad right now, and we need to focus on changing their sentiments before it escalates.

So now he was sitting in the well-lit tiny space, holding his notes with trembling hands. Benny stood beside the cameraman who gave him the sign to begin.

"To everyone that I have hurt with my stupid actions these past few days, I am very sorry." He swallowed and cleared his voice because it was shaking. "I acted irresponsibly, and as a result, caused harm to someone who didn't deserve it. I will take my punishment seriously. I will excuse myself from the duties of For-Runners while I work on reflecting and improving myself. I promise to come back better, and win your trust again. Forgive me. Thank you for understanding. Anders Quigley." He bowed.

His apology was filmed in three takes and then Benny nodded that it was satisfactory. He patted Anders on his shoulder and said, "Take it easy, go have some rest, and come back stronger."

Anders nodded and bade them goodbye.

As he walked to B House, he wondered if his apology was going to do anything to quench even the minutest bit of the rage in the fandom. The fans were very angry and had already nicknamed him "bipolar ingrate." It was the worst thing he'd ever been called in his life and it hurt. He prayed that the police would find who spiked his drink, maybe it would help calm down some bad-tempered fans. He felt bad for his actions, but was grateful that he was the only one who was targeted in the band. In fact, the fans were supporting the other three much more. He couldn't complain. They were working hard.

Veronica stayed with him for two more days in B House. Twine gave up his room willingly for the time being. She played games with him, did his laundry, cooked some dishes with the ingredients that the housekeeper purchased for her. She tried to make it so that Anders didn't feel so alone, as the other boys were busy and barely at the apartment. Calls weren't coming in like when he'd had to show up at the headquarters for an appointment. He tried the best he could to stay off the internet, and reading wasn't appealing. He hoped that he would feel the urge to work on something because when Veronica left, all he'd have to keep his mind busy for a few hours would be therapy and community service. He needed something else to occupy his time.

He wasn't going to see her off to the airport, so before she left with the chauffeur that Mr. Rob sent for her, she gave him a parcel. "No one would blame you if you decided to quit this and come home," she said to him. "I'll support whatever decision you make, okay?"

He nodded, emotional and couldn't speak.

She hugged him as the chauffeur took her suitcase to the trunk. Then she got into the car and off they went. He stood outside for some time even after the vehicle had disappeared. There was no need to rush back into the empty apartment. When he entered the living room, he sat down on the couch and then opened the parcel.

It contained his dad and mom's rings, now as pendants on a silver chain, a cell phone that belonged to his dad, a CD, and a letter.

He rubbed the rings with his fingers and closed his eyes. He couldn't help the tears that flowed from his eyes. He was sad, but it was a different kind of sadness. The anger he felt the past few days seemed to have dissipated. He remembered when his dad had lost weight once and said his ring kept falling off, and his mom had joked that he didn't need to change the size because he would gain all the weight back with the holidays approaching, and all the baking he was going to be doing. He did gain back the weight.

He turned on the cell phone and clicked on the gallery. His dad's cell phone was the epitome of an electronic album. He took pictures and filmed any and everything. He was surprised that the cell phone had survived the crash. He knew his dad had it with him because he didn't go anywhere without his phone. He opened the letter, which was a copy of his parents' estate. He wasn't interested in looking through that.

Then the CD. He played it and held his breath, knowing that he would see them. A kid with a large smile and missing front teeth appeared. Anders laughed as he saw the kid fumbling with a plain T-shirt.

"Hi, my name is Philipa and I will be teaching everyone how to design a T-shirt. I have many helpers here, Mr. Quigley, Mrs. Quigley, Tiana, Robbie, Farren, Trisha, Louis, Kimora..." She named everyone as the camera panned through the room, showing their smiling faces. These were Everest's students, and they made a video of their designing T-shirts for For-Runners. Anders was so attentive, waiting for moments when his parents were filmed. Their laughter was comforting. They made so many mistakes trying to use stencils, and Feng suggested buying an iron-on to stick the letters on the T-shirt. Dad and his short-cuts, Anders thought. He couldn't help grinning eye to eye as he watched the video.

Chapter 17 (The Mirror Reveals)

Yesterday was the last day of his community service. As always, the librarian smiled when he returned the keys and checked out.

"Well done!" Said Mr. Kho, who was very grey and very old, but had eyes as bright as headlights. On the first day Anders met him, he thought Mr. Kho looked like a hawk. Anders knew not to mess with him because he gave off the impression that he could see all that happened in the library. Anders was taxed with archiving old works from paper to digital format and he was very happy to do it. It was community service, but he was also keeping his mind occupied and learning so much. So on this day as he finished his work for the last time, a deep sense of loneliness engulfed him. He was going to have spare time that he didn't look forward to.

Today, his therapy session had seemed a bit odd. Dr. Kim had frowned so much with each answer he'd given her. He'd been honest, that was the point of getting help. Then she'd constantly asked, "How are you feeling?" He'd answered the best he could to explain it. His fellow band members were barely at home. Trance and Twine were working abroad; Alphonso was on a movie set in another city. The only people he could chat with sometimes were the housekeeper, Benny, and Mr. Kho. Now he wasn't going to get to chat with Mr. Kho anymore, and he'd been the most interesting of them all. Yes, he felt a sense of accomplishment for finishing community service, but he wished it were longer because he'd now have to look for something else to do.

"But I hear you've started getting song-writing assignments again," she'd said. He'd answered affirmatively.

"That could occupy you plenty," she'd said. He'd agreed.

But her frown got deeper and he couldn't tell what he'd said that made it so. Now she continued.

"You've come a long way and I think it is now okay for you to think that you can get back to where you used to be. You know where that is, right?"

He didn't respond.

"I mean getting back to the fun singer-songwriter who had many admirers."

He sighed and then said, "I don't think it will ever be the same."

"Says who?" she countered. "I can give you a list of examples of people who had a falling-out with the public and voila, they're back and all has been forgotten."

Anders studied his fingernails without responding.

"Don't you feel that the nastiness that was directed at you months ago has now lessened?"

"I wouldn't know. I don't go online or pay attention to people."

She nodded. "Let me give you a simple example. When we began your session and you had to walk into this building, what did it feel like? I guess my question is, how did you feel with people around?"

" It was uncomfortable and nerve-wracking. They were always looking at me and saying things. I didn't listen to them, but I would guess it was mean things."

"Fast-forward to today. How was it when you came in?"

"Not as bad. I guess people are now used to seeing me so they don't care anymore."

"This is the point I'm trying to make, Anders. We will start working slowly on getting you back to what used to be normal to you."

He shifted in his seat.

"It seems like you don't like the idea."

"That's not it. I just don't know how to face the fans. I think they hate me now."

"Anders, they don't hate you. When people look up to someone, they see them as people who can't commit any human mistakes. This is why they react intensely when their idol does something that they think he should be above doing. But guess what? Time changes things. Their reaction to you won't be as intense."

"But I think they'll still remember."

"Of course they will. But their reaction is now watered down. The anger has dissipated, I can assure you. When the police released the statement that you'd been aggravated, and that part of the video had been edited, and that your injuries were sustained when you'd passed out, some of your fans reacted strongly in your favor."

He still didn't look convinced and she noticed this. She placed her notebook and pen on the coffee table that was between them.

"Why are you called "cool mystery?""

"Excuse me?"

"The official For-Runners fan site nicknamed you "cool mystery.""

He frowned. "Um, I have no clue."

She nodded. "Well, you would want to find out about that some time – when you're on speaking terms with your fans," she laughed.

He was still frowning.

"Anders, on a deeper level, fans will be fans. They will dislike you when you act human, but some will still remain loyal. Unless you commit such an atrocious act that would even shock the devil, they'll rethink their loyalty to you. It's a good thing that you're not active online, stay that way for now. But I think you should know that the hurtful posts about you have been taken down, and there are some comments from people who say they miss you."

He looked up in surprise. He didn't think he'd heard her correctly. *Did she just say they miss me?*

"Anders, Anders…"

He stuttered. "Did they really…"

Yes, some fans missed him, but not all of them. He'd been too hopeful, and was hurt when he read some comments. *What was I expecting? That they'd just open their arms wide and say, "Anders, we totally forgive you. All is forgotten."* Well, that wasn't the case. Some out there still held him in contempt, and some said bye to him, that it was nice knowing him. The only thing that kept his heart from total annihilation was that For-Runners' music was still appreciated.

He saw the "cool mystery" term that seemed to be associated with him, but he had no idea why. Online, the fans who still supported him called him that, and what he understood after reading most of their posts, was that they thought he was cool and mysterious. And this phrase happened to take effect now that he was not seen in public anymore. They were contemplating on what he was doing at the moment, and speculating that he was writing songs that would no doubt be number one on music charts. He was flattered. It was a good thing they didn't know that wasn't the case.

He took in a deep breath. The laptop tasks popped up just in time to remind him of the deadline for music he was supposed to write. The assignment had said, in this time of sadness and despair, pour out your heart. The funny thing was that the two songs he'd written had nothing to do with sadness. In fact, they were the opposite emotion. One was a dance song without a clear message, and the other was a ballad about falling in love. It was laughable. It sounded like a poem written by an eighteenth-century romantic. But his eyes lingered on the pop-up and something in him stirred. Was he ready to pick up the mantle from where he'd stashed it? Was he ready to go back to who he'd been? He was still saddened by how unforgiving his fans had been. While he'd thought that they should have been on his side, he realized that it was his arrogance that had been speaking. Anybody, no matter who, should get repercussions for being a nuisance. He deserved the backlash, but he thought the magnitude was still unfair. He had been treated like he'd killed somebody. Then he reminded himself that it came with the territory of being popular. He sighed again and shut down the laptop.

The apartment was quiet, but he didn't feel as alone as he'd expected to. He walked past the kitchen door and walked back, looking at his reflection. He went into the bathroom and looked in the mirror to see his face more clearly. He wasn't shocked at how much he'd changed physically, but it was unsettling to see how everything had taken a toll on his appearance.

He didn't like his protruding cheekbones and the dark, almost purple, circles under his eyes. The thing that bothered him the most was his hair. It wasn't what it used to be. It was now dull and tangled. A bird's nest looked better. And so he picked up a hat, left the apartment and went in search of Benny. He needed a haircut.

Trance yelped. "He cut his hair! Oh my god, he cut his hair!"

Anders was watching TV when they opened the front door noisily, pulling their luggage behind them as they'd just returned from the trip. He looked at them and smiled and noticed that Alphonso was also with them. Twine and Trance had been abroad for a week and Alphonso had been out of state almost a month. They must have rendezvoused at the airport. Now he saw Alphonso's eyes widen as he noticed the tattoo on his arm.

"I see it's your mission to surprise us," Twine said.

"The tattoo is temporary. I just did it because I got bored."

"You drew that?" Trance asked in awe.

"Uhuh."

"Looks cool, Man," Twine said as he tugged his luggage along to the bedroom.

Anders couldn't help grinning. He'd missed his roommate, but more importantly, he'd missed the friend who had warmed up to him, and later became distant again. Suddenly, he wanted to jump up and go ask about their trip, but he held himself back. He was just happy to see that things were getting back to normal.

Trance continued to stare at Anders.

"What?" Anders asked.

"Why did you cut your hair though?"

Anders shrugged. "Felt like it."

Alphonso, who was busy searching for something in his suitcase which he'd opened in the living room, said without looking at them, "He's done with the old and bringing in the new."

"That's not it," said Anders. "I just felt like getting a haircut."

Trance seemed okay with the response. "Still, it looks good on you," he said, before he left.

"Found it!" Alphonso said in excitement. He then threw it toward Anders, and Anders caught it. Then he zipped up the suitcase and pulled it along with him without saying anything about the item he'd just given Anders.

It fit in his palm, and had been wrapped in an irregular shape so he couldn't guess what it was, but it was slightly heavy. He unwrapped it and found a blue square box. Inside the box was a crystal cube that he carefully took out. Then he peered into it, and noticed that there was something in it. It was the shape of a mountain that he would recognize anywhere. The top of the mountain gleamed with snow-like powder and at the base were tiny words, "Always by your side." Anders was stunned. It was a gift that reminded him that he needn't feel alone. He wanted to run to Alphonso's room and scream that he was thankful for such a thoughtful gift, but he knew he'd frighten him because he began to weep. Alphonso had gifted him with Mount Everest, and made him think of a few jokes Everest and Feng had exchanged over her lovely name. "Thank you," he murmured.

He brushed his hair with his hands. He couldn't deny the change he saw in the mirror. He was beginning to look better, and he had his brothers to thank for it. The week before, they'd forcefully dragged him to the studio and after just a few minutes in there, he almost cried for joy. He'd missed the instruments. He'd missed the sounds. He'd missed the vibration. He'd even missed the smell.

Those three boys knew him well, and they'd purposefully made mistakes like singing out of tune or playing the wrong note or saying the wrong words to the lyrics. They knew that Anders wouldn't ignore them. That was all it took. He was here and there, coaching, correcting, suggesting, and then a light bulb went off. He got it. He started to laugh. "Good one, guys, you got me."

Next thing, he went to his favorite corner and logged onto the computer. For the first time in a while, he had an idea for a real song and didn't need to be told to compose it.

A few days later, Anders felt the change within himself and it seemed to manifest on his face. He looked healthier, and the scowl that had threatened to be imprinted on his face had vanished. He noticed, on his way to Headquarters for this session, that people were actually looking him in the eye and smiling at him. He wasn't dreaming. Two people called his name and said hi to him. He entered Dr. Kim's office with a grin that he didn't realize he had. It was when she smiled widely that he caught himself, coughing to hide it even though it was too late.

"Have a seat, Anders. I think we're going to have a good session today," she said.

Chapter 18 (Slack)

For-Runners' official social media page was re-vamped and the fandom noticed it. It hadn't been given a major update since Anders' scandal, but the week after Twine, Trance, and Alphonso returned from their various scheduled tasks, For-Runners' social media page was updated, and schedules for their upcoming events weren't just on FFQ's website, but theirs. The fans couldn't be happier.

Although one thing was apparent, the only updates Anders had were photos of events he'd attended before the scandal. Some fans didn't mind this. In fact, comments concerning Anders were complaints of his scarcity. They missed him.

The biggest surprise of all was when the boys got packages from the CEO and they opened them up to find brand new phones.

"No way!" Alphonso screamed in excitement.

They all turned their attention to Benny, who had perched on the arm of the couch, grinning ear to ear.

"Is this for real?" Twine asked.

Benny nodded.

"But there's a catch, right?" Anders asked.

"You got that right. Mr. Rob thought it was okay to give them to you all, a gift from one of our sponsors, but there are rules, of course."

"Let's hear them," Twine said.

Benny went ahead and read a bit of information he'd noted on his phone about what was expected from the boys concerning the usage of their cell phones. They were allowed to make and receive calls from approved family members and friends. They were allowed very minimal social media engagement, which had to do with updating their group social media page. Their posts would be moderated by managers and then approved or disapproved. This was a big step since they didn't used to be allowed to make any contributions to their page. Failure to abide by the rule would lead to the return of the phone.

"I think it's fair," said Trance.

"It's a miracle," Benny said. "You guys seem to be getting a different treatment. It seems like Mr. Rob gives you all a lot of slack."

"How?" Alphonso asked.

"Well," Benny cleared his throat. "I'm not saying he favors your group more, but he has been doing stuff differently for your group. You guys have got more work than most of the groups combined, you got B House, you have more visitation days, and now the phones. Okay, I admit that you deserve it because you guys work so hard, and have gotten to a point that often takes other groups years to get to. So, definitely well-deserved."

"Of course," said Twine.

Alphonso had already begun to test the apps on the phone.

"One more thing," Benny said when he saw Alphonso. "If you run up your phone bills, it comes out of your paycheck."

They chuckled. "Tell us something new," Twine said.

"Wait a minute, they approved it," Alphonso said in surprise.

"No way!" Anders responded.

"Yes. Look," Alphonso said.

It was Anders' photo all right. Alphonso had been attached to his phone, literally, since he'd gotten it the afternoon that Benny brought it from Headquarters. He had been taking nice photos with it. At first, the guys had whined that he should stop, but they soon got used to it because it seemed like it was a new-found hobby for him.

He'd taken a photo of Anders, who was in a dimly-lit part of the studio, playing on the piano. He was so taken by the music he was playing, that the photo captured his perfect posture, fingers on the piano keys and eyes closed.

This was one of the photos that Alphonso had posted on their social media page, which had been awaiting moderation. Then a spike in the traffic on the page alerted them to the fact that fans were very busy on it. They'd wondered what caused it. Lo and behold, it was the photo of Anders. It had been approved and posted with the original caption that Alphonso had included, which said, "Leader of For-Runners doing what he does best. Don't you just love his pretty face?"

While some fans were thrilled to see a current photo of Anders, his haircut was the major topic of almost every comment.

"He looks younger."

"NOOOO! *Sad face emoji*"

"Nice haircut."

"Wow, he looks great!!!"

"I missed you so much."

"Grow your hair back."

"Please talk to us. We forgive you."

"Love you, Anders!"

The comments were endless, and most noticeable were the minimal number of hurtful comments. Anders felt emotional, but he reminded himself not to continue to read the comments. It looked like the fans were on his side again, but there were the usual mean comments that still popped up, and he tried not to let them get to him. He was still trying to trust his fans. He knew that human nature was such that a friend today could be an enemy tomorrow. The hurt he'd felt when they turned against him was still ripe in his memory, and as he worked to better himself daily, he reminded himself that he had to try to be at ease with his fans again, but not forget the repercussions of scandals. He'd learned his lesson.

"Wow, Anders, I'm so happy to see this, you have no idea," Alphonso said, his grin still in place.

Anders nodded, taking up his notebook from the coffee table. He was feeling a certain way and needed to pour it out in words.

"I'm so surprised they approved this post. I guess we just assumed they wouldn't post any of your pictures yet. I'm glad I added it."

Anders smiled. "I'm surprised too. I guess Benny's slack theory is true. Remember it took up to a year for A-Plus to be included back into his group activities and his scandal wasn't even as bad as mine.

"True that!"

Chapter 19 (You)

"You" by Anders Quigley

Hair like summer night
Eyes like salt water
Lips like autumn clouds
Neck like lighthouse

How you stun me
How you strike me
Who are you?
I don't know but you know

Tell me who you are
I want to know, I want to know
Tell me who you are
Please let me know, let me know

Always in my heart, you are always in my heart 2x

Stare like laser
Voice like soft raindrops
Smile like sunlight
Feel like cool breeze

How you make me wish
How you make me feel
I know you
I remember you

Tell me how you've been
I want to know, I want to know
Tell me how you've been
Please let me know, let me know

Always in my heart, you are always in my heart 2x

Scent like spring night
Touch like cotton
Kiss like buttercream
Dance like waves

Even if you walk away
Even if you go
I'll be here
I'll wait for you

It was exactly ten months to the day since he'd recorded his apology.

It was exactly ten months to the day that he knew he'd screwed up big time, and might be abandoned by those who once said they were his fans.

Ten months ago he'd felt an overwhelming shame, but today, he'd heard that *You* was number one on the music charts and was stunned.

It was his comeback song. A solo that was green-lighted by Mr. Rob, because he thought it was the perfect song for him to re-introduce himself to his fandom, and remind them of what they'd missed.

Anders prayed that he wasn't dreaming because it would be a very cruel dream. He couldn't have imagined that *You* would be in the first top-twenty music category, let alone number one. He'd put so much into the song, but he'd still believed that the fans were still angry with him and didn't want to hear his voice. He'd composed it without meaning to, and then arranged it and then recorded it. No one put a stop to it. They encouraged it.

In fact, Benny had called him a couple of months earlier to say that Mr. Rob wanted him present in their team meeting. He'd attended nervously, wondering if he'd done something wrong again. Up until that moment, he hadn't been included in For-Runners weekly meetings. The invitation was terrifying, until at the mid-point of the meeting he realized that he had nothing to worry about.

He was reminded of what it felt like to be part of For-Runners. He'd missed this important feeling of belonging to something substantial. When the managers talked about tasks on the calendars of his group members, he'd felt hollow and left out. And when Mr. Rob called his name, he was startled.

"What are you working on?" he'd asked Anders.

"I'm in the process of recording a song."

The only emotion Mr. Rob showed was in the tapping of his fingers. It drummed twice on the table and then he asked, "solo or with For-Runners?"

"Solo. They're all busy," he responded.

"Does the song work better as a solo or group?"

Anders was about to say solo, but he paused, giving thought to the question. The truth was that it could work both ways, but he preferred the song to be sung by himself alone. It was a project that had started as a forceful way to get out of his head and stop wallowing. Then thinking so much about the verses he'd written, tugged so hard at his drive and willingness to get back to his normal self, that he found himself focusing on making a good song. Soon he felt he was onto something better than he'd imagined, and became super-focused on making a masterpiece.

Anders was not new to creativity or feeling accomplished at the end of his projects, but it had been a while since he felt motivated to write a song, let alone record it. *You* was special and he wanted badly for it to be a solo work from him to the fans. He owed them a great deal.

"Anders?" one of the managers called.

He'd zoned out and forgotten that a question had been posed to him.

"Sorry," he said. "The song can work both ways."

Mr. Rob nodded and that was the end of the conversation about what he was working on. The meeting took the usual form that Anders recalled, and also closed the usual way, with comments of encouragement to the band and the managers, and for everyone to continue to work hard.

A sigh of relief could be heard because the complaint section of the meeting had been short. The boys had done well with all their scheduled activities, and their evaluations from the people they'd worked with were satisfactory. If it had been a different result, then after the meeting there would have been a separate meeting with the managers and the band wouldn't have been spared easily.

As everyone filed out of the room, Anders heard his name. He waited until Mr. Rob pointed to a seat. "You will get a comeback in a few months and I want to know if you're prepared."

This was so unexpected that Anders didn't know what to say. Mr. Rob continued. "Dr. Kim's report, without violating doctor, patient confidentiality, states that you have improved so much. But I'll like to get the confirmation directly from you before I call on the team to work with you again."

When Anders exhaled the breath he hadn't known he'd been holding, it was shaky with nervousness. Mr. Rob undoubtedly heard it, but didn't react in any way and just continued talking.

"Keep up with what you're doing, and I'll call upon you again to find out if you think you're ready to return to the stage. You may go."

That was all. Anders' brain ran hundreds of miles a minute, replaying all he'd heard, and searching to see if he was anywhere near ready to go back to singing. When he realized he'd walked the wrong way, he decided to push all the thoughts away from his mind and just focus on working on *You*.

Now, *You* was making people talk about him, anticipating his return to the spotlight, and he was excited about the great response to his song, but scared to return and face the fans. Mr.

Rob would be contacting him any day now, and he didn't know if he was ready.

"It's so good to see you."

"Thank you for having me," Anders responded.

He was noticeably pale, but he looked healthy. His hair was growing out, now at an awkward length falling around his cheekbones, but this made him appear edgier than people remembered his looking.

The eye-liner that he'd refused, but the makeup artist had painted on his eyes anyway, made him resemble someone who had walked off a rock-n-roll band stand.

He was dressed completely in black, a black tank underneath a leather jacket, black jeans, and black hefty-looking boots. The only other color he had on was a red wristwatch.

He looked formidable and reserved, but if anyone had stood very close to him, they could have heard his heart beating loudly. It was his first time back in the spotlight and he was beyond terrified. He'd taken a sip from his cup of water twice, to compose himself and it had helped him think of answers to the questions.

The interviewer chuckled as she recalled Anders was the For-Runners member of few words.

"Is that a new tattoo?" she'd asked as she noted the dark drawing on his wrist peeking out from his cuff.

He'd shaken his head, no, and shown her the drawing of wheat. He'd done it for fun with ink that was temporary.

That paved the way to more questions about tattoos, and he revealed that he didn't think he could get a permanent one because he'd get bored with it easily.

"I digress," she said. "Back to your new music, *You*. It's been speculated in the music blogosphere that *You* is about a girl you used to know. Do you have anything to say about this claim?"

"No."

She laughed. "So you're not denying it?"

"I will say it's a song dedicated to someone out there who let someone go and is reminiscing."

"And there is another claim, a very interesting one I might add, which said that during your difficult time, there was a girl who helped you through it, and you wrote this song sort of as an apology because you couldn't date her, but you're open to it in the future."

He smiled. "Can I meet her?"

This made the interviewer laugh aloud. "You're really good, Anders. I'm happy to see that you're back with spunk. It was nice having you on our show."

"Thank you," Anders said, looking a bit embarrassed.

Two months after "*You*," For-Runners was back with three new songs, and one of them was written by Anders.

It was an understatement to say that people had missed their being all together. It seemed that the group was seen in a new light after Anders rejoined them. They were complete. They were flawless. They looked like they'd done another makeover, but if people paid attention, they'd notice that the boys were more mature, probably because of their workload, and the experiences that they were adding to their list of accomplishments on a daily basis.

Anders was different. It wasn't just his adoption of a darker look that made him seem brooding, but it was his behavior. He used to be quiet because of the language difficulty, but now he was guarded, and if he had something to say, his presentation was cautious. He used to be attentive and interpreted things literally. But now he listened to find the underlying meaning of everything. To some, it came across as though he were lost in thought, but he just processed things a bit longer. This new quirk was something he'd picked up during his therapeutic sessions. To others, he was just being very careful with his actions.

Alphonso now appeared to be a more carefree person and a goofball. He'd taken to acting so well that his comedic personality began to shine. His style wavered a bit as he reverted, not completely, but a bit, to his old style. The baggy tees were back, but they were usually graphic tees. He knew that it wouldn't be long before the wardrobe department switched his look back to the one they preferred, cool rocker with slimmer-cut graphic tees. He was enjoying the liberty of wearing baggy T-shirts while it lasted.

Trance was his stylish self with his blond tips bleached even lighter. When Anders was indisposed, he was the "face" of the group. He was the band member who represented them at functions, while the other two members were busy with other solo scheduled activities. This added more likeability points for him because of the friendly vibes he gave off. Also, in one instance where he attended a show with his brother, Togo, their cat-dog squabble was so relatable that fans responded favorably to him. It was a good move to always let Trance show up first when For-Runners was called upon, because the fans always brought down the house with their screams and cheers.

Twine's intensity seemed to decrease as his sexual appeal increased. His muscles were still the usual conversation starter when he was anywhere, but lately, people talked about how chiseled he was beginning to look, and the girls weren't lying low. He was the member of the group who got the most fan mail from older women.

Now they stood on the stage of The Eve Show, a TV talk show that aired at 9:00 pm on Mondays, showcasing artists of all works. Anders was a fan of this show, one of the TV programs he'd watched during his time away from the public eye. They'd been led from the waiting room to the studio of the show. The audience had screamed in enthusiasm. Anders was a bit emotional; he'd certainly missed performing on stage with his group members.

This was his first televised performance with For-Runners since he'd returned. He tried to look composed, but he knew his misty eyes were a dead giveaway. He blinked the tears back. Then the host, Dan Lotus, came over to chat with them just before it was time to announce the show. They were his first act of the night, and he was thrilled because it had been predicted that the rating of his show was going to sky-rocket due to Anders' return. And another large bonus was that For-Runners was going to perform one of their new songs with backup dancers.

It was time. Dan Lotus introduced them, and then the sound of the drums and guitars took off. Anders voice came in and filled the room. He sang the song he'd written entitled, "*She was Dancing in the Rain.*" Two dancers were flanked by his side, and then Alphonso and Trance were behind them, and then Twine behind Trance. They formed an interesting trapezoid shape.

When Anders had first sung this song in its entirety to the boys, Alphonso's jaw was on the floor. Why? This was not Anders' usual music style at all. They were all surprised. If they were asked to describe Anders' songwriting style, it would be slow tempo and brooding. This song was very unlike him. Twine said it was proof that Anders wasn't depressed anymore.

When Anders made his case for this song to be picked by Mr. Rob, he said he wanted the fans to see an energetic side of the band after the gloom he'd caused them. This wasn't the first groovy For-Runners song, but it was the first of its kind written by Anders. On the day of its release, the reception wasn't great, and it seemed like it was going to flop on the music charts, but within three days, it was anything but a luke-warm reception. It started to rise in the charts with a speed that was exciting and a bit scary. It was like a child that had an overnight growth spurt.

When they finished performing, the buzzing excitement could still be felt in the air and Dan Lotus was grinning in delight. He said to them, "I spoke to Anders earlier about the inspiration behind the song, but he didn't say anything helpful. Do any of you know?"

They all shook their head no as though it had been rehearsed. They noticed this and burst out laughing along with the crowd.

Then Anders said, "Well, I got caught in the rain once, and it was futile to run because I was drenched. I wasn't happy about it and was grumbling. Then I saw a girl without an umbrella, who didn't seem to mind the rain at all. In fact, she was smiling and skipping, she skipped and kicked in puddles, and at some point was twirling. I just stood there, and I guess I was blown away by how she'd managed to change my earlier irritation at being in the rain into something beautiful."

It was quiet.

Dan Lotus' smile that was plastered on his face increased and threatened to split his face. "Did you all notice something?" He addressed the crowd, but didn't wait for their answer and continued. "He talked, I mean, he just went on and on."

Anders dropped his gaze in embarrassment.

"No, Anders, that was an amazing story. It shows how great an artist you are, because you managed to turn something you saw, into music that got us wondering which dancer you wrote about. But before I move on to ask Alphonso about his upcoming movie, a part of the song said, that at first it seemed like she was angry and looked up at the sky, and when she saw that the rain wasn't going to let up, it seemed like she made up her mind to make the best out of the situation and dance instead."

Anders smiled. "I just added the angry part to make her human. I've never seen anyone so happy to be drenched in rain like that. Her hair wasn't puffy and frizzy either. That was my own addition. In fact, her hair was sleek and shiny and she was laughing."

Chapter 20 (Rumor Has It)

Twine wasn't thrilled about being scolded in the midst of other members, especially when the issue was a rumor. Anders, on the other hand, thought the issue he was being scolded for wasn't as bad as the one he'd faced four years ago.

In boy-band universe, if a group lasted more than five years together, all members intact, they deserved a special award. For-Runners was now at five years and still going strong, but it seemed like there were beginning to be endless rumors that made people think the end was near for them.

Hardcore fans pleaded daily in their posts online that the members should work out all their issues and never break up. Fans of other competing boy-band groups reveled in the possibility of their breakup and made fun of them.

While management within the Agency knew that these were baseless rumors, it still worried them and they had to act fast in order to quench them.

The rumor of For-Runners impending breakup started, when a girl, who coincidentally popped up in a couple of photographs with Twine, said he'd told her that if he dated her, he'd have to leave the group. And that he also had said if she'd have some patience they'd become a couple. Twine swore that he'd never said that to her or anybody.

This girl, Pamela, happened to be a former trainee of FFQ. The Agency had dropped her after two years because she was not improving her skills, and didn't show signs of wanting to be there. When this supposed conversation happened between Pamela and Twine, he hadn't gotten approval to date yet.

There was a clause in the FFQ contract that forbad trainees of a certain age to date. This had to do with their focusing on getting good enough to debut, and to stay focused on excelling as artists. Dating and owning phones were major distractions that FFQ was strict in its prevention. When the Twine and Pamela rumor went around, it was investigated because of the magnitude with which it became public. They soon found that there was no proof.

Apart from photos at parties held at FFQ that put them in the same vicinity, and the fact that they'd once shared the same practice room space, when Twine had to practice choreography for a solo variety show program, and Pamela was a backup dancer for another band, there was no proof that they'd had any kind of relationship.

This rumor started after Pamela had been let go, and FFQ suspected that they were being targeted by her for malicious reasons. It wasn't a surprise that she'd targeted one of FFQ's most successful groups.

"I want to know why she told them this lie," Twine said angrily. "I only spoke to her once or twice!"

His clothing was strewn on the floor of the bedroom, and he kicked it angrily as he vented his feelings. Anders didn't know what to say to him.

Twine was a flirt. But he always made his intentions known. Anders knew this and so he knew the rumor was baseless. Twine had just turned twenty-two, and while he was still at an age that FFQ still frowned upon on his dating, he'd posed the dating question playfully, and Mr. Rob didn't respond with his nasal-sounding, "No." In fact, it was such a surprise that Twine asked again and Mr. Rob ignored him. One thing was well-known in FFQ, if Mr. Rob doesn't voice out his opinion on something or refuse it, the answer to the question could go either way. That was confirmation that Twine could get into a relationship without getting his head bitten off.

So, here he was, thinking he could ask out one of the beautiful judges from the music competition he'd hosted for one episode, and Pamela's rumor was going to ruin everything.

They'd been summoned to a conference room and he and Anders were the focus of the meeting. Mr. Rob was saying he'd let a lot of things slide, but it was time for him to bring out the shackles since the boys chose to act stupid when they were given freedom.

Anders had seen Twine angry time without number, but he'd never seen him so angry that the anger seemed to rise visibly in his body. His neck turned red and then it seemed like the redness was spreading upward.

Twine wanted to talk back, but he held it in. He knew that if he did, what he'd say would be disrespectful and he'd get in big trouble.

"Contrary to what you may have heard about me, I am not opposed to love. I am opposed to stupid distractions that can be avoided, and young boys get easily distracted. You can throw away years of hard work with one night's mistake, and forget that you aren't just working for yourself. So as long as you are contracted to this Agency, you will be reminded of your duties."

Twine caught Anders' eyes on him and looked away. Elvira was not a mistake and it hadn't happened at night, he thought.

"You claimed earlier that you never had any conversation with her that could have led her to believe you were going to leave For-Runners. I'll assume you're being truthful. Now, this is exactly why we have the laws we have in place. Relationships that turn sour, affect the parties involved, and indirectly affects those around them. This is supposedly a relationship that never happened, yet, we're here because of it," Mr. Rob said, looking everyone in the eye, one by one.

Twine exhaled loudly.

"Anders, like I said earlier to you, it doesn't matter what your sexual preference – "

Anders cleared his throat, swallowing the discomfort that was there. *Mr. Rob knew he wasn't gay, right?*

"FFQ doesn't discriminate. But if your actions are just for a group of fans, then you need to correct it to be more inclusive.

Your fan-service seems to be causing a few uncomfortable talks arising from your actions, and we would prefer that you tone it down a bit."

Anders frowned. Earlier, he thought he'd been scolded for his I-don't-care attitude but this sounded off.

He raised his hand.

"Yes, Anders," Mr. Rob said.

"If I may ask, I'm a bit confused. I thought earlier you said the reason why I was called out was that I wasn't doing more for the fans, and I needed to get past the past, and work on focusing on all of them."

Mr. Rob paused, looking at Anders, who was wondering what was so hard that he seemed slightly uncomfortable talking about. Then the movement of his eyes made it known that he was going to say it anyway.

"The fans think you're more focused on the gay community than everyone else."

Trance went on a coughing feat.

Alphonso tried not to chuckle, but he couldn't hold it in.

Twine couldn't keep a straight face either.

Anders was, well, not shocked. He was just a bit taken aback that this was actually a complaint.

Mr. Rob continued, "I found it necessary to address this because a board member made a complaint. He wants his daughter to feel the same attention you give to the boys."

Now, Trance could not be stopped. He had to excuse himself.

"She said I pay more attention to the boys?" Anders asked, this time a bit surprised.

"As uncomfortable as this might seem, I want you to be aware of this. Apparently, she's not the only one who thinks so."

"How is that? I sing to everyone. I don't think I've ever picked out a boy in the crowd and serenaded him," Anders said.

It was now Alphonso who developed a cough.

"We're not joking here," Mr. Rob cautioned. "For-Runner is a fan favorite, both boys, and girls, men and women, and we want to keep it that way."

Anders sighed. "Were they specific about their complaints so that I can be more careful in the future?"

Now, it was Mr. Rob who looked highly uncomfortable and couldn't look Anders in the face anymore. He nodded at Benny, who sniffled to hide his amusement and started to read off a sheet of paper.

"Hugging your fellow band members tight and pecking them."

Anders nodded.

"Singing to them and standing too close to them."

Anders nodded.

"Drawing air heart signs and throwing kisses at them."

Anders chuckled.

"Saying 'I love you' to them."

Anders stopped Benny with his hands. "I now understand. I shouldn't act like I've lived with them for years and they are my family, got it!"

Chapter 21 (Feud)

Mama Miso went all out for Ander's twenty-first birthday. As she usually did on any of the boy's birthdays, she closed down the restaurant and presented the celebrant with a cone-shaped cake. It was bigger and better. The day had started out sad for Anders, but this event warmed his spirits. Every year_on his birthday, he was reminded of his parents. He'd started to get used to the fact that they didn't need to be present physically in order to celebrate with him.

As usual, Veronica sent him a card filled with updates. It was her way of letting him know all that was happening with her. Sometimes she added extra pages and this year wasn't an exception. The biggest news of all was that she was going to have a baby. Anders was over-joyed to hear it. This was an issue that she'd struggled silently with, and he was thrilled for her. She also sent him a box full of edible items from home. Anders actually looked forward to this box of items on his birthday like a kid waiting for a present from Santa on Christmas day.

They all sang happy birthday to him, and were now eating and chatting while he played a game of arm wrestling with Elvira. She was all limbs at seven and didn't take after Twine's stout-like stature. Over the years, Elvira formed a bond with Anders that sometimes made Twine jealous. She always sent him a present through Mama Miso whenever she visited Twine.

Anders had a collection of beautifully drawn cards, paper dolls and other miscellaneous items given by her to him. When she was five years old, she'd baked some cookies for him, which were colorfully designed, but hard as rocks. Anders took a picture of them before he sadly disposed of them.

He, in turn, made sure he brought presents for her whenever he visited Mama Miso and Maya. She may not have taken after Twine, but she reminded him of Twine. He felt sorry that Twine couldn't share his relationship with her openly, but she was a well-adjusted kid and well-provided for. That was enough for the moment.

As Anders ate quietly, his mind reverted to the events of that morning. He had discussed with his girlfriend that he'd like to make their relationship known during his party, but she'd said no. He'd expected it, but had tried anyway. Now as he ate, he looked up and saw her at the far end of the room, chatting animatedly with Trance. He had asked her out three months ago, and she'd slipped her response to him in a note when he went to Mr. Rob's office for a meeting. She'd responded after four days.

Now as he took a bite of his meal, he remembered the day it happened. He couldn't hold back when he saw Jiju at the cafeteria. He'd just picked up an energy drink and turned to see the bright red hair and those large green eyes staring at him. Then she smiled and said, "Are you okay, Anders?"

He heard himself respond, "No."

Her smile had vanished and she'd dropped her tray on the counter, walked the few steps that were between them and stood on tiptoes to touch his forehead. "Your head is warm. Maybe you should go now and get yourself checked. You guys have a show tomorrow," She'd said.

He'd smiled and held her gaze. Then he'd whispered quietly, "Go out with me."

Those eyes of hers which were already large grew even larger. She'd taken a step back from him, remembered where she was, and tried to compose herself. She'd laughed a high pitched laugh that sounded nervous to Anders' ears, but probably friendly to others who thought he'd said something funny to her. She didn't pick up her tray. Instead, she turned around and walked away, leaving him looking longingly after her.

Four long days later, he'd walked into the reception area. She'd looked up and seen him with a quick smile on her face, and her attention back on the monitor as she told him to take a seat and she'd inform Mr. Rob that he had arrived.

"You can go in now, Anders," she'd said a few minutes later.

He'd looked up, searching her face to see if she had anything else to say, but that was it. He would try again, he'd thought. Just as he passed beside her, she'd caught his arm, given him a folded light blue paper, all the while keeping her gaze on the computer screen. He'd put the paper in his pocket.

In the meeting with Mr. Rob, it had been difficult for him to pay attention. He felt the weight of the paper waiting to be unfolded.

After the meeting, he'd come out of the office and unfolded the note immediately and he saw, "YES!"

He'd looked up from the note and at her. She still busied herself with her work. She'd known he was there and had read the note. The small smile on her face was the telling sign. He'd walked out of the reception with a large grin on his face.

Fast-forward to today, his birthday, dating Jiju hadn't been an easy feat. At first, it was all sparks and butterflies for them, doing things in secret and playing coy with others. Anders knew that he wasn't allowed to date, but he hadn't planned on asking her out. It just happened. They were going to date in secret. He knew of a few other agency-mates that were dating in secret, evading public knowledge, and making it less obvious within the Agency. It was also an unwritten agreement not to snitch on fellow agency-mates about their relationships. People acted like they didn't know, and if discovered by management, they had only themselves to blame. So it was, date at your own risk.

But Anders woke up one morning feeling convinced that he could date her openly. He would approach management and state his case. The secret was weighing on him and he was feeling deprived of a lot of things that he wanted to do with his girlfriend.

"Are you crazy?" she'd asked. "Anders, they will end it the moment you mention my name. Firstly, your age. Secondly, your fans. Thirdly, my brother-in-law. Should I go on?" Even though she spoke in anger, Anders was taken by her sing-song voice and couldn't help smiling.

She exhaled aloud when she saw his face. She suspected it would be futile to argue with him so she stood her ground. "I'd prefer to date you secretly. If you don't agree, let's end it." She said this with her fingers crossed behind her back.

Anders facial expression hardened. "Got it," he said with a small voice. He looked up to see her staring at him, her face had softened and she looked like she was holding back tears. He reached out to take her hands, but she walked toward him and embraced him. "I'm really sorry. I truly am. I was being stupid when I agreed to date you. We'll get in trouble, I know, but I really like you."

He hugged her tighter. "We'll make it work," he had promised.

Trance straightened her collar and from where Anders sat, he saw her stiffen. She smiled tightly and took a step back. She said something and started heading to the restroom. She swept the room with her eyes, which landed on Anders and stayed on him, until she reached the door to the hallway that had the bathrooms. Anders relaxed his hands. He'd been clutching tightly to his silverware. Something told him that he was going to break soon, but it couldn't be helped. He had to hide his relationship with Jiju for as long as he could until it was okay to go public.

"It's not Jiju's fault," he said to Mr. Rob.

"Anders, this is not the time to be a knight in shining armor. She has worked here long enough to know this. The only reason why I haven't suspended her is if the news gets out, then we would be admitting that you were both in a relationship."

"Thank you," Jiju murmured.

"Do not thank me, Jiju. You know better. Leave my office."

She turned around and walked slowly to the door, her head still down and her face still swollen from crying.

Anders stood, feeling cold from the space that had just been deserted. They'd been called into Mr. Rob's office and stood side by side in front of his desk as he reprimanded them for being so stupid.

Anders had automatically tried to protect Jiju, at first denying the relationship, but Mr. Rob provided a photo that shut his mouth. It was in a gossip magazine. Jiju and Anders were holding hands, and the title above the photo said, "Is the For-Runners' Frontman Playing on Both Teams?"

Now that the story was out, FFQ would do reconnaissance work as to how much the story was believed. It was going to be expensive. But they had experienced publicists who would take care of it. They were lucky that the photos weren't as scandalous as a kiss photo would have been. Mr. Rob was certainly not in a good mood, and he wanted to get the point across to Anders.

"You will end the relationship."

Anders wanted to ask for leniency. What if they were more careful? But with one look at Mr. Rob's face, he swallowed his question.

"Leave!"

He opened the door to the living room and saw Trance frowning at the laptop screen. "You guys were dating?" he asked without looking away from the screen. Anders was too angry to respond to the question. He just could not believe that Mr. Rob expected him to end his relationship with Jiju so easily.

"They're calling her a beard online. They think you're gay."

He didn't say anything and headed for his room. He slumped on his bed. He couldn't get the teary image of Jiju's face off his mind. She knelt down as soon as Mr. Rob showed them the magazine, pleading and crying. She talked about not wanting to lose her job because she had nothing else.

They've been dating for five months and he barely knew anything about her. That was the down-side of secretly dating. They couldn't meet whenever they wanted, and they couldn't do whatever they wanted. When they'd managed to meet, they spent the little time catching up about what was going on around them. There hadn't been enough time to know about their families, or even know about situations other than work. He was ashamed to see her cry so much, and wondered why she'd said she had nothing else. What was her story? Mr. Rob's face confirmed that there was a story, and when he gave the flimsy excuse that she was allowed to keep her job to save face, he knew it was bigger than that. Mr. Rob had never been one to buckle out of terminating somebody who clearly went against the rules. Anders was surprised that his only punishment was to end the relationship. He'd expected more, but this was very painful.

As Anders thought more about it, he realized that this was indeed a worse punishment than anything else he could have been given. He liked Jiju so much, and still refused to get it into his head that they had to end their relationship. Whenever the thought of ending the relationship recurred, it showed up with a pain that he didn't want to feel, and so he quickly tucked it away and acted like nothing was wrong.

Then Trance walked into the room and said it aloud, "You two were really dating? How long? Why did you hide it from us?"

Anders growled and got out of the bed. "To avoid all these questions." He left the room with Trance following behind.

"Did Mr. Rob end it?"

Anders turned and faced Trance, his irritation apparent on his face, but he tried to hold it all in, after all, it wasn't Trance's fault. He turned around and headed toward the kitchen, Trance still following behind. He fetched a small bottle of orange juice from the refrigerator, and was making his way to the balcony outside the kitchen, when Trance grabbed his arm and put a finger on his mouth, stopping him from saying a word. Then he beckoned to Anders and pointed for them to return to the living room. This was odd, but Anders went anyway.

"What?" Anders asked when they went back to the living room.

Trance smiled. "I think Twine needs some privacy."

Anders' eyes went wide. "Why?" he asked cautiously.

Trance chuckled. "He's with a girl."

Anders was a bit relieved to hear that, because he'd thought of something else, but it quickly dawned on him what Trance said. Twine had brought a girl to B House and it was a no, no. But what escalated Anders' irritation wasn't that per se, it was just the fact that Twine had gotten out of hand lately. He couldn't ignore it anymore.

Anders headed for the balcony and Trance did not stop him this time. He knew better than to block Anders' way. As he pushed open the kitchen back door, he saw them making out noisily, a sound Anders wished he couldn't hear. The girl faced the door while Twine faced the yard. So she was first to notice Anders coming out. She pushed Twine away from her hold, but she knew she'd been caught and couldn't pretend.

Anders stopped short when he recognized her. Zara, the other twin. He couldn't believe his eyes. Just a week ago, Twine had hooked up with Zoe, her twin sister. Anders walked toward them.

"Zara, go home," he said.

"Excuse me?" Twine said, looking at Anders with narrowed eyes.

Zara was about to leave, but Twine held her back.

"Zara," Anders called.

Zara got out of Twine's grip and hurried toward the kitchen door.

Twine was pissed. "I don't get in your business. Why are you getting in mine?"

"Are you seriously asking me that question?" he said to Twine, walking closely toward him with his eyes burning in anger.

"Mind your own business!" Twine warned.

"I would if that sweet girl hadn't asked me about you recently," he shot back at Twine. "You've been messing around lately with this girl and that girl, and if you want to hook up with everything in a skirt go ahead. But while you're at it, find time for your kid!"

Twine swung at Anders, but his knuckles only grazed his nose. Anders swung back and got Twine's jaw. Both of them groaned with pain, Twine clutching his jaw; Anders rubbing his knuckles.

Trance ran toward them, pushing them apart. He was surprised. "Er, what's going on with you guys?"

Twine looked angrily at Anders, his eyes hot and moist.

Anders shot back a dirty look, eyes sharp and jaw clenched.

As Anders turned away, Twine said, "How is Jiju? Huh? You can hook up with a girl and I can't?"

Anders turned back, fuming. "You compare your one night stands with my relationship? Look, Man, if it's gotten into your head that everyone tells you how good looking you are, milk it and make the most out of the opportunity. But remember what's important while you're doing all of that. I saw her face and she misses you. One month, Twine, one whole month and you haven't called her." He looked disgusted as he turned and made his way to the kitchen door.

"Who's he talking about?" Trance asked.

"Mind your own business!" Twine spat.

"Okay, okay, no need to be angry, Bro," Trance responded, hands up in mock surrender.

"Guys, I can feel the tension between you two and we're going to be filmed. We will be on TV. They'll notice. Please loosen up," Alphonso said.

They walked in as the host called their names. Good thing that they were on opposite ends. The audience was so thrilled to have them there that the screams lasted a while. Anders took the time to collect his thoughts. Twine had called Elvira that night after their fight, and even after a week had passed, they still weren't talking to each other.

Now For-Runners had to do a TV interview, and they had to make sure that no one detected their feud.

The show went on well, with Alphonso's funny remarks and Trance's shy answers. Twine was usually nonchalant during interviews, so he didn't seem out of character when they asked him how long he worked out in the gym, and what his diet was like.

Then it was Anders' turn. "Will you ever wear any colors other than black and gray?" the host asked?

Anders smiled, biting his lip as he thought about the question. The audience responded with cheers and giggles.

He pointed to the hairband on his hair that he'd used to tie his bun. "It's rainbow colored. I think that's enough color, don't you?"

There was laughter.

The host then fetched a magazine and said to Anders, "There are many single people in the audience, and I'd like to clarify something with this question…"

There was a photo with Anders and a group of people from FFQ. They were attending the concert of one of FFQ's boybands. In that photo, they'd circled Anders and Jiju, whose hair could not have made it more apparent who she was. Anders swallowed, and tried not to feel the pulling sensation in his stomach. He'd gone twice to Mr. Rob's office and begged Jiju to reconsider. He'd promised to be more careful. He couldn't endure the breakup because it was so painful.

She'd pleaded back that while she liked him, she wasn't going to go against Mr. Rob's wishes. She was helping her family through her job with the Agency. She'd gotten away with so much already and didn't want to blow it. She would not date him anymore. She was sorry.

Anders inhaled. The host had asked him if the picture with his rumored girlfriend was a coincidence and what his relationship status was.

He mustered enough courage to hide his pain and smiled. "We're not dating and never dated. In fact, she's a family friend."

The host smiled as though he'd discovered a long lost treasure. After all, he'd gotten Anders to talk about something personal on his show. That was a rare occurrence."

The audience loved the answer. They screamed in excitement.

"So, are you dating someone presently?"

Anders shook his head, "No, I'm single."

Chapter 22 (Notice Me)

Anders returned home for his parents' memorial service. Veronica had found something in one of Everest's shoe boxes and wanted Anders to see it. She'd decided that it was best to wait for him to come home and then she could hand it over to him. This was something that he needed to see closer to where his parents were laid to rest. That way he'd get the chance to stop by their graves afterward if he needed to. Veronica suspected that he'd want to when he saw the video.

Whenever their memorial drew near, Veronica always went through a few of Everest's belongings that she'd always said she'd donate, but never had. This year she was determined to follow through with her plans, and had started sorting the items a month earlier before the memorial day.

She'd opened one of the shoe boxes in the past and glanced through it. It had contained miscellaneous items like CDs, batteries, phone chargers, and cases. But this time, she took her time while looking through them. She poured out the contents on the floor, and it was then she'd noticed a flash drive among them. The flash drive was the shape of a pen so that's why she'd missed it before.

She abandoned her tasks and made her way to the sitting room, in search of her laptop.

She plugged in the flash drive and opened the folder that was entitled, "My Talented Baby." It was a video that Everest had recorded with her cellphone. Everest had recorded Anders secretly in his make-shift garage studio. She'd perched awkwardly near the crack of the opened door and filmed as Anders said into the mike, "I will be singing an original song called, *Notice Me*. But first, let me tell you a bit about this song."

He cleared his throat and said, "My mom is a teacher and she told me something about one of her students once, and I wrote this song because of the question I had about why people chose to do what they did. Her student wanted to be an actress, but she didn't think she was pretty enough. During the conversation, my mom realized that her student was talented, and could honestly make it in the movie industry, and was actually beautiful even though she didn't think so. But there was a draw-back. She wanted to be an actress for the wrong reasons. The conversation between her and my mom revealed a deep longing to be noticed. It was the fame and not really the art. So I wrote this song as I thought about the reason why people do what they do. Were they honest with themselves? Why did they worry about awards and fans and money, if it was just about the art?" He laughed. "I think this is the longest I've ever talked about my music." He cleared his throat and then began to sing.

Everest, where she perched, tried her best to keep her hands steady. It wasn't about muscle fatigue, but deep emotions upon hearing her son's voice and the passion in his music. When Anders finished and said, 'thank you,' she turned around quietly.

"That was my baby. Isn't he talented?" She whispered as she walked toward the living room, out of Anders' hearing. "The cool thing is he doesn't know how talented he is, so his momma, me by the way," she chuckled, "will show people out there what he can do. His voice is God-given, and I wouldn't be doing my duty as a loving mom, if I let him hide out here and not show the world what he's got." She laughed, "Okay, I admit am being silly suggesting the world needs to hear his voice, but I just want others, beside his dad and me, to enjoy his songs. Okay, bye for now."

Veronica was in tears after hearing Everest's voice again for the first time after so long. It seemed like it had been only yesterday that she'd talked to her about her troubles with finding the right man. Everest always had the right words, and such a carefree spirit, that Veronica sometimes wanted to incite a quarrel just to get her sister to look bad for once. It never worked. Everest was not cut out for drama. She liked everything to be simple and fun.

Veronica went to pick up Anders from the airport herself. They'd planned to lay low, as Anders was now so well-known that he couldn't risk announcing his arrival. She'd been given instructions as to the particular exit that was reserved for celebrities who wanted to stay out of the public eye. When she arrived, a man asked her for the verification code Anders had given her before she was allowed to drive in.

Anders took no time putting his luggage in the trunk of the car and getting into the passenger side. "Sorry, Aunt, I'll give you a hug when we get home." The he did a double take. "Wow, you are, um, big!"

"It's called pregnancy, Anders," she said with a smile as she started the car. "How was your flight?" she asked, taking a quick peek at him. He wore a fisherman's hat and sunglasses that concealed his identity perfectly.

"Not bad," he responded.

"Hungry?"

"No."

"Well, I made your favorite soup."

"Not going to say no to that," he said.

She chuckled. "Good."

They were both silent, a commonality they shared and were comfortable with. Veronica turned on the radio and tuned it to a jazz station. Anders closed his eyes, not to fall asleep, but to let his mind wander with the sounds created by geniuses who appreciated the true art form of music.

The day before, he'd had his soup and gone straight to bed when he and Veronica had gotten home. He hadn't thought he was tired, so he was surprised when he had to be waked up in the car when they'd arrived. Veronica had advised him to eat something and go straight to bed. He'd done as she'd suggested.

Today, he awoke to a beautiful sunny day. It seemed too bright for the solemn occasion that was going to take place in a few hours. Anders, over the past couple of years, had adopted a memorial style that was foreign to his country, but traditional in his adopted country, as he now called his country of occupation.

Memorials were usually sad, but they toasted to the departed with food and drinks. At first, he thought it an odd practice, as there was no reason for a memorial to be celebratory. But he went back on that thought, when he realized that some people celebrated the life of the departed; the life that they had led were worth celebrating and being thankful for. Anders thought it was nice to adopt that attitude for his parents' memorial. They'd been great parents and he was thankful for every day he'd spent with them.

He came out of his room to see that Veronica had prepared the meals. She was bringing out dishes from the refrigerator and oven. His parents' memorial was attended by just two of them and they usually made too much food, so they carried it to a shelter afterward. There were times when they met friends of his parents at the grave site, and a few always visited with them afterward to have some refreshments.

"Morning, Aunt," Anders greeted.

"Good morning, Anders," Veronica responded, without taking her eyes off the bottle of punch that she was pouring into a jug.

He moved around her to the coffee pot and helped himself to the steaming brewed coffee.

"Do you need help with anything?" he asked.

"No, I'm good to go."

He leaned on a counter and sipped his coffee. He didn't know if it was the right time to ask, but she sensed it and beat him to it. "It's right there on the top of the rack," she said as she put down the bottle carefully, and pointed in the direction where the flash drive was.

He exhaled, placed the cup of coffee on the counter and turned toward the flash drive. When she'd said flash drive he'd had an idea that it had to do with his mom. After all, she was the one who liked to record videos and save them on her flash drive, which she liked to wear around her neck on a lanyard. He recalled telling her that CDs were going to be obsolete, and she should save the videos online instead, but she'd laughed and told him to spare her his computer lessons. She'd stopped burning CDs, and started saving the content on her flash drive and carrying it around instead.

He picked up the flash drive and now looked long and hard at it. Then he muttered to Veronica that he'd be back.

He walked into his bedroom still feeling the warm object in his hand, as though Everest had just handed it to him after saving a video. It was always warm. He stopped beside the desk where his laptop was placed.

I don't know if I want to do this, he thought.

He soon felt overwhelmed and sat on the bed, now looking at the flash drive with his mom's handwriting scrawled on it.

His eyes welled up and he found his finger tracing the words on it. Gosh, how he missed her. He'd promised himself not to cry this year. He had to get a grip, and convince his parents, who were undoubtedly watching him, that he was okay. That he could manage without them. He wiped his eyes and plugged the flash drive into its port on the side of the laptop. He clicked open the folder labeled "My Talented Baby" and clicked on the video.

It was shaky at first, but then it focused on him as he spoke into the mike. He remembered that day vividly. He was never one to say anything before singing, but on that particular day and for that particular music, he felt he wanted people to understand the context of the song. His mom had made it happen and that's why it was special to him.

He couldn't hold back and sobbed bitterly when his mom turned the recorder on her face as she bragged about him. He missed her so much. He tried to be quiet so as not to make Veronica uncomfortable, and covered his face with his pillow to drown out the sounds. "Dad, I know you're taking care of Mom. I'm so sorry I wasn't around in your last moments together."

It hadn't been a ruse. The weather was brilliant with brightness and heat. He was sweating under the three-piece suit he wore, which he'd purchased for the occasion. He had to look his best for his parents. Everest would be proud of him because she'd tried to no avail to get him to dress this way sometimes, and to lose the hoodie and converse.

He stood like a statue in between his parents' graves. They'd been well-taken care of. Some people had already been there to visit because there were fresh flowers near the stones. He bent and touched Everest's headstone. He took in a deep breath and exhaled.

"Mom," he said, swallowing, and then continuing, "Mom, how are you doing? I saw your face today, so beautiful." He cleared his throat. "I saw the video you sent to Mr. Rob. You did such a bad job with the recording," he smiled. "But the sound was good. I now understand why Mr. Rob liked the song." His attention was drawn to a small crack on the edge of the stone. He'd have to fix that as soon as possible, he thought.

"Mom, I can't sing '*Notice Me*' without thinking about you. Fans want me to sing it all the time even though it's an old song. Sometimes I get sad when I sing it, but sometimes I'm happy to sing it," his voice faded as he tried to hold on to his will not to cry.

"I miss you, Mom," he said quietly. "I'll try to do better. I'll try to make you proud."

He sat on her stone and then faced his dad's. "Mr. Feng, the baker," he called out with a smile, "there is still no bread out there as soft and delicious as yours, Pops."

He stood up and rubbed the headstone, as though he were touching his father's head. "I miss you. I miss you so badly. I can't —" He lost it. Maybe next year, he thought as he bawled. Maybe next year I won't cry.

Chapter 23 (Reva's Day)

"Cursed, I am!" She screamed as she rolled on the bed from one end to the other and back again.

"You are not cursed. You are a girl," Reva said, as she put on her Elmo T-shirt.

"Why? Why? Of all days, I hate my life!"

"Stop yelling!" Reva hissed. "If anyone hears you they'll think the end of the world is near." She rolled her eyes in irritation.

"It is the end of my existence, as far as I'm concerned. Do you know how long it took me to save enough to get the VIP package? Do you?" She growled, looking like a rabid dog that was ready to attack. Reva decided it was the wrong time to tell her roommate to brush her hair because it was sticking out in all directions.

"So do you want me not to go? It seems like you're angry about it."

"I'm obviously not angry at you or else I wouldn't have given you the ticket. I'm angry at my stupid period for crippling me and making me retch like an idiot. Now I have to miss this concert that I've looked forward to for the longest time." She huffed. "It's so painful, Reva, I mean it."

Reva turned around and looked at Mabel-Agatha. She looked so sad and deflated, as though she'd just lost all her belongings in a fire. "Mabel, I'll make sure I get you your autograph. I'm sorry you won't be there to give a peck to Anders."

Mabel-Agatha screamed like Reva had poked her with a red hot burning metal. Reva shook her head at her reaction. She understood why Mabel-Agatha was angry. This was For-Runners. She'd been looking forward to their concert for quite a while. She'd purchased one of their best seats and VIP packages. She was a die-hard Anders fan, and had even designed a cardboard for the concert that read, "I Have Definitely Noticed You!" She'd waited for this day, but then she gotten hit hard by a very painful menstrual cramps.

She'd been crying since early this morning, and then Reva had volunteered to attend on her behalf, and make sure she got an autograph for her. Mabel-Agatha's mood turned slightly better after knowing that her hard-earned ticket wasn't going to go to waste.

She was happy to have a roommate who would attend a concert that she wasn't interested in, well, Mabel-Agatha thought so. Reva always had clever and annoying rebuttals when Mabel-Agatha drooled for Anders. She'd mentioned once that if she were interested in the band, Twine would be her pick.

"Sheesh," Mabel-Agatha had scowled. "With Anders there, you'll pick Twine?"

"Just saying," Reva had responded, but she couldn't deny that she'd stared long at Anders' face on her roommate's laptop screen, and forgotten where she was for a moment.

The fan-meet looked like a market crowd of crazy people. Reva pitied the security men, who were trying their best to control wild teenage girls. She wasn't one of them, of course. She was there for her roommate's autograph.

She took her place in the front before the rope that separated her from the members of For-Runners. It was good to invest in VIP tickets because she was in the front row, away from the pushing and tugging, and she suspected that if she stretched forth her hand she'd be able to touch a band member. But she wasn't that desperate and just calmly watched.

Then, it was as if her eardrums exploded. The band members started to walk out from behind a curtain and the screams got out of hand. Why hadn't she purchased earplugs? she wondered. She used her fingers to block her ears, and breathed a sigh when the screams became muffled. *Which one is Anders?*

Then she saw him. He had a pained expression for a moment, as though the screams had hit him hard, but his face composed itself and wow…

Reva took a moment to drink in what she'd just seen. She heard herself say, "I get it now, Mabel." He exuded charisma in his steps and even in the way he pulled out his chair to take a seat. The way he sat, putting both elbows on the table, his head a bit low and then letting his eyes rise to the level of the crowd. If this was acting, he was doing a fine job and she totally believed him.

He looked shiny, she noticed in amazement: his hair, his skin, and his eyes. His facial expression was calm and attentive, his eyes narrowed, as though he was listening to someone talking to him from the crowd. If Reva could describe him, she'd say he was such a juxtaposition that he looked like a living statue.

She swallowed and shook her head clear. She looked at the other members, who by contrast had smiles on their faces. They looked more human and alive. She settled her eyes on Twine. She knew Twine because of his popular sports drink commercial. He'd been a runner in the advertisement, and she had admired his body, form and speed. She'd seen his photo in a magazine and recognized him as the runner. That was when she'd found out that he was in a band. It was cool to have such an athletic person in a boyband, she'd mused.

But her eyes roamed back to Anders, who was now chatting with the band member to his left. She watched his fingers tap on the table and his mouth move. She watched him slant his head a bit, and then allowed a small frown on his forehead before it disappeared. Then he nodded and sat up. She exhaled loudly.

Twine picked up the microphone and said, "Hello *Forever*, it's so wonderful to see you all."

The responding screams could wake up the skeletons of the dead.

Twine laughed into the microphone. "I'm glad you're happy to see us. Today, we have an amazing show prepared for you all, and we hope you'll enjoy every minute of it."

There were cheers, whistling, clapping, hooting.

"As you all know, this moment is for the top ticket holders. From all of us we say, thank you for buying them, and we'll make sure we serenade you with some love before our big show tonight."

Screams of excitement.

"But first, an acapella version of the first and second verses of our number one song, *She's mine.*"

The screams continued until Anders sang the first note. Then the song ended too soon to the dismay of the fans. They began to chant, "More, more, more!!"

"We'll give you a lot more this evening," Anders said, and caused a screaming session when he winked at them.

The fans were now called upon to line up for autographs. The VIP ticket holders came in three groups based on how expensive the package had been and Reva was in the second group. The signing went efficiently, even though there were some fans who lingered to chat, or tried to get a hug. The security team made sure the line moved.

Then it was Reva's group's turn. She was behind four people and she fetched the photos she needed from her backpack. Mabel-Agatha had given her a photo of Anders and a group photo of all of them. She'd instructed Reva to present the group photo to the other three to sign and Anders should sign his solo photo. Reva had purchased a solo photo of Twine outside the Arena. But as she stood in line, she cursed herself silently for not buying one of Anders.

She got to the first band member, whose name she didn't know. She gave him the group photo and he smiled at her before signing it. She nodded and waited awkwardly as the girl in front of her was talking so quickly to Anders about how much she loved him. She rolled her eyes, thinking that if Mabel-Agatha were here she'd probably act the same way.

Then it was her turn and she placed the solo photo of Anders in front of him. He took his time and looked up slowly at her.

Her heart began to thud quickly, and she held on to her stance and focused on not flinching. He was still looking at her. *Please look away, please look away,* she said inwardly. It was bad enough that it took all her might to appear normal as though she weren't about to crumble, but his stare wasn't wavering. Did she have a giant booger in her nose? she wondered.

Then he cleared his throat and asked for her name.

"Make it to Mabel-Agatha," she said.

He reacted the same way everyone did when Mabel-Agatha introduced herself. It was an odd name combo and it took some getting used to, but now Reva preferred to just call her Mabel.

"Nice names," he said.

Reva didn't think so though, but she clarified that it belonged to her roommate and she couldn't tell her to her face that her names didn't go well together.

He smiled. She almost passed out. *Stop,* she thought. *I don't want to embarrass myself.*

He was writing something else after signing his name. Now she almost beat herself for not having another photo of him. He was the generous kind of celeb who took his time to make his fans feel special. *At least Mabel would be thrilled,* she thought.

Then he looked to the side and saw that the line was being held up. The others in front of Reva had already gone through. He gave her the photo and she hurried on to Twine.

Reva could not hide her excitement when she saw Twine. He smiled the same smile she'd seen on TV, and that made her fumble as she tried to fetch his photo. When Twine signed his autograph, he acted as though he wanted to give her the photo and then drew it back. Reva was stunned for a moment, and then tried but failed to conceal her excitement. He was so handsome and she was so overjoyed to get more time with him.

She took the photo, and walked to another line that directed them to where they were supposed to sit and wait to be called upon for photos with the band. She was still in a daze with her ears buzzing with excitement. Twine was so good looking in person. Even Anders, whom she never paid attention to before now, was very attractive and eye-catching in a delicate way.

She missed the photo ops. There had been a misunderstanding when she'd left the hall to use the restroom. She wasn't allowed back in for security reasons, even though she'd tried to explain that she had been there only minutes ago.

"Look, here is my ticket. They also signed an autograph for me."

The mean-looking men at the door ignored her.

"I paid for the package and I need to be there for the photo ops."

"Let's see your receipt," one of the mean-looking ones said.

"I don't have my receipt, but I have the ticket pass. See?"

They ignored her.

She cursed under her breath and gave way to a mass of people who were struggling to get in. They didn't have the right tickets. Those were the people who were making it difficult for her to re-enter. She soon gave up and went to look for a kiosk to get some snacks. She decided she would wait until it was time for the concert. They wouldn't deny her that expensive seat.

She made her way later to one of the entrances into the Arena. She was let in after her ticket was scanned and she was patted down. People were already trickling in, and she was thankful that her seat was easy to get to, even though it was far down in the front, and she'd just entered through an entrance near the back.

She finally got to her seat, with the people beside her already seated. There was music in the air and a projector already playing videos of them. When Anders appeared above, she felt her stomach lurch in excitement. She let out a giggle, noting that she could do it safely in the crowd and not feel embarrassed.

She listened to people chatting around her about their favorites in the band. She heard about one called Trance and how cute he was. She thought she knew who they referred to, because she remembered someone she thought was cute beside Twine.

She tuned out every sound around her and focused on the projector, letting herself smile when she saw Anders and Twine. She couldn't wait for the show to begin.

Chapter 24 (Performance of Redemption)

Right before they took to the stage, an introduction played on projectors around the Arena. "For-Runners has been in the music scene for some time now, and they were considered to have made it big, when their second album became the fastest selling in the country, and topped music charts internationally.

"Their efforts as a band, and as individual artists when they do solo activities, have continued to be praised due to their high musical capabilities and talents other than music. Anders is known to write and produce music for other artists, and is also a detail-oriented tattoo artist. Fun fact: he only tattoos exclusively, and his designs are very intricate and complex. Another cool fun fact about him is that he doesn't have a permanent tattoo on his skin. He explained on one occasion that it's because he's an indecisive person and gets bored easily."

These fun facts got *Forever* laughing. The hard-core fans already knew all this, of course, but it was fun for newbies like Reva.

"Twine is known in the fitness scene for his athleticism. Apart from music, he now owns gyms, and guest stars in shows that promote fitness and sports. He is the face of two new protein powder brands, and advertises exercise equipment. He doesn't believe he's a playboy, but we know that he has caused a lot of heartbreak in the reality-show business, where he enjoys being a guest-star."

Forever cheered despite Twines' being called a playboy. Reva scowled.

"Trance is known as the baby-face of the group. He's the youngest, with fingers that were sculpted for the electric guitar. We argue that his personality doesn't fit his musical instrument of choice, but that's the fun of it. His shyness doesn't take away from the energy and skill he puts into his music. The younger *Forever* can never get their fill of him when those fingers create haunting sounds that put them in a trance, get it? Trance is favored by clothing lines because of his model stature and tends to appear in fashion ads along with bandmate, Anders."

The screams were really loud when Trance's face appeared on the projectors, but Reva suspected that it was because they'd mentioned Anders.

"Alphonso aka 'sun ball.' He is the sunshine and clown of the group. With his guitar, he composes funny songs for *Forever* at fan-meets. *Forever* looks forward to what their 'sun ball' prepares for them whenever they meet with the band. Alphonso is also the actor in the group. He has been in many movies and TV shows since his debut."

There were cheers and claps in support of the 'sun ball'. Reva smiled at the funny nickname.

"All four band members, although different, consider themselves brothers, and cannot imagine For-Runners without each other. Their bond is always appreciated by *Forever* because of the fact that their love and support for each other can be genuinely felt. They have had their share of rumors of disbanding, but it has never happened. They always say that it is the uniqueness of each of them that makes their band stronger, because they each have so much they bring to the table, and instead of viewing themselves as solo talents, they see themselves as branches that form the tree that is For-Runners."

The screens turned white and then the music changed. The show was about to begin.

The stage platform on which they stood was going to rise up from the bottom, and level up with the stage of the Arena as all four of them took their places. Hearts thumping, and fans chanting their names: it was showtime, and Anders knew he couldn't afford to fumble on the lyrics of one of the most emotionally complex songs that he'd ever written. They'd been on hiatus for about a year. Their fans had missed them. They'd promised a hell of a come-back. They were performing in the Arena, which was an honor. Their album was doing much better than they'd expected. They were still in the top spot after four consecutive weeks. They'd heard the buzz for their album-of-the- year nomination. All they had to do now was defend the fact that they were number one, and Anders wasn't going to let them down. And just in case she'd be watching, Anders had to impress her the most.

The lights were blinding. Their voices filled his ears, giving him the familiar energy that came with performing for a crowd of such magnitude, only this time the crowd was unimaginable. The Arena was new. The one that had previously stood on the same spot, had been torn down and rebuilt due to damage it had sustained from mother-nature. It was a chance to rebuild and make it bigger and better, and the construction, which had taken almost four years, had ended the year before. For-Runners was one of the first ten musical acts to play in the new Arena. It was reserved for those who could sell-out and they did just that.

Anders could feel his legs shaking, but he concentrated on focusing all the nervous energy on the face he longed to see again. The stage began to rise, the chants became even louder, and then, the twangy sound of the electric guitar like only Trance could create, started to play. Anders took the two steps he usually did to get to the mouthpiece of his silver-plated microphone that stood on its chrome stand. Right hand on his chest, one huge inhale and exhale and he started to sing. The crowd went mad with excitement. It had definitely been a while since that angelic, yet tormented, voice was heard live.

He did it! He did not forget the lyrics. He delivered and knew it was epic. He had pictured the smile on her face, even though it wasn't his to claim. He had pictured the girl that had given him a temporary loss of functionality just by staring back at him. 'R,' the name he called her in his head, just because he had seen the letter on her choker, was his focal point, the person he sang to. He knew that because of this, his performance would be overly emotional, but that was what their fans, *Forever*, liked.

When he took a step back for Twine, who left the drum set and came to address the crowd, he watched the monitors that screened the crowd. He knew it would be futile to check if she was one of them. The crowd was too large and the bodies were too small. He scanned it anyway and didn't notice when Twine called him back to the microphone. It was when Alphonso tapped him on his shoulder with a wide grin, that he knew he'd missed something.

He plucked up the microphone with a smile, trying to cover up his flop for not paying attention. "I'm just so amazed by you all, that I had to take it all in there for a moment. Sorry about my temporary freeze. Are you ready?"

"Yeah," the crowd roared.

"I said, are you ready?"

"Y-E-A-H!"

"Our last song tonight is *Just Know*." The responding scream was piercing. Every band that has made it, has one song that fans go crazy over. *Just Know* was that song for For-Runners. It was the song that put them on the map. It was the song that went global. It was the song that won them numerous awards. It was their number one most downloaded song. It was their chart-topper, and the song that seemed to have been played in all TV shows. *Just Know* did wonders for the group, and whenever they got to sing it on tour, the fans were always beyond happy.

It was still one of Anders' pride and very special because Trance had gotten the chance to contribute to it. It was only recently that Anders admitted to the fans, that there was a relationship he'd had in mind when he'd written it. People still thought that the song was about his past love, but he revealed publicly that it was about his mother's relationship with his father from the eyes of a six-year-old. He put it out that that was how he'd seen love, until he'd grown up and lost the innocence and purity as a child. As a grown-up, he saw some faults in his parent's marriage, but at that time in his life, all he'd noticed were the bliss and fairy-tale moments. It was with that eye that *Just Know* was composed.

Now he sang the song with a new meaning. This time, he was living it even though it was make-believe, because the object of his affection had no clue that he was singing to her, and he didn't know if she was near or far.

"Thank you!" and with a blowing kiss from For-Runners to the crowd, the stage darkened.

When the platform lowered to the basement level of the Arena, Twine tapped him on his shoulder and said, "Man, who is she?"

Chapter 25 (Turns Up With One 'Like')

Fifteen venues, done. He'd had less sleep after the first show because of his frantic search for 'R' afterward. Now he had more time on his hands, but his search wasn't fruitful. He was becoming more frustrated daily, as he browsed online on different social media looking for a 'Mabel-Agatha.' It was soon evident that she didn't use her real name if she had a social media page. He then searched for Mabels and then Agathas to no avail. This task was more frustrating than the times he tried to make two difficult lines rhyme.

"Man, I can't sleep because your laptop is too bright. It is 3:00 am."

Anders had no clue that it was that late, and so he apologized to Twine and shut down his computer. His search would continue the next day as it had done for the past several days.

Just before he slept, he wondered where she was and what she was doing. She'd looked like she could be in university. Then he drifted into a deep sleep.

He'd been in the studio all day and he was extremely tired. But he didn't want to slack off on his search for the girl whose friend was called Mabel-Agatha. Anders had come up with a new way to hopefully find 'R.' The managers were to alert him when they posted photos on their social media and he would try his best to search through the 'likes' that came in.

The first couple of hours were like hell, because of the speed at which the photo was liked. He couldn't keep up, but he managed to search profile pictures that had a female in them. This could also be a waste of time, as he knew that not everyone used their images as their profile pictures. In fact, he noticed that some were pictures of him, which made him grumble when he saw them. He still hoped and never gave up.

This evening, as he ate his hot noodles at the dining table near the kitchen, he got a text alert that a photo was going to be uploaded in five minutes. He abandoned his bowl of food, and ran to the bedroom, mouth full of food, hoping not to choke. He opened the social media page and waited. In four minutes he refreshed it, and then the photo appeared. The likes started to pour in immediately and he clicked away.

There was a profile picture that got his attention. He clicked it quickly, and lo and behold, it was the photo he'd autographed for Mabel-Agatha. He recognized it easily, because he'd composed the poem around his head in the photo.

He started to cough because, in his excitement, the peppery remnant of what he had eaten went the wrong way. He needed to drink some water, but wasn't willing to get up and get a cup. He clicked on the profile, and thankfully it wasn't set in the private feature.

He scrolled on Mabel-Agatha's page and saw a photo that could be she. The comments underneath confirmed that she was the one. People either called her Mabel or MA. He was so beyond excited that he almost screamed.

Now he searched desperately to find 'R' and came up with nothing. Maybe they've not known each other for long, he thought. *Please, please, please.*

Then he clicked back to the profile photo, and underneath was the caption thanking the best roommate in the world, 'Reva,' for bringing back an autographed photo, with a possible original poem from no other but cool mystery, Anders of For-Runners.

Anders held his breath as he realized that 'R' could be Reva and the name had a hyper-link. He clicked it, and then clicked on the profile picture. It was a selfie with the caption, best concert ever. He knew the concert to which she referred, as she was still wearing her Elmo T-shirt, and her large, dark, almond-shaped eyes smiled at the camera. He feared that he would have a heart attack, and mused that it wasn't a bad way to die.

Chapter 26 (One-Sided Meeting)

It was past midnight and Anders was still on Reva's social media page, smiling sheepishly at her funny pictures and laughing aloud at the captions.

"She's so witty," he said to himself.

"Who?" Twine asked, rolling on his bed to face Anders.

"Oh, sorry, didn't mean to wake you up."

"You sure about that? Because you've been laughing out loud for the past hour. I know you don't like sleep these days, but Man, am tired."

"Sorry. I'll go to the living room." He got up from the bed and picked up the laptop.

"Who is she though?"

He acted like he didn't hear Twine's question and quickly left the room. The living room was quiet, and the others were already in their bedroom. Anders went to the comfortable love seat in the corner, placed the laptop on his lap and continued his exploration.

He clicked on an album that was dated the year before and the first picture left him stunned. It was Reva with long hair. Her hair color was still the same with the different shades of brown, but her face was a bit rounder and bare. Bare, with freckles that he hadn't remember seeing when he was signing the autograph for her. She may have worn makeup, he thought.

He stared at her eyes, lost in them as his thoughts jumbled up to form nothing in particular. He just stared at her for a while. He was roused by the sound of a waking refrigerator, and his eyes moved low on the laptop to the time, which was now twelve to two in the morning. He needed to go to bed, but he didn't want to move away from his comfortable position.

He clicked on her recent activities and found a photo of her with Mabel-Agatha. They were in a café, sipping on frappes. Reva looked so cute with her hair packed up in a bun. They had some textbooks beside their drinks on the table, which confirmed that they were university students. He scrolled down to see the comments, and there wasn't any reference to a school, but someone had called her, "Reva Santana." *That may be her full name.* He scrolled up to continue with her recent activities and stopped. He almost cried for joy. She'd actually 'liked' a few photos on For-Runners' page, but he'd missed it. She'd liked their group photos, three of them. He grinned widely after discovering this. Now, he could go to bed.

As he closed her page, Mabel-Agatha's page tab was the next one that opened up. He was about to close it when he saw a link referencing a school. He saw that they were second-year students in university. A smile grew on his face as he pondered the possibility of visiting her campus. After all, it was just a couple of hours flight away from him. He had an idea. He closed Mabel-Agatha's page, shut down the laptop and headed for his room.

He opened the door quietly, made it to the desk in the dark, and carefully put down the laptop. Then he went to his bed and took his cell phone from the nightstand. He texted the social media manager.

"Here is a photo. Please approve and post."

It was a photo from a photoshoot taken with his phone. This version was not the official copy that was printed. It was a behind-the-scenes photo after he'd been dressed and ready for the shoot. He liked it because he thought the lighting was right.

If approved, which he thought likely, it would be posted sometime tomorrow. He'd watch out for Reva's 'like.' Hopefully, she'd 'like' it. This was his thought as he tried to sleep. It took a while, but sleep came eventually, despite his anxious energy and excitement.

She 'liked' it and Anders was on top of the world. He was like a kid who was high on sugar. He caught the attention of his bandmates, who didn't know if they should be worried about how overjoyed he looked and acted. It was unlike Anders to show such extreme emotions, they were used to gloomy and straight-faced Anders, not the grinning talkative one.

"I'll ask again, who is she?" Twine said as he took a seat on the floor, gulping a protein shake.

They were in the living room waiting for Benny, who was on his way from Headquarters. He had a briefing for them, concerning their next singing and advertising gigs.

Trance and Alphonso were playing a game, and Anders held on tightly to his phone, peering at it and laughing aloud.

"I so knew it was a girl," Alphonso said, clicking the pad with such speed that it threatened to snap. He was losing the second battle. "Who is she, Bro?"

Anders paid them no heed. He was browsing Mabel-Agatha's page now, laughing at her amusing comments about For-Runners. She's been a fan of theirs, a part of *Forever* from about the time they'd come onto the music scene. She'd declared Anders' her 'bias' from the get-go, and he was happy to see that she'd stayed with him through his shameful moments.

In fact, she'd shown support for him by making a collage of his photos and writing encouraging words on it. She wrote that he was supported and loved no matter what. He should take care of himself. He should take a break and come back stronger. He was always in her heart.

In a perfect world, Mabel-Agatha was the one he should fall for. She was beautiful and smart and seemed to like him very much. She had a sexy side to her that guys noticed almost immediately. She let out a diva aura, yet she seemed approachable too. She wore heavy makeup that made her look doll-like, but her smile seemed sincere. Her killer body shape could not be ignored because she showed it at every chance in her photos: chest out, hips raised. But it was her roommate Anders had eyes for. She wasn't as vocal as Mabel-Agatha concerning loving For-Runners, but he was okay with it because she had 'liked' his photo.

There was another activity on For-Runners' social media page, and the managers had posted a photo of Twine after Anders'. He suspected that they were going to post solo photos of all of them, after all they were a team and that was how it was meant to be done.

But then, something caught his eyes as the 'likes' and 'comments' on Twine's photo came in. She commented. Reva commented on Twine's photo. His heart sank.

He went back to her page to see her activities and sure enough, she'd 'liked' his photo. However she'd 'liked' Twine's and also left a comment.

He closed his eyes and inhaled, trying to hold in the annoyance that was now beginning to rise in him. What was he doing? He questioned himself. Was he really jealous? He exhaled again. *Get a grip, Anders.*

Then he clicked on her social media page to see what she'd written on Twine's photo comment section. It wasn't worded. It was an emoji with hearts as eyes.

"Eff it!"

Twine looked at him with rounded eyes. "Er…" he said in confusion. The face that had been laughing just minutes ago now looked red in annoyance.

Alphonso paused from the game, and both he and Trance turned to look at Anders. They didn't need to ask him if he was okay because his facial expression said it all.

"Are you reading comments again?" Trance asked.

Anders closed his eyes as he inhaled audibly, calming his facial features, and trying to appear expressionless.

"It's nothing," he said and was about to close the page when he recognized Mabel-Agatha's profile ID in the comments section.

"Whacha doing here?" it said, tagging Reva along with her question.

"Hehehe roomie, you're here too," Reva responded, tagging Mabel-Agatha.

"Sheesh, is it surprising? I'm just happy you're now a *Forever*…I see it's still Twine. Don't worry, you'll soon become an Anders bias."

"I don't know. I like the real man *muscle emoji*"

"My Anders is a real man too," Mabel-Agatha defended.

"Sure," Reva responded.

Anders swallowed. He waited, five minutes went by. Their conversation had ended. Now he could feel a small thump repeatedly on his forehead. It was the beginning of a headache that he wasn't looking forward to. Once again, his effeminate style was going to cost him something big; a girl he liked. He was not happy at all, and he turned off his phone, stood up, and said, "Call out for me when Benny gets here. I'm going to take a nap."

"You have to stop reading those comments," Twine said, looking pitifully at him.

He didn't say a word and headed to the bedroom.

He didn't dare go to the comments section again. He reveled in the photos that Reva posted, reading her captions and imagining more from it. She was a self-proclaimed geek, and he found himself keeping up with her book recommendations, and visiting blogs that she subscribed to. His bandmates were surprised to see this new part of him, as he'd not bought any books in the five years they'd known him.

"Never thought I'd see this day," Alphonso said when he walked into the studio and saw Anders crouched in a corner near a lamp, oblivious to his environment, and completely focused on a book.

Twine laughed, "If only he'd studied this hard when he was learning our language, he wouldn't have had such a difficult time talking to people.

"He's having a more difficult time now. He's not talking to anyone."

"What are you reading, Bro?" Trance asked.

Anders didn't respond.

"See?" Alphonso said.

They let him be and went on about their business.

He'd had enough of stalking her online. He knew where she went to school. He could afford the flight ticket. He had some free days before the photoshoot for his new wristwatch campaign. He made up his mind. He bought the plane ticket.

They knew he was going to be out, and of course, he got briefed about staying under the radar since he'd refused a bodyguard. He didn't tell them that he was flying out of town. Flying as a celebrity wasn't new to him so he made the necessary arrangements to fly quietly without rousing the attention of the paparazzi and fans. He couldn't afford to get discovered.

Now he stepped out of the taxi and was on her campus, happy with the fact that he wouldn't be easily made because he fit right in. It was a rainy day, so it was normal to be hooded, wearing a backpack, and bending low because of the weather.

He had done his research and inquired covertly and found out that Reva Santana was a second year student studying psychology. He had also deduced from Mabel-Agatha's posts the name of the campus housing where they lived.

He didn't have a real plan, but just wanted to see her again in person. He'd arrived on a weekday and it was late for lectures. He knew she worked in a campus café, but he didn't know where it was located. He soon found a directory and found out where to go.

The rain was now beginning to pick up and so he walked faster. He hurried under the shade of a building and waited.

Students ran in the rain, but those with umbrellas and in raincoats didn't hurry. Some used their bags as shields and some used jackets. He watched them all with lowered eyes, paying attention to their backpacks. Reva had a gray backpack, and one of her recent photos showed that she still carried it. It was the same one she'd had on the day of the concert.

It was getting darker and he was getting worried. He would have to call for a taxi and stay at a hotel for the night. But he had hoped to search and find her. Just as he was feeling a bit down, he heard a voice which he recognized. The person was actually standing beside him. She'd come out to see if the rain was still heavy, and laughed saying, "I should have taken my umbrella from Mabel, gosh, not again."

He couldn't believe it. He didn't have to look to confirm. He was stunned.

The excitement he felt compared to none, and he tried his best not to turn around and scream his presence, and then confess that he was there for her.

Before he could do anything, she walked into the rain. She didn't run, just walked. She had nothing on her, save a jacket that was tied around her waist and she didn't untie it to cover herself.

He'd seen that play out before, like *dejavu*, but this time, he knew who this person was and she was more beautiful.

Anders also walked in the rain and followed, staring at her as she went.

What were the odds that in a busy campus, on a rainy day, she would show up where he waited? If this wasn't fate, he didn't know what it could be.

The rainfall didn't impair his sight and so he saw her clearly. The darkening sky was no match for how clearly her skin shown. He could see her so well that it was scary. He thought was probably because his senses were heightened in that moment.

"She's so beautiful," he had chanted twice as he watched tendrils of wet hair fall on her face and how her hands wiped them away.

Then something magical happened. The squishy sounds that her steps made became a beat that his head created. Then "she is so beautiful" became a whisper and then a line in a song that was beginning to form.

As she walked fast, he missed his train of thought and only focused now on catching up with her. He made sure he didn't lose her as she started to jog. He didn't want to increase his pace with hers and draw attention to himself and startle her. But he kept up and saw where she went. It looked like a residential building, and he was glad that he remembered enough to find the building when he showed up the next day.

He couldn't show up the next day. He was sick and lay in the hotel room feeling angry. He only had that extra day and would have to return the next day. Walking in the rain had been such a bad idea, but deep down he didn't regret it.

He caught his flight the next day, and tried not to pay attention to his raging emotions. "I'm going to visit her again, soon," he consoled himself.

Chapter 27 (E)

Anders was in a good mood. For-Runners' latest music release was doing well, but that wasn't the reason why he was smiling widely. He'd noticed since the week before, that Reva had stopped posting photos of her boyfriend, and Mabel-Agatha's random comments had confirmed that they'd broken up.

This moment outweighed the moment he'd found out that she was in a relationship. He felt betrayed, but had no right to because he'd never asked her out. He'd spent three years pining for her from far and near, without letting her know. It was his fault, but he still felt let down.

Now the song that she'd inspired, which was about the first time he'd seen her on that rainy day on campus, was trending. He thought it was a good sign. He wanted her, but he was still afraid that she would refuse his proposal.

He'd named this new song, *Lightning Girl.* Critics called it the fraternal twin sister to, *She was Dancing in the Rain.* Although quite similar in context, *Lightning Girl* was a sharper tempo and not as playful and groovy as, *She was Dancing in the Rain.*

This time when questions about the song were posed to For-Runners on a talk show, Alphonso answered. He knew about the origin of the song and noticed that Anders was unwilling to say anything about it.

"Twine has a tendency to trespass," Alphonso said.

"I do not," Twine responded.

"Yes, you do, and that's how you found out about *Lightning Girl.*"

Twine smiled.

"So, Twine was using Anders' laptop and then opened a folder. He saw an unfinished song that was slightly similar to *She was Dancing in the Rain*, but the lyrics were different even though they shared almost the same story.

So Twine talked to Anders about it, and was pressuring him to finish the song. He didn't realize that Anders already had, and the completed version was on his personal hard drive. It was because of how interested Twine was in the song that Anders played him the finished song. He'd written it for fun without the intent of making it public since we already had *She was Dancing in the Rain.*"

"But we really liked *Lightning Girl* because it's a complete story, and the way he describes the day and what she did was very detail-oriented," Trance said.

Anders was asked about the mystery lady behind the song because of its vivid lyrics, and he'd shrug saying there was no lady. Unlike his enthusiasm when he'd talked about *She was Dancing in the Rain* years ago, this time he was quiet, which made people more convinced that there was a lady.

FFQ liked when their celebs held their tongues on matters relating to relationships, and Anders was good at doing that. He always wrote songs that got people talking, and they were happy that he had a quiet attitude. FFQ had suggested ahead of the promotion of the song, that it was better to keep fans guessing. Even though Anders was now the age to start dating, they wanted to avoid scandals as much as possible. But it didn't hurt to get fans talking, because that was what made the band relevant in the music scene.

"Tell us something about the song, anything, Anders."

He bit his lip in thought. "I guess I can say it was easier to write *Lightning Girl* because the picture was clearer."

On their way back home, he continued to read the novel he'd purchased after seeing the book cover on a blog that Reva liked. The book was a fast-read, and while sometimes he couldn't stand the behavior of the protagonist, he related well to the story. It was a contemporary romance novel, and he wished Reva would take to him like the protagonist took to the main male character in the book.

He liked the writing style of the author, and he searched online to see if she'd written anything else. He found out that she had and ordered another book of hers immediately. Soon he found himself on her social media page, admiring her tenacity in her clever advertisement of her books and the fun captions that went along with them. She was cute, he thought.

They reached home and retired to their bedrooms. Twine was on the phone with a friend, who was a realtor looking into houses for him. At twenty-seven, he wanted to buy a house and Mr. Rob agreed to the idea. Anders was not ready for that yet. He was just set on getting the girl that made his heart race.

He finished Author E's book and had so much he wanted to say to her. He was restless and needed an outlet for what he'd read. He couldn't just comment openly on her social media page or website. He didn't like the idea of sending an email either. So he settled for a weird option, creating a new social media page for the sole purpose of communicating with the author.

He created the page with the name John Smith and followed her social media page. Then he proceeded to leave her a message about his disappointment with the protagonist that had started out promising. He started his message with compliments that praised the fact that her book was a page-turner and that the story was unique. He smiled when he hit the 'send' button.

Not long after he'd sent the message, he received a response from her and he read it with excitement. For one thing, he wouldn't have guessed that she would use such vocabulary to a person who was just critiquing her book. Sure, he may have used some distasteful words in his critique, but he hadn't realized how hurtful it had been. She was not a happy camper, and she defended the protagonist like she was her best friend.

Anders couldn't help smiling when he read her response. He read it twice, repeating the phrase, "egotistical nonentity." She was definitely a writer. He thought about going to bed and sending her a response the next day, but he was buzzing from the excitement of chatting with her and he started typing up a response right away.

He wrote about the next book of hers that he'd already read, toning down his compliments, but still letting her know that he had enjoyed the book immensely. He contemplated deleting the part of the message that stated that no one had the guts to direct such insulting words at him in real life, but he decided at the last minute to let it be. He wrote about actually getting more hurtful comments on his social media page by people who weren't his fans, but he never responded to them. Then he confessed that he'd pondered writing to her for weeks and eventually succumbed. He advised her not to change her writing style because it was unique.

He got a response from Author E, apologizing for how she'd replied to him earlier. Then she thanked him for his comments about her second book that he'd read. At this point, Anders was struggling to keep his eyes open, and before he knew it, he was being roused awake by Twine in the morning. He had dozed off without meaning to. It took him a minute to remember that he'd been chatting with Author E before he slept. He fetched his phone, which was in need of some charging juice and clicked open his fake social media account. She'd sent a message to him asking who he was. He smiled, knowing that he couldn't tell her. He got out of bed, plugged in his phone to get it charged and headed to the bathroom.

He continued to check the inbox of his fake account, but Author E didn't write to him again after asking for his identity. It was no wonder because the situation was weird. He didn't accept any friend requests, because the account was solely for the purpose of chatting with her, and he didn't bother uploading a profile photo either for obvious reasons.

He didn't want to tell her who he was, and he knew that if he wrote that to her, she would not continue chatting with him. He had to think about it, and then a week and a half later, he saw that she'd released a new book. It was the sequel to the first book he'd read: the one that he'd written a hard-to-hear critique about the protagonist. He ordered it immediately and couldn't wait to see if the protagonist was still annoying.

He was ready to chat with Author E. It'd been a while and he'd finished her third book. He had to admit that the character development of the protagonist was impressive. He wondered if his comments had had anything to do with it, but he doubted it since the book was released just weeks after their chat. The main reason why he wanted to resume his chat with her, was that Reva had written a review on her social media page and recommended Author E's book. Author E had a small fan base and could easily chat with Reva. Anders started to imagine ways he could connect both of them in order to hopefully get Reva's attention. He couldn't think of an easy way without causing Author E to be suspicious so he decided to start small. He sent a chat message. It had been a month now since she'd asked him that question. He ignored the question and delved into her new book, complementing the growth of the protagonist.

She responded almost immediately, saying that instead of ignoring her question about who he was, he should have just replied with "no comment."

Anders smiled as he typed asking her if she'd missed him.

She replied that he shouldn't flatter himself.

They went on and on and Author E mentioned how weird and creepy it was, chatting with someone who was clearly using a fake account. Anders denied being a creep. Then after they chatted a bit, Author E decided to take her leave, but he stopped her with an interesting proposal, offering to give her a story and to eventually tell her who he was.

That captured her interest and she responded, "I'm in."

Chapter 28 (E Finds Reva)

Hearing Anders' story from him was fascinating to me from the get-go. Who gets the chance to hear something first-hand from a well-known celeb and not through gossip sites and bad tabloids? Almost no one. Celebrities wouldn't be reckless enough to seek a random person online, and spill juicy details to clarify the tabloid stories that had holes and questionable facts. That's what the ears of trusted family members were for. But that's what Anders had done when he reached out to me, and I still get goosebumps remembering when he confirmed who he was.

After hearing him out, and filling in the blanks on stories of him and his band that I knew were a bit off, and also correcting the lies by the media, I didn't envy him at all. It was so hard to live in the public eye without being scrutinized on every move you made, and being judged on every mistake. I hoped that at least celebs got immense happiness from their work because it didn't seem worth it at all.

Anders, to me, needed something out of his world of glitz and glamour; something normal. That is why I was supporting the idea of his dating Reva Santana. She seemed like she'd bring him a different kind of happiness, one that wasn't encased in the hyped life of famous people.

As I continued to chat with him day after day, my heart broke for him. I recognized a silent cry for him to be noticed by someone real and out of his bubble. I wished his parents were still around, so maybe he wouldn't feel this type of loneliness. He seemed like he was getting to a breaking point that needed immediate mending, not the band-aid kind of fix. He wanted to be loved and appreciated by someone whom he didn't pay.

At twenty-five, he now had leeway to make some important decisions on his own, and he knew it was the right time to move forward with the next phase of his life. The problem was, he wasn't sure that the person he wanted would want him back. That was why he didn't want to proceed and was stuck in a loop of "maybes."

He needed help, but this wasn't the help he could get from his bandmates, who he considered his brothers. Sometimes he laughed so hard he cried because he had the money and the fame, but those things couldn't buy him the heart he wanted. He usually felt pathetic when he heard love stories of how others approached their girlfriends easily, or had the perfect blind dates, but the closest he'd gotten was visiting Reva's social media page on happy and sad days and loving her from afar.

He'd even upped the number of photos posted of him on For-Runners' page just so he could smile at her 'likes,' and when she didn't hit the 'like' button, he had sleepless nights.

I had asked myself, why me? Why had he chosen someone like me who was nowhere near his reality, or even understood his lifestyle? But the answer began to unravel. I would listen and I would certainly understand. I was a writer with a curious mind, one who stuck to reality and dealt with contemporary issues, and was able to separate them from fantasies. One who was knowledgeable in tabloid affairs, but didn't take the same train as the gossips. That wasn't all. Reva Santana was a fan of mine and he wanted to appeal to a like-minded person.

Anders' action, which seemed careless, confirmed something to me. He was done fantasizing about Reva and was ready to talk to her face-to-face. He was done wishing that she was his. He was done being jealous when she commented on Twine's pictures. He was done making excuses that being in her life might cost her privacy and leave both of them full of regret.

He was done thinking that the beautiful geek was too good for him. He was ready to give her a chance to say yes or no.

I didn't tell him that I knew the main reason why he'd sought me out to chat with. I probably would have told him if I hadn't like his story, but he had been good at his word; his story was juicy and I was writing it.

When I confirmed Reva's name from Anders and I went in search of her, to my surprise she was very easy to find. In fact, she followed my social media account. At first, I thought it couldn't be she after all, since she was from another country and spoke another language. This was certainly a different Reva Santana. Then I opened her page, and I knew she was the one. Anders confirmed it when I sent a snapshot of her to him.

I didn't mention that she'd followed me on my page, a fact that I would later realize that he'd known all along. I looked into her a bit, and found out that she was American-born, and had moved away with her parents when she was eight years old. She still kept up with her roots even though she now identified as a citizen of her current place of home.

She was a fascinating person and I understood why Anders liked her. She was single and it seemed like the perfect time for him to approach her. I found myself thinking really hard about how I could assist him, and then it came to me to find out first if she would even consider dating him. It wouldn't be great if he were to find out that he'd been right all along, and that she only had eyes for Twine. If she had reservations, then I'd tackle that problem later. I'd have to try to convince her somehow, or maybe set up a blind date and viola...but I hoped it wouldn't come to that. I wanted it to be simple.

I made a plan. It was going to be a series of questions posed to my followers using examples of three popular boybands with three to four members in each of them. I was going to disguise my real intent about finding out if Reva could see herself dating Anders, by saying it was a poll to help me with research for my next book that was about a boyband. I laughed when I read the questions I'd written. After all, I really was writing a book about a boyband. I hoped Reva would participate as I uploaded the questions, because she'd done so in the past when I'd asked questions on my page.

I had to develop a certain level of willpower in order not to look like someone with OCD, because to an onlooker, I just kept opening the same page and clicking the reload icon. It could be disturbing after doing that for five minutes straight.

My followers started to answer the questions, even going as far as giving reasons why they thought Anders or Leon or Twine or Ezra…was going to be the perfect fit for a first love in my book. I'd written that I was having trouble making a scene realistic. I wrote a short bio of my female lead, which I described with Reva Santana's looks, making sure to change her eye color. I even went as far as to making her a smart college sophomore with a music interest.

Reva wasn't a music major, but I found that she appreciated a wide range of music. I gave a bit of context with what we knew publicly about the members of each boyband. I wanted one of them to be my inspiration to pair up with my female lead.

This was a big gamble because Reva could choose Twine. I already made up my mind that if she chose anyone else, I wasn't going to share the results with Anders. I just wanted to say the right thing or claim something that would result in a push for him to approach Reva.

When Anders first mentioned Reva, it was his description of her that made me wish for them to meet. He didn't describe her the way that a guy who only had one thing in mind would describe a girl. He seemed to have seen more of her in depth. That was attractive to me. But I didn't settle for his description because I thought he could be biased. And then I saw her photo and thought, "Wow! He was whipped."

From his description, I'd pictured her almost perfectly. I even heard her voice the way he'd described it. I didn't even do due diligence to check if she had an inkling of interest in him, but I thought that the fact she liked his photos was a start. She didn't detest him.

Then something happened. It was the tiniest of comments, but any female who commented that on a photo definitely has some interest in the person. "Yum," was the comment. Anders had definitely missed that because that would have been the ego-booster, arrogance-steamer, cocky-high that he would have needed. I saved a screenshot of the comment.

Reva didn't participate after day one of my post, but the post was still garnering more traffic as fans were answering questions and tagging friends to know their opinions.

Two people were leading and I wasn't surprised. They were Anders from For-Runners and Ezra from Shooter Spade. My readers thought that the female lead character of my pretend-book seemed like their type. I could actually show Anders this, I thought.

It was on day three that Reva left her answer and she'd chosen two people; Leon and Anders. She'd chosen Leon because he'd mentioned liking geeks and she thought my lead character was a geek. And she'd chosen Anders because she thought they'd be a perfect fit. That was all I needed. I took a screenshot and prepared myself to write a lengthy message to For-Runners' frontman.

Chapter 29 (The Dreaded No)

"So, is it going to be a blind date? Or are you going to meet her randomly?"

"E, I'll like to keep this part of the story to myself if you don't mind."

"What? Nooo! You can't be serious. This is when it gets really juicy. Come on, Anders, after all my help."

"*Smiling emoji* and I am grateful for it. But you know she hasn't said yes yet. Heck, she doesn't even know that I'm interested in her."

"Oh, I see. So, blind date it is."

"No."

"You're going to surprise her and just appear right in front of her?"

"No."

"You're killing me. Spill something, please. I promise not to tell."

"*Grinning emoji*"

"Anders, please?"

"I have a plan, but I'm not comfortable sharing it yet. I'll tell you how it went later."

"Not fair."

"Life isn't, E."

"Sheesh, whatever."

"Don't be mad. I'm freaking out here and I don't want to jinx it, so I can't say anything until it's over."

"Sure, okay. I'll wait."

"Ttyl."

"You still haven't explained who she is and how she's been helping you?" Benny said, printing Anders' boarding pass.

"She's just a friend that has been giving me advice about girls."

Benny's eyebrows shot up. "You mean like a relationship expert?"

Anders chuckled, "Nothing like that." But he didn't say more even though Benny was clearly expecting him to explain. It was Anders after all, when a conversation was over, it was over.

Benny had been looped in a week ago by Anders to help set up his meet with Reva Santana. At first, it was difficult for him to relay the message to Benny without sounding like a stalker who was ready to pounce on his prey because he was starving. But he managed to explain to Benny in simple terms that he liked a girl who he suspected liked him back, and he needed help in planning a subtle way for them to meet without shocking her too much.

Benny was the one who was shocked. Anders liked a girl, and he's making him set up a meet for them. Why? The boys were certainly not aware, because this wasn't something they'd shut up about, especially Alphonso. But Benny had to give it to Anders for his wonderful timing, because Trance was out of the country on a solo gig, Twine was visiting his family, and Alphonso was lending his producing skills to an FFQ girlband for their music video shoot. Anders was supposed to be wrapping up some music mixing sessions, but had canceled.

Benny had to admit that he liked that Anders was thinking of a relationship. He needed one, if anyone asked his opinion, so even though it was weird for him to be helping with this, he was happy about it.

"So what am I supposed to do again?" Benny asked, now enthusiastic.

"Simple. Just get a hold of the person in charge of food and drinks on variety show day. Reva will be working at the food stand, and I'd like to have a face to face meeting with her during the second half of the games."

"Okay," Benny looked a bit confused.

"While the games are going on, her boss will tell her to go pick up some more items from the van. The van will be parked at the loading dock and I'll meet her there. The loading dock is in the back of the building where they unload foodstuff for the cafeteria.

"And you're sure about the layout…"

"I am," Anders answered quickly.

Benny nodded.

"Here is the boss's contact info. She's going to listen to you when she hears you're from FFQ. Please just tell her that it's a surprise and don't mention my name. The students are there for a variety show organized by *Caesar Entertainment*. I don't want to cause trouble and mess up their turnout if they know I'm on their campus."

"Got it. Talk to the boss. Boss sends Reva to the back. You meet Reva and ask her out. Sounds like a plan, but a bit complicated. Why do you have to meet her on this day?"

"Because it's the best time. I'm free, the others are busy, and Reva will be within reach without her roommate or other friends around her. And if she says no to me, then I won't die of embarrassment since there won't too many eyes out there in the loading dock."

"Ah, well planned!" Benny said with a smile. "What's her last name?"

"Why?"

"So that she'll send out the right Reva."

"I doubt if there is another one, but we never know. It's Santana."

"Cool."

"I know, right?"

"Reva, did you hear me? Go and bring some more fish sticks from the cooler in the van."

"I heard you, Ms. Qiqi, I'm still frying the egg rolls. I'll go as soon as this batch is done."

"Leave it. I'll take care of it. We need the fish sticks."

Reva set the spatula aside and removed her gloves. She could hear laughter from the school baseball field, where the variety show was being filmed. The place was packed with students, those who wanted to be on TV, those who hoped to get scouted by *Caesar*, and those who were there just for fun. She was all about making extra cash and the school paid well during agency-funded programs.

There had been a rush for her food stand before filming began, and she was happy to be one of those who were behind-the-scenes. Her group made the snacks from scratch, and then another group picked them up to go and sell them out on the field. She didn't envy those who had to be out there in the canopies and tents, catering to wolf-like university students who were insatiable and rowdy.

She got to the loading dock, which was deserted and only had parked cars, food trucks, and vans. She fetched the keys from her pocket and proceeded to open the back door of the van.

She climbed in and was rummaging among boxes that held frozen snacks, trying to find the ones that were labeled, 'fish sticks,' when she saw a shadow in her peripheral vision. She stopped and turned slowly. Although there was no need to be scared in daylight, she swore that she'd been the only person around and she should have heard someone coming.

It was a tall figure and she thought it was a 'he,' but she wasn't too sure. Then he looked both ways before looking into the van, where she now crouched facing him and trying to feel around for a good-sized object that she could use if he stepped into the van.

"Hi, Reva," he said as he pulled down his hood.

She was sure she was seeing incorrectly. Then she walked slowly to the door and no, her eyes weren't deceiving her. It was freaking Anders looking at her. Did he say Reva? she thought, as her jaw fell to the ground.

They stayed where they were, looking at each other in amazement. One was so stoked to see large dark almond-shaped eyes trained on him. The other was hoping it wasn't a dream.

"I'd come down if I were you. You'll end up with back pain if you continue to bend like that."

"You'll have to step away from the door if you want me to get down."

"Oh, right, my bad," he said, looking down in embarrassment as he moved out of the way.

She still didn't move. She was still staring at him in amazement, wondering what on earth he was doing there dressed like a burglar. His agency wasn't hosting the variety show, and even if they were, he wouldn't be at the back of school, but in the spotlight on the baseball field. She shook her head to clear her senses and slowly stepped down. He stepped forward with his hand out to assist her and she took it without thinking. When she realized it, she withdrew her hand and missed her footing.

She yelped as she staggered, dreading the moment, because she'd already pictured how badly she was going to land on her face or if lucky, her knees, but that did not happen because Anders acted fast. He caught her by her waist and managed to turn her as they both fell awkwardly. He was the one lying on his back and she was also on her back, on him. He smelled good, she thought and then she got up quickly, apologizing profusely, and took both of his hands without asking. She pulled him up and said, "Nice watch," after checking to see that it hadn't cracked. Then she started brushing down the mud that caked his pants.

He stood still.

Then she stopped.

"Sorry," she apologized, watching his Adams apple bob in a fit of swallowing. He looked uncomfortable.

"It's okay," he said quickly. "I'll give them a good wash when I get home," he smiled, not taking his eyes off her face.

She looked back; seeing him so close was what one could call a revelation of some sort. Sometimes photos didn't do justice to a person's features, and this was the case for Anders. She'd thought he looked carved because he was all lines and angles. But it was the way he gazed back at her that made her stare at his eyes. She lost her train of thought, just looking at his pupils dilate. It was fascinating, and then it occurred to her that she was standing too close to him.

She immediately stepped back to look around him. No one was there, thankfully. She'd lost it for a moment. And then she remembered why she was there in the first place.

"Fish sticks," she said.

"What?"

"Fish sticks. I was supposed to get some fish sticks for Ms. Qiqi. She's going to kill me."

He laughed.

She twirled around, eying him. "It's not funny. Why are you here, anyway?" And as she held on to the door to climb into the van again, he placed his hands on hers.

"Ms. Qiqi knows about this," he answered softly, "she sent you here to meet me."

She stopped all movement and turned slowly to meet his gaze. Their hands were still together on the door. Then she slid hers slowly away. "Don't you feel stuffy?"

He took a step back, "sorry about that."

"Ms. Qiqi planned this, you say?"

"I made the plans and she just helped with the execution," he responded with a smile.

"I see," she said, looking skeptical. "So why are you here, Anders?"

"To see you."

She nodded. "Do you know me?"

"More or less."

She nodded again. "You called my name so I know you have the right person. But how do you know me?"

He scratched his head. "Do you mind if we talk in the car? I have a nagging feeling that we'll have some visitors soon and I'll prefer not to be seen."

Her eyebrows shot up. "Ar, you'll prefer not to be seen with me."

"No, that's not what I meant."

She chuckled, "I'm joking. I'll prefer not to be seen with you as well."

He swallowed. He knew why she'd said that – the same reason why he said it too, but for some reason, it made him a bit down. He looked at her. He had to admit that she was doing well. She acted normally, as though they've been friends for a while, not like someone who'd just met a popular celeb. He'd played their meeting in his head for days now, and they all had her looking wide-eyed, speechless, nervous and uncomfortable, excited, babbling, and not as calm as she was now. If anyone was nervous, it was he, and he worried that the perfect moment to ask her out would never come.

He just had an hour to get back to the airport and he wouldn't leave until he got her response.

"Where's your car?"

He pointed to a silver Kia sports car and she stopped herself from whistling. It might be a rental, but he had great taste.

"I'll take the driver's seat," she said as she made her way toward the vehicle.

He frowned and then got it. That way, he wouldn't kidnap her. He grinned as he fetched the key from his pocket and pressed it.

They were now seated in the car that smelled of a mix of newness and whatever expensive cologne he had on. She didn't even bother wondering if she smelled of fried oil.

She turned to him. "It may not appear so, but I'm surprised to see you in person."

"No, you don't appear so."

"That's because I have a feeling I'll be seeing you sometime."

He frowned. "Er, I'm not sure I follow. We don't have any concerts soon, and I don't have any public scheduling for about four months."

She smiled and shrugged. "I've seen you around campus."

His eyes widened and he blinked multiple times trying to figure out if he'd heard her correctly.

"Wh-hh-aa-tt?" he stuttered.

She grinned.

"Really?" he asked.

"Yeah. The first time I saw you I thought I was hallucinating because there was no way you could visit our campus and nobody would know of it. So I thought it was my imagination. It was last year and you were near the greenhouse."

His eyes got even wider. "You saw me there?"

"Weren't you the person?"

He nodded, dumbfounded. And here he was thinking he'd gotten away with stalking her. He now wondered how many people had recognized him. But there wasn't anything about his visit on the gossip sites.

"Then before Christmas, I thought I saw you beside the curved tree. We have a tree on campus that is a bit spiral and…"

"Yes, that was me."

"Aha!"

He exhaled as if he hadn't known he'd been holding his breath.

"Anyway, I was sure it was you, when I saw you earlier this year at the side of the library building. Since many people had left for the holiday, the campus was basically empty, and I was there to finish up my assignment. I actually followed you."

"Huh!" Anders looked like he was going to faint.

She grinned. "Yeah, I saw you get into your car. And then there was the fan video of you at the airport. That was confirmation that I wasn't seeing things."

He was still unable to say anything and just looked at her in amazement.

"Anyway, I just wondered if you were planning on going to school here or something, or maybe you had someone you were visiting here. I wanted to tell my roommate, who adores you so much by the way, but I didn't want to turn her into a stalker and get her hopes up, because trust me, she would have set up a watch on this campus and made sure you were found if you showed up."

He cleared his throat when he heard the word, stalker.

"So you actually came to this campus all those times I mentioned?"

He nodded.

"Wow," she said, smiling. "And you didn't come to inquire about schooling here?"

He shook his head. This is it, he thought. He exhaled and said, "I came because of you."

She pouted and had a small frown on her face. "Me?"

"Yes, you."

"Wait a minute, you said you came to see me today. You don't mean to say that all those times..."

"Yes, all those times I visited it was to see you."

She scratched her ears as though she hadn't heard him right.

He sighed. "The truth is, I've been wanting to meet you since the day I signed the autograph for your roommate. You remember the concert at the Arena, right?"

Her mouth was round in surprise. "How could I forget?" she murmured and slanted her head in thought. It actually seemed like yesterday. She still remembered the high she'd felt from that concert. Now she frowned. "That was like three years ago. Then I saw you on campus last year. So why didn't you say anything to me? Her frown deepened.

"Er, maybe this isn't a good time to say this but I actually found you much earlier."

"Really?" she squealed, still bugged-eyed in surprise. "But I guess it wasn't the right time for you?"

He smiled. "On the contrary."

"Then why?"

"That's not important. I'm just glad you're single now."

Her face lost all its expressions and became still. "How do you know I'm single?"

"Er..." he cleared his throat, trying to swallow a lump that had suddenly manifested. "Er..." he tried again.

She had a no-nonsense look, but he saw something else brewing, discomfort, and he knew he had to ease it before it turned into fear.

"I asked, I asked. I didn't want to cause any problems so I asked," he said, exhaling and trying to steady his breath. He'd come so close to messing up and he knew it.

She nodded as though satisfied with his response, but her eyes still held some worry.

So he went for it, very quickly. "I like you, Reva. I've liked you since I met you at the Arena, and I've wanted to ask you out for a while." He swallowed and continued after exhaling. During his confession, she'd kept looking at him without wavering. "You may not like me, but I'm just asking for a chance to change your mind. Please go out with me."

She still kept her gaze on him intact and acted like she hadn't heard him. Then she snapped out of it, making an odd expression as though something smelled funny. He didn't know how to react to this, but he still looked at her, nervous but expectant.

"You're a good songwriter, but I have to say that that was a poor proposal."

"Er," he could feel sweat now gathering on his forehead. "I…well…I"

"I'll take it," she said nonchalantly.

He looked unsure.

"Yes, my answer is yes, Anders."

He was surprised and then he went in for a kiss, breaking the invisible boundary that had been drawn between them by the handbrake between the seats.

She pushed him away after a few ticking seconds, her eyes wide and her lips still puckered.

His eyes looked huge as well, more surprised at himself than scared at her reaction. But it was clear that he didn't think his actions were unjustified, because rather than apologizing, he said, "There's more to come."

She couldn't look any more surprised, so she just sighed, relaxed and responded, "word to the wise, Anders, it doesn't always feel like it feels in your head."

Now he looked horrified. "Was that really bad?"

She tried keeping a straight face, but failed and broke into a fit of giggles.

Chapter 30 (Cloudy on a Sunny Day)

"I think you're speeding. Slow down."

He laughed. "I'm not sure how you can tell. This car isn't even noisy."

"I just know you are."

"I'll try to slow down a bit, but I have to catch my flight. My manager made sure that they had the private gate opened so I can board secretly, and if I miss it, then it will be a hassle to set it up again. I can't afford to be seen here by the paparazzi when this visit is supposed to be non-existent."

"Well, it's all your fault. You should have planned better."

"If only you knew how hard it was to pull off this small plan."

She giggled.

Anders really liked the sound of it, but he didn't want to do the textbook new couple cheesiness where he told her he liked everything she did – "laugh again, I love the sound, or smile again, you're my sunshine…" that sort of thing. But he had to admit that the day was unusually bright after she'd said yes she would date him. It was even brighter when she agreed to fly down for their date.

"So are we a couple?" he'd asked as he held the door open for her.

She stepped out and stood so that they were standing really close and facing each other. "Aren't you being too hasty?" she'd asked. "Let's go on a date first, don't you think?"

He shook his head and then nodded in agreement.

She'd then pecked his cheek and bent to make an escape under his arm. He'd watched her run toward the van and then turned to wave. "Safe flight!" she'd screamed.

Now he drove to the airport, with her voice on the car speakers. His excuse for calling her immediately was to test the number she'd given him. He hadn't had a chance to do so when she gave him her number earlier, because she'd left her phone in the booth. She saw his call come in, excused herself and went out to the back of the building, where they'd been earlier, to answer her cell phone.

"I mean it. I'm not comfortable with how fast you're driving and you're distracted too."

"I'm not. You're on the speakers and I'm paying attention to the road."

She sighed. "Well, then, let me let you drive. Call me when you board your flight."

"Wait a minute, I just..."

And she heard him yell, "What the – ?"

Followed by a sickening combination of metal thuds, whines, scratching, and glass shattering sounds. Her mouth was ajar in shock, eyes wide as her hand clenched her stomach. Then there was a flow that made its way from her stomach to her mouth and she rushed to the plant beds and retched. She still had her cell phone to her ear even though the communication had been cut. She heaved loudly and painfully, tears running down her face, 'what the fuck?' rang in her thought.

Her phone dropped from her hands as she grabbed her hair and screamed. She didn't need to be told that what she'd feared had just happened. Why hadn't he listened?

Anders had used up more time than he'd thought. He was supposed to meet up with Reva and go straight to the point, "I like you and I'm here to ask you out." She knew who he was and would have either said yes or no. If she'd said no, he would have tried his best to convince her to change her mind, and if needed, beg on his knees. It didn't get to that, thankfully.

But it didn't play out the way he'd pictured. He liked how it had happened. Being so close to her was more intriguing, seeing that he hadn't made up how beautiful she was in his head: the freckles that gathered cutely on the bridge of her nose and her cheeks, her long lashes that batted when she caught herself looking at him in awe. Her voice did more to him than he'd imagined, and he couldn't fight his urge to hear it again.

That's why he'd called when he was on his way to the airport. It wasn't about testing to see if she'd given him a fake number. He missed hearing her talk, even though he'd heard her only just moments ago.

She was right that he'd been speeding. Benny had texted him to ask if he was on the way back to the airport, because the gate agents were waiting for him. He'd been staring at Reva so he hadn't heard the message come in.

Now it didn't matter if he was at fault, or if it was that of the other speeding vehicle that had left its lane and tried to pass him. They'd been on a two-lane road, and the car behind Anders had left its lane and drove by his side, which was the side for the oncoming vehicles. The driver had hoped to get in front of Anders' car before the oncoming vehicle reached him, but hadn't realized that the oncoming vehicle was closer than it had seemed.

Anders was driving so fast that he hadn't been able to slow down quickly enough to give room to the other vehicle that was beside his own. The other vehicle had also been speeding too fast, and couldn't slow down fast enough to return behind Anders' car. There was a head-on collision and Anders' car was struck by the impact of those two, with one vehicle pinning his car to the edge of the road. He was still conscious when shards of glass from the windshield of his car hit his face, and he heard the unmistakable sound of a broken bone that was from his leg.

The worst moment after the crash for Anders was his choking on dense, oily smoke while not being able to see or move. In that moment, he felt pain stabs from all parts of his body. It was the most uncomfortable, painful feeling of his life, and all he could think of was, "is this what mom and dad went through?"

As the smoke thickened more and he couldn't breathe, he suspected that it was only moments before the car would explode, and he thought, "You know what, I'm glad we met. Sorry, we won't go on our date, Reva."

Chapter 31 (Rumor Has It Part II)

The accident was on the news, and was blown out of all proportion within hours when the identities of the victims were revealed. Rumors of all types spread like California wildfires, and fans of Anders and For-Runners were heartbroken about each and every one of them, as the rumors continued to be bleaker and gorier as the moments went by.

Some said he'd lost limbs and amputations were scheduled to be done. Some said he looked unrecognizable, and would need facial reconstruction because he'd broken nose and jaw. Some said he had lost an eye. Some said he had a broken spine and was paralyzed. There was only bad news, because no one could picture anything better after the site of the accident was shown on TV. The shattered twisted vehicles and blood everywhere were retch-worthy, and it was a surprise that there were two survivors.

Anders and a woman had been airlifted. The man who'd overtaken Anders was pronounced dead at the scene.

Three weeks later, Benny was still telling Reva the same thing, "Anders cannot see visitors." She threw out her good-girl attitude and started cursing like a mad woman when they spoke on the phone.

Sadness had plagued her for weeks, but it dissipated a bit when she answered a call from Benny. He introduced himself and wanted to know how she was doing.

She'd asked him immediately about Anders, wanting to know how he was doing. He couldn't give anything away because he wasn't supposed to, but he told her that the doctors were doing their best for him. The location where he was being treated had leaked online, and fans flooded that hospital day and night. Reva had also gone there to leave a teddy-bear in the space that the hospital had designated for fans to leave gifts and say prayers for Anders.

Reva made it a point to call Benny's number every day. She'd begged him and promised that she wouldn't say a word to anyone, if he told her how Anders was really doing. She tried reasoning with him, telling him that she couldn't sleep if she didn't know, and she'd had a recurring nightmare of his broken and bloody appearance. Benny never budged. He stuck to company policies and didn't give her any useful updates.

Reva became more agonized by Benny's refusal to tell her anything, even when she told him that he'd asked her out on a date. Benny didn't refute her claim, but stuck to his resolve of not saying anything to her in particular. Reva soon threw out her well-mannered demeanor and started calling him in anger. This didn't faze Benny. In fact, he acted like he expected it and let her rant.

"I get it that you're doing your job, Benny, but this is cruel. I'm not just his fan, Benny, you know this. You can make it happen. I'll just be at the door. I just want to see him please."

He sighed heavily. "He's not seeing visitors."

"So are you saying he's conscious?"

"I never said or implied such."

"Then it wouldn't matter if I just took a peek. I'm going crazy here. If he hadn't come to see me, this wouldn't have..."

"Reva, if I could, I would, but I can't. Just be patient."

"For how fucking long? Do you know how hard it is to see all those speculations? Last week there was 'RIP Anders' trending and I almost lost my mind. Can't FFQ give us better updates? One news source says he's fighting for his life, and another says he's stable. That's all we get, no details. Just help me out. I promise on my life not to say a word. Just tell me. I don't have to see him, please."

As usual, Benny was silent. Then again as usual, he said, "I'm sorry I can't be of help, Reva, I have to go."

"THEN DON'T FUCKING PICK UP WHEN I CALL, IF YOU HAVE NOTHING HELPFUL TO SAY TO ME!"

He hung up.

"Go to class already or else I'm calling your mom," Mabel-Agatha whispered in Reva's ear.

She'd made the same threat for a week now and Reva didn't move a muscle. She'd been on her bed, going between sleepy and semi-awake states. She'd lost her appetite and her drive to do anything. Her studies were suffering, her weight was dropping, and her roommate was dying of worry.

Mabel-Agatha didn't know what had taken over her roommate's will to live like a human being, and she was confused as to how to approach it. At first, she thought Reva was crying bitterly due to something hurtful that may have happened at school or work, and she waited for the tears to resolve before she could ask about it. It only took three days.

Reva was swollen-eyed and hot with temperature, and Mabel-Agatha thought it was a fever of some sort that was plaguing her roommate, especially since vomiting and loss of appetite were involved. Mabel-Agatha was also in a very sad mood from hearing about Anders' accident, but her roommate's health and sanity was her first priority. If only she could get her to talk about what was wrong.

Reva refused to get herself checked out at the school clinic. She refused food. She refused to get up. Mabel-Agatha was very worried.

"Just tell me what's going on, Girl, please."

Reva didn't move a muscle and even though she faced the other way on her bed, Mabel-Agatha knew she was awake.

"You have to stop this, whatever it is!"

No response.

This behavior continued until Mabel-Agatha threatened again to involve Reva's mom.

That didn't get a response either.

Then Mabel-Agatha overheard Reva's voice on her way back from work. She was about to open the door when she heard Reva yelling and assumed she was talking on the phone. As far as she was concerned, Reva wasn't dating anyone, so it couldn't be about a breakup and she listened closely.

What she heard didn't explain anything, but it gave her some answers. Reva's behavior had to do with someone she liked. Mabel-Agatha knew that it wasn't Reva's ex-boyfriend, no way, but someone new. She was now very curious. So she opened the bedroom door quickly and caught Reva eyes. They were tearful and swollen.

"Who is he?" she asked, her lips beginning to tremble in anger. "Who the fuck is he?"

Reva bit her lips and didn't respond, so Mabel-Agatha snatched her cell phone from her and began to look through the numbers. She saw a number that had been called consistently for the past week, but it wasn't labeled.

Reva didn't make any effort to snatch her cell phone back from Mabel-Agatha, because she didn't have the strength to do so; instead, she just cried more and Mabel-Agatha got angrier. She dialed the number and the person said, "Reva, I'm only answering because Anders would want me to do so. I have nothing to tell you about his state right now. Be patient, please."

Mabel-Agatha's eyes and mouth rounded in surprise as she hung up.

She turned now to Reva, still with her surprised look and said, "Was that Anders' manager, as in, For-Runners' Anders?"

Reva's response was loud bitter sobs that escaped her.

"What? Girl, you better wipe your eyes and spill. You can cry later," Mabel-Agatha said.

"That's it, Mabel, that's it. I don't have anything else to tell you."

Mabel-Agatha was still hounding Reva for more details, one day later after Reva's tearful account of meeting Anders at the cafeteria loading dock.

"You freaking met *cool mystery* and you're only mentioning it now, what kind of bestie are you?"

Reva swallowed, still trying not to think of Anders and what he might be going through. Mabel-Agatha's non-stop yapping was actually helping because she had something else to focus on.

"What was I supposed to say? He came here, hung out, and was in a ghastly accident on his way back?"

Mabel-Agatha stopped talking for a moment and then said, "Yes, that's what you were supposed to say. You know how I feel about Anders, and you know how freaking scared I've been these past few weeks because of your behavior. You should have told me."

Reva sighed.

"You thought I wouldn't believe you?" Mabel-Agatha asked, taking a seat near the dresser that held the framed autographed photo of Anders from the Arena concert.

"Not that. I wasn't thinking. I just wanted his super-loyal manager to tell me he's doing better or something."

"Well, they pay them to keep their mouths shut. We'll just have to wait for FFQ to update us." Then she took a good look at Reva and sighed. "I'm sorry you were going through this on your own."

Reva smiled. "Sorry I didn't say anything to you."

"It's okay. I'm sure you were scared that I was going to steal him from you," Mabel-Agatha said jokingly.

Reva frowned, "No, I thought you were going to call me a traitor for stealing him from you."

"True. But I won't believe it until I see it though."

Reva clutched her stomach as a shooting pain went through her.

"Are you okay?" Mabel-Agatha rose and walked quickly toward the bed where Reva sat.

She was now swallowing and trying not to cry. "Good, good," she waved off Mabel-Agatha. "I don't care if we don't date. I just want to hear that he's okay."

Mabel-Agatha hugged her roommate, who was unsuccessfully trying to keep herself from crying.

There was an inkling of truth that was in the latest rumor. The answer to what Anders was doing in that city had finally been revealed. An unknown source said Anders had asked for a girl when he opened his eyes, and this news was met with reactions that ranged from happiness to jealousy to sadness.

FFQ had announced later in the week that Anders was awake and making conversation. They thanked the fans for their support and prayers, and still urged for continuous support as recovery would be a long road for him.

This was good news to everyone's ears, since it had been over a month now since Anders had been in an unknown state, and the rumor mongers hadn't been kind to him. But the news about the mystery girl he'd visited was bigger. Who was she?

Mabel-Agatha reveled in this rumor and laughed at all the speculations about this mystery girl, while Reva was very nervous and became jumpy at even the slightest of sounds. Her nervousness started when angry fans began to blame her for his accident, and vowed that if she were discovered, she'd be in big trouble.

Thankfully, the angry fans were nowhere near to guessing Reva's identity, because they stuck with the idea that Anders' girl was a fellow celebrity. Mabel-Agatha used the opportunity to get Reva to do a lot of favors for her, threatening to expose her, playfully of course, but Reva took the threat seriously and did whatever her roommate asked. It was funny and pitiful.

And then the call that Reva had been waiting for for over a month finally came.

"I'll pick you up," Benny said.

Her heart had been pounding fast since she'd hung up from Benny's call, and Mabel-Agatha's squeal did nothing to relieve it. She'd turned their wardrobe upside down, looking for the right outfit for Reva to wear. Meanwhile, Reva's sweat pores were over-working, drenching the neck, back, and underarms of her blouse. She was so nervous that she felt sick. She didn't know how she'd react when she saw Anders, and she was hoping that he looked nothing like the images in her nightmares, all scarred and sewn up like a product of Dr. Frankenstein.

Then she got a call that she was to meet at the driveway close to the school library. Mabel-Agatha knew Anders hadn't come along, but she couldn't stay back. So she held Reva's hand and walked together with her. Just as described, there was a black tinted standard Kia parked. A man got out from the driver's side when he saw the girls approach.

He walked to the other side and asked, "Reva Santana?"

Reva croaked, "I'm Reva," and then cleared her voice. Mabel-Agatha released her hand, but before that, whispered in her roommate's ear, "Tell Anders that I said, get well, because Mabel-Agatha needs to see you in a concert soon."

Reva nodded, wiping her sweaty palms on her jeans. She'd finally settled for a navy blue sweater and dark blue jeans; nothing fancy, but something perfect to hide possible sweat duct malfunction.

She got into the car, buckled up, and trained her eyes on her folded palms. She didn't look up to see where the car was going or even to look around where she sat. The driver was quiet and she was too.

The drive was long, but she didn't care. All that mattered to her was that she would get to see Anders.

When the car slowed down, she looked through the window and noticed where they were. It wasn't the hospital where Anders' fans had been dropping off gifts for him. They'd probably moved him to this new location to protect his privacy. The car finally halted in the garage, and Reva waited until the driver opened the door for her.

He ushered her into an elevator and they went to the fifth floor. He then led her to a desk, where all he did was nod to the lady.

"Have a seat," she said to Reva, who went and sat down.

She surveyed her surroundings and it looked more like a hotel than a hospital. Maybe it was a private facility for celebrities, she thought.

Soon a round-looking man with a friendly face who could have used a larger pair of pants came toward her. He looked around and after deciding that she was the one, since no one else who looked like a visitor was around, stretched out his hands and said, "You're Reva, I presume?"

She took his hands. "Yes. And you are?"

"Benny," he responded.

"Oh..." Her face grew hot in embarrassment. She knew she had to apologize to him for her bad manners, and the horrible choice of words she'd directed at him during her phone calls, and as she was about to say something...

He smiled. "You don't have to apologize. Anders was happy to hear about your outburst."

Now she frowned. "You told him?"

"Why not?"

She withdrew her hands and pouted.

He chuckled. "This way.'

His coloring wasn't good. He looked like the early beginnings of soured milk. His head was wrapped in a bandage. It was full of old cuts and stitches. He wore a neck brace. One hand was wrapped and the other had needles in it. The rest of his body was underneath the bedding, and Reva could guess that there were more stitches and wrappings on his torso and legs too. But one thing that remained perfect was the light in his eyes. He was so happy to see her. She knew he was in pain because of the grunting sounds he made when he laughed or moved a bit. And so she tried not to make him talk or react, but he was stubborn.

"I can't help it. I've missed you," he said when she begged him not to say anything.

"When? I thought you've been unconscious the whole time."

"Even in my unconsciousness," he responded.

"Urgh!" she made a sound as though she was going to throw up. "Stop being cheesy."

He laughed a soft laugh, making sure not to aggravate the pain he felt in his ribs. Then they were both quiet and his face relaxed. He fell asleep. Benny had alerted her that he was drugged up, and went in and out of consciousness easily, so she shouldn't be alarmed if his speech began to slur and he closed his eyes.

She got up to stretch. She'd been sitting for a while. His room was warm and the curtains were closed. A minimal amount of light came in from a crack in the curtains, and it was very quiet except for his breathing. Beside him, on a small table, was a Manilla envelope addressed to him. She looked closely to see who it was from and it said, 'from Author E.' She wondered who the person was. Then she went back beside the bed where she'd been sitting earlier and returned to her chair.

She watched him. He slept calmly and stirred, frowning due to pain. Then she carefully touched the line that formed between his eyebrows, and it cleared immediately. The next time she did it, he opened his eyes slowly. He narrowed them a bit as though it were too bright in the room.

He saw two large eyes staring back at him. He noticed this time that under those eyes were dark patches, a sign that the owner hadn't slept much.

"Are you really awake?"

He recognized her voice and it sounded even more cracked like she had a sore throat. The name came immediately, Reva. Waking up took a lot of energy due to the medication he had in him, but recognizing the person he was with took no effort at all.

He stared at her.

"Are you...maybe I should call the nurse." She made an attempt to rise.

He blinked.

"Okay, I'm going to get a nurse."

His hand that had needles in it moved swiftly and touched her just as she got up. She looked back at him and exhaled heavily, but her eyes held worry.

His thoughts were jumbled. *What had happened? He tried to recall and then it came back to him as he tried to move his other arm.*

It was painful. He tried to relax.

"Do you recognize me?" she asked, trying to hide the panic that was clearly in her voice.

He didn't have the heart to trick her. She looked deathly tired. *How long had he been out?*

"Reva," he said quietly.

"That's right," she responded, her voice shaking as though she were about to cry. Then she cleared her throat, sat down and sighed heavily. She looked at him and then straightened herself. She said with determination, "By the way, everyone now knows we're dating. It's online."

"We are?" He asked, trying to look shocked, but failing woefully."

She rolled her eyes.

"Come closer," he said.

Now he knew his good hand from his bad hand. He raised it to her face, not minding the needles, and rested it there for a bit. It started to shake due to fatigue, and she took it in her hands and brought it to her lips.

"I was so scared," she said, her eyes glistening, but she blinked back the tears.

"I'm sorry," he whispered.

A nurse walked into the room and Reva placed his hand carefully back beside him.

"How long was I out for?"

"Twelve hours."

His eyebrows shot up in surprise, and then he made a face that said, "Only?"

Reva made way for the nurse who was now examining him, checking his vital signs.

"You think you went into a coma? You're not that cool," she mocked him playfully.

He laughed, but thought better of it when a shooting pain tugged at his ribs.

The nurse frowned at him. He lay still. She finished examining him and left the room.

Anders looked her eyes and said, "I'm glad it wasn't a coma because I would have missed my chance to go on our date. I've already delayed it quite a bit."

"I would have waited for you to wake up," she said immediately.

It was his silence that made her look at him quickly. He looked okay. He just couldn't respond.

Her response had left him speechless. He stared at the girl that he'd bet was into Twine and no one else.

"Are you crying?" she asked incredulously.

"No," he responded, turning away. Then he turned back, looked straight into her eyes and said, "Someone stole Harry Potter's invisible cloak and is cutting onions beside me."

In that moment, Reva forgot that she'd been sad, and laughed so hard that she fell off her chair.

ABOUT THE AUTHOR

Emem Uko has added another brilliantly-written book to her list of works. "In *Notice me*, she takes you on a suspense-filled journey on the behind-the-scenes struggles of the lead vocalist of a boy band. A journey of growth, loss and finding a long-needed love." List of Emem's published books include, *Façade*, a young adult novel; the sequel to Façade entitled, *Janus*; and *Hers to Tell*, a suspense novel. Watch out for more books from her and get updates from her website, www.ememuko.com. Emem also blogs about different interests on Z and S (www.ukoemem.com) and you can stay in touch with her on Facebook @authorememuko and Twitter @ememuko. Emem Uko holds both Bachelor's and Master's degrees in Business Administration.

93163728R00159

Made in the USA
Columbia, SC
07 April 2018